GUTS & GLORY: BRICK

In the Shadows Security, Book 6

JEANNE ST. JAMES

ST. JAMES

———

Acknowledgements:

Photographer: FuriousFotog

Cover Artist: Golden Czermak at FuriousFotog

Cover Model: Chase Ketron

Editor: Proofreading by the Page

Beta readers: Whitley Cox, Andi Babcock, Sharon Abrams & Alexandra Swab

A Special Thanks

To Alexandra Swab for assisting me with Brick's blurb. Your help, as always, was invaluable!

Also, thank you to ALL my readers who belong to my readers' group:
https://www.facebook.com/groups/JeannesReviewCrew/
You all encourage me to keep writing!
Love to you all!

Chapter One

THE GLASS-SHAKING slam of the front door had all the Shadows shooting straight up in their chairs. Brick wasn't the only one sitting around the table whose hand automatically fell to the handgun strapped to his ankle.

What sounded like a woman's heels came down the hallway in their direction.

"Shit," Ryder muttered. "You said she was out with the sisterhood tonight."

Mercy's silver eyes slid to him. "Yeah, she's fucking supposed to be out most of the night with the rest of them."

"I knew we should've had poker night at the fucking warehouse," Steel grumbled.

"The motherfucking heat is out," Hunter said. "We would've had to cancel because of blue balls. And all the women are occupied with Bella's baby shower, so it's the perfect time to play."

"We could've worn layers," Walker muttered.

All eyes slid to him. "And your momma could've dressed you up in your fucking snowsuit and mittens, too."

Walker gave Steel the finger.

A stutter of those clicking heels was heard, a stumble, then a bang. Like Rissa had fallen against the wall.

Brick glanced at Mercy. "Jesus, is she drunk? What'd you do wrong to make her get smashed?"

Mercy frowned and surged to his feet. "Nothing. I never do anything wrong, asshole."

Chuckles and snorts circled the dining room table where their chips, cards, ashtrays, cigars and booze were strewn.

Before Mercy could go check on Rissa's condition, a woman burst into the room, her dark blonde hair—the same color and almost the same length as Rissa's—a wreck. Her blue eyes—also the same color as Rissa's—wide as she took them all in.

"Fuck," Mercy muttered and sank back into his seat, scraping a hand down his scarred face.

"You didn't set the alarm?" Ryder asked, grinning.

"You know I fucking did," Mercy grumbled, then turned to face the intruder. "How do you have the fucking code?"

"From the last time I was here. Parris gave it to me." The woman made a face at Mercy. "What? I'm her sister, not a terrorist."

Brick pursed his lips as he took in a younger version of Rissa, but one just as curvy and whose attitude, and other similarities, could make them twins.

Gorgeous, but a pain in the ass.

Or at least, that's what Mercy said. Not the gorgeous part, the pain in the ass part.

Though, Brick never had a chance to meet her in person. And he only half paid attention when Mercy bitched about her during their poker games.

Normally, Mercy wasn't one to bitch. He usually kept shit to himself and let it eat at him like acid. But apparently Rissa's sister liked to do stupid things. Or, at least, make stupid decisions.

The biggest one being, moving across the country to

shack up with a man she met on the internet after only talking with him for a month.

Mercy said she was "impulsive."

"She lets you smoke cigars in here?" Not only were Londyn's *S's* slightly slurred, but her balance wasn't so steady, either, as she wrinkled her nose and waved a hand around to break up the smoke. "Yuck."

"Rissa know you're here?" Mercy growled.

Brick read the look on Mercy's face and hoped to hell that Rissa hadn't forgotten to tell Mercy something so important.

"No, I sent her a text when I landed at the airport... For some reason she hasn't responded yet."

Brick swore Mercy rolled his eyes.

Actually, rolled his fucking eyes.

Brick dropped his head and hid his chuckle.

His chuckle died when Londyn stepped up to the table, grabbed the bottle of whiskey sitting next to the pile of poker chips in the center, removed the cap and guzzled straight from it.

While Brick had noticed many similarities between Mercy's woman and her sister, he'd also noted that her chest was just about as big as Rissa's. And Rissa had a *great* rack.

Brick's eyes swung back to Mercy to make sure he wasn't going to die for even thinking those thoughts. He swore the man could read minds.

Luckily, Mercy was too busy scowling at Londyn, so Brick turned back to her. She had dropped the bottle for a second, took a breath and then took another guzzle.

Brick noticed he wasn't the only one whose eyes were glued to her exposed cleavage in the deep V-necked pantsuit thingy she was wearing, or the way her throat moved as she swallowed.

"Bet it would look like that if she was swallowing something else," Brick said under his breath, unable to contain it.

Next to him, Steel stifled a snort and dropped his head.

Mercy surged to his feet and snatched the bottle from Londyn. "Why the fuck are you here?" He slammed the bottle down next to him and out of her reach.

"I had nowhere else to go since you made Parris sell her house in Vegas."

"I didn't—" Mercy's mouth snapped shut and he just shook his head.

"I can't understand why she'd want to leave Vegas when Michael spoiled her. You're just a big ol' grump."

Steel jerked beside Brick, and he had to turn his face away before his laughter got him a .45 bullet smack between the eyes.

Her red-rimmed blue eyes landed on the bottle next to Mercy. "I need a drink."

"How much have you had to drink already?" Ryder asked, looking more concerned than amused.

Londyn lifted a shoulder. "A couple on the plane... And... maybe..."

"Right. We can figure it out on our own," Mercy stated. "No more booze."

Londyn's lips parted as she stared at Mercy for a long, uncomfortable moment, then, as if she shook something loose, she clapped her hands together loudly and yelled, "Then I need ice cream! Your wife have any ice cream?" and beelined right out of the room toward the kitchen.

"Wife?" Brick's head rotated from watching Londyn's thick, but luscious, ass disappear around the corner to Mercy. "You get married and forget to tell us about it?"

Before he could answer, Londyn backed that caboose right up so they could only see her head tilted back, her long hair spilling down her back and the sweet, sweet ass that, if he was a dumb fuck, he'd try to tap.

But, one, he wasn't dumb, and, two, he preferred his balls to not end up on a skewer and served for dinner.

"Oh... That's right. I meant your girlfriend, *Ryan*. Over two years now and my sister still doesn't have a ring on it."

Then she set that train in a forward motion and disappeared.

"Damn," Brick whispered. He picked up his beer and took a sip to hide his smirk.

"No wonder her fucking man left her," Mercy grumbled.

"I heard that!" came from the kitchen.

"That was the fucking point!" Mercy bellowed back.

"Can we get back to the game?" Steel asked.

"Why? This is so much better," Brick said under his breath, though Mercy heard him and shot him a look that could curl wallpaper.

"Should we just call it a night?" Hunter asked.

"I'm not leaving yet," Brick announced. "This is too good."

"And anyway..." Londyn announced as she came back into the dining room in record time, carrying a heaping bowl of ice cream and dragging a chair behind her from the kitchen. She worked it around the table to shove it in between Brick and Steel.

Giving each other a look, they shifted their seats enough to make room.

"He didn't leave me. I kicked him out." She circled her spoon around the table with narrowed eyes. "Doesn't look like any of you eat ice cream."

Before anyone of them could answer her, Mercy barked out, "Notice something?"

"Yeah, a whole bunch of panty-wetting men sitting at a table *not* eating ice cream. But, *helloooo*, I've given them up. All of you. I don't care how hot you are. How skilled your tongues are. I'm done!" She shoved a full spoon into her mouth and closed her eyes like she was having an orgasm. "Damn, that's good."

Yes, it was. Brick watched as she jammed the spoon

into the frozen mountain again and lifted it to her mouth. His eyes were glued to her lips as they parted and her tongue darted out. Then the spoon disappeared again, her eyes closed once more, and she made a *mmm* sound.

Mmm. Yeah. Fuck.

His hand dropped to his lap as he wondered if she liked to eat cock as much as she liked ice cream. Though by her curvaceous figure, he guessed she liked ice cream a whole lot.

Mercy's shout of, "No women!" pulled Brick out of his ice cream fantasy.

"What?" Londyn asked as the now empty spoon exited her mouth.

"What you apparently hadn't noticed, Londyn, is there are no fucking women sitting at this table."

She raised her brows. "Well, I am." As Mercy's mouth opened and the rest of them sat on the edge of their chairs to watch this all unfold, Londyn cut off whatever he was going to say. "Where's my sister, anyhow?"

"With the rest of the women, where she belongs."

Londyn's raised brows plunged dangerously low and she dropped her spoon into the bowl with a clatter. "Where she belongs?"

Brick crossed his arms over his chest and sat back. This was better than porn. More entertaining than Heaven's Angels Gentlemen's Club.

It was...

"Why the fuck are you here, Londyn? Did your man kick your ass out finally?"

"You know *my man* didn't kick me out. You *know* I kicked his ass out." She dropped the bowl onto the table and a little bit of ice cream landed on Brick's arm.

She noticed it, too. "Sorry." She glanced around the table. "I don't have a napkin." Then she leaned over, giving him a perfect view of her tits, and licked the melting ice cream off his arm.

Rewind.

She licked the melting ice cream off his arm.

Who did that?

But that warm, wet tongue on his skin...

Shit.

"Why?"

What? Was Mercy asking her why she licked his arm?

"Didn't Parris tell you? He hit me."

The room went electric, snapping and popping circled the table. The woman, whose mouth was again full of ice cream, seemed clueless to what she just set off.

"What'd you do?"

Londyn was now licking the back of the spoon like a cat licking its paw.

Brick's fingers twitched near his dick.

"Why do you assume I did anything?" she huffed, then shrugged with a grimace. "I shot him."

Spines snapped. Jaws tightened. Eyes slid around the table. That little tongue on his skin and on the back of the spoon were quickly forgotten.

Did she just say...?

"You shot him," Mercy repeated in a scarier than normal tone.

"Well, yes." She sucked in a breath and launched into, "I first kicked him in the balls, then I shot him."

"Get the fuck out of here," Steel grumbled low. Brick wasn't sure if the man was impressed or surprised.

"He struck you once and you shot him."

"Once was all that was needed."

On the other side of Brick, Hunter released a long "*Fuuuuck*" as he dropped his head in his hands.

Mercy's face turned thunderous. And for him, it took a lot to make it so. He was seriously pissed. The man

7

normally went subzero cold when he was angry, not the other direction.

She leaned forward, jabbing her spoon toward the center of the table. "Okay, here's what happened..."

Everyone—except for Mercy, who rolled his eyes toward the ceiling and kept them there—leaned forward, totally entranced.

"Poker night's over," Mercy muttered.

"Oh no. Fuck no. This is just getting good," Brick announced. He wasn't going anywhere until he heard what happened.

"Okay, so..." Londyn started, ignoring the scary look Mercy was shooting in her direction. "I thought he was my soulmate—"

"Brick meets a new soulmate every time he swipes right," Hunter said.

Brick ignored him and kept his eyes on Londyn's lips as she took a breath to continue her story.

"It turns out he was anything but. Because you can't have two soulmates."

"Says who?" Steel asked, playing along.

"Says me," she spouted.

Brick heard a long *trying-not-to-murder-someone* sigh at the other end of the table. He ignored that, too.

"You can't have a second soulmate when you've married your first one."

Brick shook his head confused.

Londyn turned hers to look directly at him and began to talk, like he was the only one interested in her story. He wasn't pulling his eyes from her to look around to see if that was true. Because fuck the rest of them, he wanted to hear it and she also now had a spot of ice cream on her bottom lip. And, *for fuck's sake*, he wanted to lick it off, just like she licked his arm.

But just as hot, that little tongue of hers darted out and swept it away.

"Which one are you?" she asked, her eyes narrowed on him.

"Brick."

"I never met you before, have I?"

"No."

"I would've remembered you," she stated.

Before he could ask why, Steel prompted her, "*Soooo*, you found out your soulmate was married."

"Not just married but had a family. It turns out I was his side-bitch! For years! And I never knew."

"So… he then used that as an escape tactic when he finally figured out you were a crazy bitch and decided he'd rather deal with his wife?"

Londyn gave Mercy a look. "No, he didn't use it as anything. I found out by accident."

"Then he slapped you?"

"Actually, he backhanded me."

"Why?" Mercy asked with another impatient sigh.

"Because I threw a lamp at him and hit him in the face, busting open his eye."

"Hold up," Brick said, more humor in his tone than there should be. "You find out he's a cheating dog. You crack open his melon with a lamp. He backhands you. You rearrange his nuts, then shoot him. Do I have that all correct?"

"Close enough," she said around another mouthful of ice cream.

"Are the cops looking for you?" The last thing any of them wanted was the cops anywhere near In the Shadow Security or the compound owned by the Dirty Angels MC. That could bring trouble.

"Why would they be?"

Jesus. This woman. Was she for real? "Because you shot a man?"

Londyn waved a hand around in the air. "It was just a scratch. A warning shot."

"What was the warning for?" he asked, still unable to keep the amusement from his voice.

"To never hit me again. *And* to fucking pack up his shit, get the fuck out of our house and go back to his damn wife."

"Goddamn," Walker mumbled under his breath. He wasn't the only one mumbling shit.

"Do you even know how to shoot a gun?" Brick asked, finding all of this so much more entertaining than a poker game.

Londyn lifted a shoulder as the spoon scraped against the bottom of the almost empty bowl. "You point and pull the trigger."

"That you do," Brick said around a chuckle.

"Tell me, if you kicked his cheating, woman-hitting ass out, why the fuck are you here?" Mercy growled.

"Because I don't want to live in New York alone anymore. I only moved there for him. I'd go home to Vegas, but Parris lives here now because of you. So... here I am."

"Here she is," Ryder announced loudly with an accompanying snort-laugh.

"For a visit," Mercy said. "Like a quick layover before you fly somewhere else."

Londyn dropped the spoon into the bowl and pushed it away. "Until I figure out what I'm going to do."

Mercy's lips flattened out. "While in a motel."

Those blue eyes narrowed on the big man at the end of the table. "I doubt my sister will want me staying in a motel when you have a big, beautiful home here."

"Along with that big, beautiful ring she has on her fucking finger, which you apparently had forgotten earlier."

"Oh, is that an actual engagement ring? Or a *just-some-thing-to-appease-her* ring?"

"She isn't fucking needy like you," Mercy said tightly.

"Fine," she surged up, grabbed an empty plastic cup, moved around the table and snagged the bottle from next to Mercy. "Sorry if I'm going through some tough times and I'm *needy*. I'll wait for Parris elsewhere."

"Like at a motel," Mercy yelled over his shoulder as Londyn rushed out of the room. When Brick didn't hear the click of heels, he realized she was now barefoot.

He dropped his head and saw her heels under the table. They were fucking hot as hell. He had no idea how women walked in shoes like that, but he did not care.

Then he pictured Londyn sprawled on his bed, her dark blonde hair spread over his pillow, her blue eyes on him, while wearing a black lace negligee that hugged all her curves and those red fucking heels.

Fuck yes.

He lifted his gaze from the shoes to Mercy, just to jerk his chain. "You should be a little more supportive of your future sister-in-law."

"You're welcome to go console her."

Brick pushed to his feet.

Mercy pointed a finger at him. "Sit the fuck down. You're not getting a piece of that. She's buzzed and in a position to being susceptible to your man-ho charms."

Apparently, Mercy hadn't been serious about his suggestion of consoling her.

"His perfect type!" Steel said, laughing and smacking Brick on the back.

"Rissa would kill me. After she killed you. So, sit the fuck down."

"But—"

"Sit the fuck down!" Mercy shouted. "Don't even think of going there."

"I thought you said poker night was over," Brick said.

"It is. It was. *God-fucking-damnit*," he shouted, then scrubbed a hand over his hair. "I need a fucking drink and she took the whiskey."

Brick leaned over, plucked a can from his six-pack of Iron City. "Beer?"

"I'm not drinking that swill," Mercy grumbled.

"Suit yourself," he said and popped open the can, the beer sliding down his throat. His eyes sliced to the doorway where Londyn disappeared. "We playing poker or are we done?"

"Poker," Steel, Hunter and Walker said at the same time. "We're women-free tonight, so we need to take advantage of it."

"A-fuckin'-men," Ryder said, sitting back in his chair and lighting a cigar. "And who knows when the next time we'll get to do this again. Women and children make life complicated."

"You don't even have kids yet," Hunter said. "I'm the only one sitting at this table with kids."

"Kid," Steel corrected him.

Hunter smiled.

Walker whacked him on the back and laughed. "I was starting to think you were shooting blanks, old man. Congrats."

"It's getting to the point where we only have poker games when they're all at a baby shower," Steel complained.

"As long as one of them in the sisterhood keeps getting knocked up, that should be pretty fucking often," Mercy grumbled.

"I keep saying that the club needs to start a fucking daycare," Ryder stated, watching the smoke roll toward the ceiling from the tip of his cigar.

"Soon they're going to need their own school district," Steel said.

"A-fuckin'-men to that, too," Ryder answered.

"Z's talking about the club running a daycare," Mercy said, shaking his head. "A fucking strip club and a daycare. Not in the same building. Thank fuck."

"Well, Moose's strippers could probably use it, too."

"We all could," Hunter said.

"Speak for yourself," Mercy stated.

"Okay, Frankie and I could."

"Jesus fuck, we're turning into the fucking women here! Can we just play fucking poker, smoke cigars and scratch our damn balls like the men we are?"

A few grunts were heard in response to Mercy's outburst, and Brick began to shuffle the deck of cards that had been abandoned in front of him. "I'm dealing, fuckers. Ante up."

Chapter Two

BRICK STEPPED out the front door, his remaining two beers hanging from the plastic rings hooked over his fingers. With Thanksgiving approaching, it was actually cold enough Brick could see his breath as he watched Walker and Ryder cut across the lawn to their houses in the same cul-de-sac. And Hunter headed down the dark sidewalk circled occasionally in light from a streetlamp since he lived a couple streets away.

Steel pounded him on the back and snorted, "Good game. Thanks for donating to our new place tonight."

Brick's eyes automatically went to the empty lot to the right of Ryder's house. Steel and Kat would be building there. Just a week ago they bought the lot from the DAMC with the winnings of Kat's last fight and once spring came, they'd start breaking ground. That left one lot in the cul-de-sac to the left of Mercy's house.

Diesel told him it had his name on it when he was ready.

Brick had no problem with his current pad. He was renting the Dirty Angels VP Hawk's old place in town and it was plenty big enough for him. It had a huge master bedroom perfect for entertaining the ladies. And he didn't have to worry about remote-controlled gates, concrete walls and security codes to get them in the front door. Or out of it, either.

Easy in. Easy out.

Steel's phone pinged and he glanced at it. "Kat's home. That means the baby shower's over. That also means Rissa will be pulling up soon and finding out her sister has invaded Shadow Valley unexpectedly."

"Unless she knew," Brick said distractedly as he stared at the dark empty lot to his right. *His* lot. One he wasn't sure he wanted or would ever need.

"If she knew and kept it from Mercy...?" Steel shook his head. "I doubt it. Mercy said Londyn's impulsive, so I could see it being a complete surprise. Though, if Kat's sister decided to just show up at our front door, I'd be torqued as fuck."

"Yeah, but they aren't close like Rissa and Londyn."

"Right. Gotta go home and make my Kitty Kat purr." Steel grinned. "I'm out." He jerked his chin at Brick and headed toward his Jeep, which was parked next to Brick's TUV. Even though Steel's custom Wrangler was not small, it was still dwarfed by Brick's Rezvani Tank.

Because bigger was always better. Right?

Fucking-A right.

Bigger rifle. Bigger vehicle. Bigger dick.

He snorted, shook his head at his own asshole thoughts and climbed into his tactical urban vehicle. Like his bedroom, it was also perfect for impressing the ladies.

Brick waited until Steel pulled away and hit the start button on his Tank, letting the growl of the engine rumble through his chest.

"You must have a really small fucking dick."

He had the Glock 19 that was stowed in an under-the-seat holster pulled and pointed toward the back seat and at the intruder's forehead before the last word even trailed away.

His heart began to beat again when he realized his target wasn't a threat. At least the kind that would kill him.

"You gonna shoot me?" Londyn asked.

"I should," he lowered the gun and turned around, tucking the Glock back into its holster, "for breaking into my vehicle."

"I didn't break in. It was unlocked. Unlike the Jeep."

"You were a finger twitch close to dying, Londyn." He twisted to face her again, even though she was hidden in the shadows of his back seat.

"I doubt your fingers ever twitch. Parris said you're a sniper. Bet you have some really steady hands."

"Former."

Londyn belted out a laugh. "Sure. Former. Wink, wink."

Was Rissa running her mouth? "What'd she tell you?"

"No secrets, if that's what you're worried about. Just general information. But I have a clue to what you all do... I'm not stupid."

If she was anything like her sister, she certainly was not stupid. She just did dumb things on occasion. But then, they all did. Like by him not kicking her ass out of his vehicle the second she revealed herself. Especially since she'd been drinking.

She wasn't only slurring slightly, her U's were being dragged out. However, she didn't appear to be sloppy drunk from the little he could see from where he sat.

"Why are you sitting in my Tank?"

"This is a tank? I've seen tanks in movies, and this does not look like one of those."

"It's the name of the vehicle."

"Is it bulletproof like Mercy's?"

While he loved his Tank, he hadn't liked writing the

check for it and a bulletproof model was twice as much. "No."

"Have you tested that theory?"

"Londyn, why are you in my back seat?"

"Because Mercy doesn't want me inside and I'm waiting for Parris to come home." That declaration ended on a sniffle.

Oh fuck.

"I'm just..." *Sniffle, sniffle.* "I..."

For fuck's sake. He was not used to being around emotional women. He never stuck around long enough for them to become emotional. He did hookups, not relationships.

There was too much variety out there to be limited to one type. He was sure monogamy could get boring fast.

Another muffled sniffle drew him back to the woman in his vehicle. Who was *not* a hookup, he reminded himself. "Did you finish off that bottle?"

A soft "maybe" drifted toward him.

He sighed, took a whole two seconds to decide what to do, got out of the driver's seat and opened the door to the back. With a quick glance back at the house of the driveway they sat in, he climbed in and she scrambled to give him room.

As he closed the rear driver's side door, he quickly glanced toward the house again, feeling a little bit of an asshole pucker. Was he going to die in his beloved vehicle?

He just needed to keep his hands to himself. That was all. Easy.

She was buzzing big time—if not totally smashed—on whiskey. Since he didn't know her, he wasn't sure what her current level of pickling was. But no matter what the level, he wasn't going to die tonight. There was plenty of other pussy out there without that threat attached.

But, *hell*, pickled or not, Londyn was hot as fuck. Even in the limited light of his back seat.

"Are you still barefoot?"

Her face turned toward him; her brow furrowed. "What?"

"You left your..." *sexy-as-fuck,* "shoes under the table. Did you put on another pair?"

"No."

"It's chilly as hell out here. Are your feet cold?"

"A little."

He pushed past her and leaned over the console to the front of his TUV to turn up the heat. "Are you going inside once Rissa gets here?"

"Yes. I just can't take... *him* right now. He doesn't understand."

Brick winced at the little bit of whine in those words. "What he doesn't understand is why you'd move across the country after meeting someone online."

"I've been with Kevin for years."

"Yeah, but you didn't know him before you moved in with him." And apparently, she didn't know him after that, either. But now was not the time to point that out.

She groaned. "I know, I know! I thought my life was getting on track. I thought I was finally going to be happy. He said all the right things. I thought..." She shook her head. "Why am I telling you this?"

"Because you're sitting in my vehicle and you like to talk?"

She sniffled, sighed and wiped a hand over her eyes. She twisted in the seat to face him. "My sister is the strongest woman I know. She got freaking kidnapped and could've died and didn't even cry once when she told me about it. And here I am crying about a man. One fucking man. An asshole who tricked me into thinking he loved me and that I was his one and only. And I wasn't. I never was."

"Londyn—"

"I need my sister. I need to figure out where to go from here. I have nowhere else to go and she's all I have left."

The last part sounded pained and raw, causing a strange feeling to fill Brick's chest.

It was like he almost... cared.

Huh.

He wasn't sure what to think about that. It could be just a fluke.

"Like you said, Mercy's just a 'big ol' grump.' Ignore him. I'm sure he won't mind you staying a few days."

"You're really nice."

No, he wasn't. If he was nice, he wouldn't be thinking about peeling that outfit off her and having her ride his cock in the back seat of his vehicle like a drunk chick on a mechanical bull.

Both jumped when a pounding on the window startled them.

"Your dick better be in your fucking pants," they heard before the door flung open and Mercy's scarred face appeared. "Get in the house, Londyn."

"You don't want me there."

"I sure as fuck don't want you in the back seat with Brick."

"Why? He seems nice."

Brick grinned.

Until he heard Mercy's parting shot. "So did Kevin."

BRICK SWIPED LEFT, groaned at the next photo that came up and swiped left again. He was going to have to find a new app soon, the pickings on his current one were getting slim. He'd either already tapped it or would never tap it, even with Steel's dick.

And last night's hookup went horribly wrong.

The photo and bio he'd swiped right for ended up being fake.

Maybe not fake, but the photo had definitely been outdated. And the bio was total bullshit.

The hot blonde he expected to show up at their neutral meeting place?

Wasn't so hot.

Or blonde.

And Brick even wondered if she was female.

Luckily, he'd spotted her before she spotted him and did a quick reverse, then sent a message apologizing for canceling because there was an emergency at work he needed to deal with.

He lifted his head from his phone and wondered why no one was talking around the table.

Oh, wait. Maybe they had been, and he hadn't been paying attention.

Fuck.

Hunter was saying, "So, the client whose daughter was murdered..."

"Allegedly," Mercy stated.

"Allegedly murdered," Hunter corrected. "By the husband..."

"Allegedly," Mercy repeated.

"Allegedly by the husband."

"We now have a bead on where he landed," Walker reported.

"And surprise, surprise..." Hunter added with dramatic flair.

"He's shacked up with a woman," Steel guessed.

Walker jabbed a finger toward Steel. "Bingo. Not only shacked up with a woman—not six months after his wife was *accidently* killed—but they bought a huge fucking house together nine months ago."

"Huge," Hunter echoed.

"That was quick," Diesel grumbled.

"Not really. He killed her—*allegedly*—a couple years ago, but they hooked up six months after," Hunter clarified. "And then he moved them out of state. My guess is to escape the suspicions from the wife's family."

"Still. Only six months before replacin' her? No wonder why Dad thinks it was foul play instead of an accident," Ryder murmured.

Walker nodded. "The investigation showed it was an accident and not homicide. The detectives couldn't point to anything proving otherwise and neither could the medical examiner. So, for them, case closed."

"Right, which is why Daddy Warbucks is payin' us a fuckton of scratch to find out the truth," Diesel announced. He was leaning against the wall of their "meeting" aka conference room with his beefy arms crossed over his chest and no little girls to be seen. But then, he didn't like to talk business in front of his daughters if he didn't have to.

Especially dirty business like this.

"Did he say what he'll do with any info we dig up?" Brick asked.

Diesel grunted and shook his head. "Gonna hand it over to the pigs."

"No action is needed on our part other than the investigation?" He was a bit disappointed he wouldn't be able to dust off his MK-11.

"For now? No," Mercy said.

Well, he just lost all interest in that fucking job. "Okay then, who's taking this job? And where's it at?"

"Somewhere warm," Mercy stated.

"Fuck. Vegas?" Steel grumbled and grabbed his crotch. "My nuts are still dehydrated from that goddamn heat."

"It's November, asshole. The heat's gone," Diesel said.

"No, out there your balls hang low during the day and then hide at night. It's fucked up."

"Well, it ain't fuckin' Vegas," Diesel shouted at Steel. "Jesus fuck. You guys are turnin' into a bunch of fuckin' pussies. Too much whinin' about jobs. Grow a fuckin' set or get gone."

Brick's gaze slid around the room, noticing everyone else's brows were held high, too. "Jewelee got her tubes tied so I know you aren't cranky because she's pregnant again."

"Got four fuckin' females in my house an' don't need to have six more fuckin' females in this room, too. You're makin' me fuckin' cranky."

"Okay, then," Brick said, clapping his hands together, trying to get them back on track. "Who all's getting this assignment and where's it at?"

Walker shifted in his chair. "The job's going to take a while since it'll be mostly surveillance and undercover work. We found a house for sale two doors down that isn't getting any bites, so we talked the sellers into renting it to us temporarily and leaving it furnished for now. They jumped on it since they're sitting on two mortgages. Whoever goes can set up there. Watch, reach out, make friends with the couple. Do a little recon. You all know the drill. Gather evidence and once we got enough either way, get out."

"How long is a while?" Ryder asked with a frown.

"Figuring at least a couple of weeks. Maybe a month. Could be longer depending on what's found or not found," Walker told him.

"Fuck," Steel groaned.

Diesel's eyes slid to him, his dark eyebrows drawn low.

Steel raised his palms up and grinned.

"I think it should be a couple." All eyes landed on Walker. "With the neighborhood they're living in, it's mostly couples and families. Well-off ones, too. I think a single guy or even two of us going in and out of there might catch unwanted attention. I also think a couple would be able to befriend them easier."

"A couple... You expect us to get our women involved? Drag them along for a job?" Ryder asked. "If so, then Steel and Sarah Connor would be the best choice."

"Fuck, brother," Steel groaned, shaking his head.

"What? It's a compliment, not an insult," Ryder stated. "Kat's a badass in her own right. She could handle a job like this."

"Can't be us," Steel said. "Kat's got two fights coming up in the next few weeks. She's in the middle of getting ready for those and I plan on flying to both of them with her. That means we're out."

"We're out, too, because Frankie's pregnant and I'm not getting her involved in this type of shit while she is," Hunter announced.

"And Ellie needs Frankie here to help get the Walker Foundation off the ground. Because of that, we're out," Walker announced.

"That leaves Mercy and Rissa, or Ryder and Kelsea," Brick said with relief, glad he was out of the running. Surveillance was the most boring assignment.

"No, it doesn't," Mercy grumbled, surprising them all.

"It doesn't? I doubt the boss man's going to do that job," Steel said, twisting his head toward Diesel.

"Not him. Brick."

At Mercy's words, Brick glanced up from his phone again where he had just swiped left ten times in a row. He still wasn't having any luck with finding a hookup for tonight. "Me? I'm not a couple, I'm a single. You just stated it should be a couple."

"Doesn't have to be a real couple. Men and women go undercover together pretending to be a couple all the time," Mercy reminded him.

"What woman do we know who could handle an investigation like this beside Kat? And also would be willing to put their life on hold for maybe a month?"

"If not longer," Walker reminded Brick.

Brick swung his head toward Mercy when he didn't answer. "Oh no."

It wasn't the scar pulling up the corner of Mercy's lip. Oh fuck no, it wasn't. It was a real fucking smile.

"Oh fuck no. I know you want her out of your house..."

"Yeah. It's been a month. It's fucking shit up."

"How can two hot women living in your house be fucking shit up?" Brick asked. "It's called the perfect fantasy! Especially two sisters."

"Because one he probably wants to gag but not with his dick," Steel said, then burst out laughing.

"This would kill two birds with one fucking bullet. One, we get her to play your wife and two, it gets her the fuck out of my house. And, bonus, she loves to fucking talk, so she'd be perfect to get friendly with the murderer and his woman."

Murderer.

"So much for that 'allegedly,'" Brick muttered.

"Alleged murderer," Mercy corrected.

"Will Rissa be all right with puttin' her sister in danger?" Ryder asked.

"At this point, yes. She's..."

"She's a distraction during your romantic interludes?" Steel finished for Mercy with a smirk.

Mercy frowned. "She puts a damper on things."

"What kind of things?" Brick asked, fighting his own smirk.

"She can earn her fucking keep by doing this job, since all she's doing right now is sitting in front of the TV and eating all our goddamn ice cream." Mercy's silver eyes pinned Brick to his seat. "Doesn't mean you guys need to share the same bed. You get me on that? I don't need her stay at my house extended because she's all broken up about you next. Bottom line is, keep your dick out of her and I'm going to tell her the same."

"And what the fuck am I supposed to do for those weeks?"

"Fist it," Steel suggested next to him.

Oh no. He'd find another way. He couldn't become a monk for the next month or so. "Doesn't Rissa and Londyn have to agree to this?" Brick asked, not liking this whole scenario at all. "Don't I?"

"You? Fuck no. Don't like it? You know where the fuckin' door is," Diesel said, jabbing a finger toward the actual door. "Mercy'll work on the women." Diesel leaned over the table, planting his knuckles onto it and locking gazes with Brick. "Daddy Warbucks said he heard we're the best. Let's not fuck that rep up, asshole." With that, the big man lumbered out.

Steel clapped his hands together. "Well, glad that was settled!" He surged from his chair and left the room in a hurry.

Everyone else filed out after him.

"Wait! You never said where this fucking assignment was!" he yelled to the empty room.

Chapter Three

"THE SWEATY ARMPIT OF HELL. That's where this assignment is," Brick muttered as he hauled his bags and a long hard case—which Londyn guessed concealed a long gun—onto the front porch of the two-story house.

She stood in the driveway next to the rented Ford Explorer and stared at their temporary residence. It was freaking huge.

At least for her.

The house in Syracuse she and Kevin had was half the size and the house she grew up in in Vegas wasn't much bigger.

On the other hand, Parris had owned an awesome house in Vegas. With a pool and everything. Which she gave up. To be with Mercy.

Londyn frowned. She was happy her sister was happy, but she didn't understand the attraction to such a cold, closed-off man.

She wondered if this house had a pool. She hoped so, because she packed her suit and it was sweltering hot there, even for November. However, she also hoped she still fit in it after eating her way through Parris's fridge and pantry for the last month.

This "assignment" couldn't come at a better time and she'd jumped on it when Mercy brought it up, even against Parris's objections. One, it gave her a purpose, which she needed badly right now. Two, she needed to get out of her funk.

And three, she was going to do some badass stuff with a badass hottie.

She watched that hottie as he dug into the pocket of his cargo pants, looking for the house key, noting he had a really, *really* nice ass.

And that wasn't even his best asset.

But hot men with large guns and even larger vehicles usually had a micro penis. She wouldn't be surprised if he was overcompensating for that.

And anyway, Mercy—and Parris, no less—had warned them to keep their hands to themselves. Quite a few times, actually, which, to be honest, began to get insulting.

However, it wouldn't be a problem, since she'd sworn off all men. Forever.

They were all lying, cheating dogs.

The one unlocking the door and going inside probably wasn't any different.

So, for the next couple of weeks, she and Brick were going to "play" a married couple in an attempt to get access to one of the neighbors' life and house.

That also shouldn't be a problem since she'd had a small part in a play in junior high. How hard could it be pretending to be McHottie's wife?

Except... Maybe people wouldn't believe someone like Brick would be with someone like her? Maybe they'd expect him to be with someone in shape like GI Jane similar to Kat, Steel's girlfriend.

Or sweet and innocent like Ellie, who also did not drown her sorrows in frozen dairy products.

Shit.

"Are you just going to stand there in the blistering sun?" she heard come from the dark interior of the house.

"My luggage," she murmured.

"Grab it and let's go. I just turned on the A/C to cool down this fucking sweat box. I need to close the door if that's ever going to happen."

Londyn pursed her lips and stared at the open rear hatch of the SUV. If she would've known she'd have to haul her bags inside herself, she wouldn't have brought so many.

Who was she kidding? Of course, she would've.

Like Parris, she liked nice clothes and shoes. And purses. And all the rest of that.

She didn't need to have a lot, as long as it was quality.

She frowned at her luggage. She should've asked if this was a paying gig. She could use more clothes since she left most of hers behind in New York when she threw some bags together quickly and hopped on a plane to Pittsburgh without much thought.

And now here she was. In a gated community in Florida. With a man named Brick.

That was a weird name for parents to name a baby. She wondered if it was a family name. Maybe he had a brother named Mortar.

She stifled a giggle-snort when she noticed McHottie heading her way, a frown on his face, along with a bead of sweat running down his temple and a ring of sweat starting to form at the collar of his T-shirt.

He stopped at the rear of the vehicle with his hands on his narrow hips, took a good look at her bags, then a good look at her. "They're not going to grow legs and walk into the house on their own. Moving bags usually takes a little effort."

McHottie had morphed into McSmartAss.

With a sigh she grabbed a bag and dragged it out of the vehicle and onto the driveway before grabbing another.

"Four bags," he muttered. "Totally unneeded."

Londyn sighed. "You told me that when you picked me up at the house. You told me that when you loaded them into your Tank. You told me that when we checked in at the airport. You also told me that when we waited at the luggage carousel. I think I got it now. Not everyone can fit all their necessities in a duffel bag, a backpack and a rifle case."

"It's a rucksack."

Londyn rolled her eyes. "It's a camo-colored backpack."

She didn't miss his lips twitch, or his eyes drop to her shoes. "Who travels in heels?"

"We're going to do that again, too? Like I told you the other dozen times, someone who likes to look good." Yep, his lips twitched for sure that time. "And don't tell me that men don't like to look good." She waved a hand from his head to his feet. "Just look at you. I'm sure you work your ass off to get that body."

"I need to be in shape for my job."

"Bullshit. There's in shape and then there's *in shape*. You do it to attract women. You're like a Venus Flytrap. You look pretty on the outside to lure us in and then, *bam*, we're your latest victim."

The man finally smirked, which made him look even more handsome. *Damn it.* "You think I'm pretty?"

Londyn snorted, extended the handles on two of the suitcases and began to roll them toward the house.

Until she almost broke her neck when one of her heels snapped. Large hands—not indicative of a micro penis—caught her by the elbow and hauled her back to her feet and against an overly warm, broad chest.

As she caught her breath and her heart slammed back into her chest, he released her like he'd been burnt.

"Shit. Those shoes cost me a small fortune."

"They're useless," he grumbled, quickly putting space between them.

"Well, now they are!" With a curse, she kicked off her heels and stuffed them into the front pocket of her suitcase. "Damn this pavement is freaking hot!"

"Hopefully you brought something other than heels with you," he said as he followed her inside, hauling in her two remaining bags.

She hesitated in the dark, cooler foyer, letting her eyes adjust, as he shut the door. "Sandals and flip-flops. Does this place have a pool?"

"I have no fucking clue because this isn't a vacation."

"But we should live the part, right? Married couple. Totally in love. Making goo-goo eyes at each other. Can't keep our hands to ourselves?"

He cocked one eyebrow at her. "We promised to keep our hands to ourselves."

"You know what I mean."

He grunted and pushed past her, leaving her luggage in the foyer next to his stuff. She followed him into the kitchen at the back of the house and he opened the refrigerator door.

"Someone is going to need to go grocery shopping," he told the interior of the apparently empty fridge.

"You mean the house didn't come fully stocked with food and beverages?"

He lifted his head and shut the refrigerator door. "Very funny."

She smiled. "I'll make you a list."

"You expect me to go shopping?"

She lifted an eyebrow. "Is that not in your skillset?"

"I'm skilled at having groceries delivered. There's an app for that."

"I'll make you a list of necessities."

"Do you cook?"

Londyn paused in her trek to the doors leading out to the back of the house. She ran her hands down the sides of her body. "Does it look like I don't know how to cook? How do you think I keep this figure?"

"I heard it was ice cream."

Londyn smothered her laugh and continued on the path to the sliding glass doors. She pulled open the blinds that covered them and smiled with relief. "There's a pool," she announced.

She jumped when his heat hit her back.

"Hard to miss that," he murmured.

Yes, he was.

"You swim?" she asked, now distracted by his presence so close behind her. He smelled really freaking good. Like a snack.

Damn it.

"I can manage not to drown," he answered, reaching past her to unlatch the slider and open it. The obscene outside heat immediately hit them like a wall.

She wandered out behind him. "Ooooh. It's huge!"

His step stuttered and he shot her a blinding grin over his shoulder.

Damn, his grin. How can any man be so stinking good-looking?

I gave up men. I gave up men. I gave up men.

Even super-hot, hellishly sexy, former Navy SEAL snipers.

Londyn squeezed her eyes shut at her screw up. *Ah, shit. I asked a SEAL if he could swim. Way to go, dummy.*

She wandered over the Olympic-sized in-ground pool as he headed toward the covered outdoor kitchen with a built-in grill and what looked like a brick pizza-oven.

"Guess I'll be ordering some steaks," he announced.

"Get on that. I'm hungry."

They went back inside to get out of the heat and spent the next twenty minutes ordering groceries from the nearest Publix. After that they wandered around the rest of the house, pleased that they would be wanting for nothing, then went to check out the upstairs.

After going their separate ways at the top of the steps, they both wandered in and out of the four smaller bedrooms and ended up in the massive master suite at the very end of the hall, which took up the whole second floor of the three-car garage.

The en suite bathroom was a woman's dream. Double sinks, Jacuzzi tub, huge shower with an oversized rain shower head and also a handheld jet shower head, which could be a woman's best friend. It was also beautifully appointed with soft lighting over the large mirrors to make anyone look good, even at three in the morning after kicking a half bottle of tequila and a quarter mile walk of shame.

She was claiming this room. He could take one of the other rooms down the hall since he was probably used to sleeping on a cot in a tent.

Their eyes hit each other's as they both said, "mine," at the same time.

Londyn frowned. So did Brick.

She set her jaw. So did Brick.

Damn it. They might have to arm wrestle for it.

Brick suddenly looked at her suspiciously when she snorted at her own thought. "What?"

"If you were a gentleman, you'd let me have the master bedroom."

"The key word was *if.*"

She tried again. "Shouldn't the lady have first choice?"

"What sexist bullshit is that? You women want equal rights unless it's inconvenient for you. So, no, you don't get first choice."

"Then don't expect me to cook. Equal rights and all that."

Brick shrugged his broad, *broad* shoulders. "There's a grill and a coffeemaker. I'm good."

"A man cannot live on steak and coffee alone."

"I can grill more than steak. I won't starve."

Damn it. "Should we do rock, paper, scissors?"

"The room's large. We can share."

Londyn left the bathroom with him on her heels and pointed to the king-sized bed. "There's only one bed."

He actually managed to keep a straight face when he asked, "What side do you want?"

"You want the side in one of the other rooms."

"We're supposed to be married, Londyn. You mentioned downstairs we needed to act like it."

"Will we be giving tours of the marital bedroom? And anyway, I've given up on men, including lying awake listening to them snore."

"I don't snore."

"How would you know? If you're snoring, you're asleep and unaware. Plus, we promised to keep our hands to ourselves," she reminded him.

"I can if you can."

That could either be an insult or a challenge. She hoped it was the latter but still... It was one she wasn't sure she was willing to take him up on. She glanced longingly over her shoulder at the bathroom. The one down the hall was nothing like that. This bedroom also had a cozy corner that was set up like a reading nook with a plush recliner. *And* it had a walk-in closet, unlike the rest of the rooms.

She sighed. "I'd prefer the rock, paper, scissors route."

"Don't think you can keep your hands to yourself?"

She pursed her lips and ran her gaze over him from top to toe. From the full head of dark hair—Kevin had thinning hair and was developing a bald spot—to the blue eyes and sexy scruff along his chiseled jaw, all the way to his muscular shoulders and flat stomach—unlike Kevin's slight pooch since he liked to eat as much as she did. She ran her eyes over Brick's lean, belted waist, narrow hips, and thick, muscular thighs that filled out his camo-colored cargo pants.

And that ass.

The man had an ass that might be hard to resist touching.

When she lifted her gaze, she saw his lips were curved into a wicked smile and those observant eyes hadn't missed a thing. Like her licking her lips as she checked him out.

The man was sexy as hell and knew it. There was no doubt he used that appeal to his advantage.

"I can resist touching you," she lied.

His smile expanded and warmth shot from her center down to her very *center*.

"Left or right?"

Shit. "I'll pick one of the other rooms."

"So, you lied," he said matter-of-factly with a tilt of his head and amusement in those baby blues.

"Left," slipped from her lips before she could stop it.

With a grin, Brick nodded. "Then left it is. Left sink, left side of the bed, left side of the walk-in closet."

She was going to regret this.

Oh, was she going to regret this.

The man had "player" written all over him.

And she had a feeling she was going to lose whatever game they were about to play.

———

YEP, she was going to lose the game she shouldn't have agreed to. It wasn't too late to change her mind and pick another bedroom, but she also wasn't a quitter.

Plus, she had a feeling Brick would ride her ass—and not in a good way—about it if she caved.

Which meant she was determined not to cave. Kevin had always accused her of being stubborn.

She never once denied it.

After the groceries were delivered, Brick had announced, "First thing first, we need to check out the neighborhood. If they're outside, we'll introduce ourselves. If not, when I go for a run in the morning, I'll make sure to run directly in front of their house. If, after a couple days, we haven't accidentally run into them, we'll make a point to go over there and meet them. Tell them we want to meet all the neighbors."

So, they had a plan and they were putting it into motion not even a few hours after landing in Florida.

She had dug out some shorts, sandals and a sleeveless button-down blouse to wear for their walk. Luckily clothes that would fit in this upper-class neighborhood outside of Ft. Myers. She might not be rich, but she knew how to shop a good sale.

"Can we do this after we eat? Maybe by then hell might drop a few hundred degrees."

"No."

No. Just *no* was his answer.

She was starting to regret how quickly she agreed to taking this "assignment." Probably for no pay and a whole bunch of heartburn. And she couldn't forget restless nights.

Or lots of private time with that handheld jet shower head.

But the satisfaction she got from his short, bossy "no" was due to him now being ready to expire from heat exhaustion as he walked beside her through the well-maintained neighborhood, wearing those damn camo pants and boots.

She had to say, he did not fit in.

Also, he had insisted they hold hands while they walked. Unfortunately, his palm was sweaty against hers.

One interesting point she had confirmed during all that, his hands were not small. And as they walked casually, pretending to like each other a whole lot, she made note his feet weren't small, either.

Maybe his penis wasn't so micro...

"Don't you have any shorts?" she asked under her breath.

"For running and working out," he mumbled under his.

"Walking is working out," she told him.

She could feel his gaze on her and looked up. Not that she had to look far. She was pretty tall for a woman, even in her sandals. "What? It is!"

"Walking is a leisurely activity, not a workout."

"Well, I disagree since you're sweating like you just ran a marathon." His plain tan T-shirt now had a huge sweat ring around the collar and even the fabric at his pits was soaked.

"Gated playground of the devil," he muttered.

"Just be glad it's November and not July."

"Who decided this is a good place to live?"

"People who hate snow." She realized they had circled two blocks and were now headed back. "I don't get it. If someone was a murderer, wouldn't they go into hiding?"

"Not if your victim's death was ruled an accident. And you're a confident motherfucker."

True. "Which one is their house?"

"See our house?"

Our house.

Like they were a real couple or something.

"Yes. The one that probably costs a fortune to keep cool."

"To the left, two houses."

Londyn counted to the left of their temporary abode. One. Two. Another house way too big for only two people. "Must have been a nice insurance payout."

"A couple mil."

Londyn stumbled, pulling Brick to a halt. "That didn't raise a red flag?"

"Why do you think the father hired us? It was a huge waving red flag. The previous policy was five hundred K."

"They probably spent a good chunk of it on that house." The houses in the gated community were probably close to a million each, if not more. It was certainly not a neighborhood in which one laid low.

So Brick was right, the man was either overly confident he'd gotten away with murder or he was innocent.

"I doubt it. Maybe a small portion of it on the down payment. But my guess is it's financed to the gills."

"Why?"

"He's a trader."

"A trader?"

"The stock market. Short-term. Day trading. All of that shit. He's probably using most of that money for the market, hoping for an even bigger payout. Problem is, the market is like gambling. You can win big or you can lose it all."

"What does she do? This woman who shacked up with the grieving widower?"

"My guess? Gives great head."

Londyn pulled him to a stop again. "What?"

Brick grinned. "I don't know what she does because we don't know who she is. It's only his name on the house and the cars from what we could find. It'll be your job to make her your new best friend and get all the deets."

"Deets," she echoed.

"Details."

"I know what *deets* are. Sheesh."

He dropped his head and squeezed her fingers with his *much larger* ones. "Londyn..."

"Yeah?"

"You fucking slay me."

She blinked. That was an odd thing to say. "I'm going to take that as a compliment."

"You do that."

Then he tugged on her hand, propelling them forward again.

"They're not outside," she whispered. "No one sane is outside but us. There's a reason for that."

"I have two eyes in my head, baby. I can see that."

Did the man just call her... "Baby?"

"We're married, remember? I'm practicing."

Kevin had always called her "honey," which she hated because it made her feel like they were in their eighties. Now she realized he probably did that so he wouldn't accidentally call her his wife's name. Or vice versa. *Asshole.* "What do I call you?"

"Stud."

Londyn just about tripped when she burst out laughing. "Brick..."

"Yeah?"

"You freaking slay me."

"I'll take that as a compliment."

"You do that, stud."

Both of them started walking faster in their race to get into the air conditioning since their first mission was a failure.

"We need to formulate a story," he stated when he finally let her hand go to unlock the front door. "Like where we're from and why we moved here and—"

His left hand caught her attention as he opened the fancy front door. "Wedding rings."

He hesitated on the threshold, glancing over his shoulder

at her, his eyebrows raised in question.

She shoved him inside. "Wedding rings. We don't have any. That could draw some questions."

"Fuck," he muttered as he locked the front door behind them. "Never even thought of that."

"None of you did, apparently, because none of you are married. Including your boss who knocked up his... his *ol' lady*, or whatever he calls her, three times."

"A piece of paper doesn't change the way someone feels."

"Uh huh. Just like Parris and Mercy."

"Don't knock their relationship. It works."

"Whatever you say."

She went to push past him, and he stopped her by grabbing her arm. "Do you think a marriage license makes a relationship better?"

He was making a point and slapping her upside the head with it. "Apparently not. Thank you for reminding me what a fool I was."

His grip loosened on her arm, but he didn't let go. "You didn't know."

"I should have."

"How?"

"When I look back now, there were plenty of signs."

"You didn't see them for what they were."

"Or I ignored them," she countered.

"You said you wanted to finally be happy."

Yes, but that wasn't all. "I just wanted someone to love me," she whispered. Suddenly, the sting in her eyes was becoming unbearable and she could feel a sob forming in her chest.

She was not going to break down again.

Not again.

Kevin, that bastard, did not deserve any more time than she'd already given him.

But it was too late.

"You need to let me go," she said thickly, pulling at her arm. "If you don't, you'll be dealing with a crying, overly-emotional woman in a second."

"Londyn," he started softly.

"Please. I already feel like a fool and you seeing me cry will make it worse."

"Londyn..."

Jesus. He was a smart-ass one minute, and nice the next.

She pulled her arm again and he let her go.

Keeping her face diverted from him she said, "I'm going to change and go for a swim." At least she could hide her tears in a big pool of water.

Without another look at him, she went upstairs.

Chapter Four

BRICK LAY in bed wondering how the hell he was going to keep his hands to himself. Yesterday afternoon, he watched her swim for a half hour from inside the house and when he came out to grill steaks, she had a towel wrapped around her and was curled up in a lounge chair.

She'd hardly said a word during dinner and picked at the meal he made, so he didn't push her.

When he had settled in to watch Monday Night Football, she had gone upstairs and never came back down.

She was being hard on herself for her life decisions. Or, at least, one particular decision.

He could understand that only too well.

Turning his head, he studied the way her long dark blonde hair spread out over the pillow. Her blue eyes were shut and, after lying awake for most of the night, she was finally out.

He knew it because...

She snored.

While it wasn't obnoxious, it was still enough to wake him. Especially since he wasn't used to having overnight company in his bed.

In fact, he never had anyone stay the night.

A temporary visitor? Yes. A long-term occupant? Hell no.

In truth, it was weird waking up to a warm body next to him. But if it had to be someone, Londyn wasn't a bad choice. Especially after seeing her in her bathing suit. Even though it was a one-piece, it had emphasized every one of her curves, especially when wet.

But now, lying next to her, he let his gaze roam from her hair over her relaxed face, parted lips, over the line of her throat. He paused on the slight lift and fall of her more than generous tits.

She reminded him of Rissa so much, but with one main difference. Mercy wasn't attached to Londyn. Or, at least, in the way that would ensure a long, torturous death.

When Brick had finally climbed into bed last night, he had noticed she was wearing a gold loose silky top with thin straps over her shoulders but had no idea what she was wearing under the sheet. He'd taken a peek as he lifted the covers to slide in.

After seeing the matching silky shorts that did nothing to cover her thick, soft thighs, he had flipped to his side, facing away from her.

She was too tempting.

That outfit she slept in was a good reminder that he needed to keep his hands to himself, but realistically he knew that might not happen. He wasn't sure he could stay celibate for the next couple of weeks.

Maybe he could find a local hookup while they were there. Just say he was running out for...

It didn't matter. He'd find an excuse.

Not that he needed one. They were only *pretending* to be a couple.

He also reminded himself they were on an assignment

and the sooner they could find out the information they needed, the sooner this job would be over.

He rolled out of bed and, since her eyes remained closed and she was still snoring, he didn't even bother to go into the walk-in closet when he changed for a run.

———

HER ASS WAS DRAGGING. It had taken her almost all night to finally fall asleep. But this morning she decided she'd wallowed in self-pity long enough.

She was done with it. This assignment was supposed to be a fresh start, a new attitude.

A new independent Londyn, free of men.

No man was needed to make her happy. That's what she told herself and what her sex therapist sister told her.

Though, ironically, Parris had a man who apparently made her happy.

Her lips flattened out as she came around the corner following the scent of freshly brewed coffee. A direct infusion of caffeine would be welcomed.

Not that she needed to be perky this morning, she had nowhere to go. She wasn't sure what their plans were for the day since she had no idea how to do the "spy" stuff.

If it meant being a typical nosy neighbor, she could do that. But she had a feeling Brick would require more. He wanted to make contact and that would take more than peeking out around a curtain.

The kitchen was surprisingly empty, the coffee pot full. She was tempted to grab a mug but something else caught her eye.

Moving closer to the sliding glass doors, her eyes slid to the large round thermometer hanging on the pool shed. Low 70s. After living outside of Syracuse, New York, for the past four years, she was used to cooler weather. While the

Florida heat would be overbearing later, she could live with the current temp.

Her eyes quickly went back to what—or who—first caught her attention.

A shirtless Brick was on the concrete, laying on a thick towel, doing sit-ups.

Londyn pursed her lips. Should she stay inside and watch without being detected? Or should she go out and get up close and personal?

That was a no-brainer. Outside, her view would be unhindered. She slid the door open and slipped out, closing it as quietly as possible behind her.

As she studied him while he effortlessly did sit-ups— counting out loud, no less—it hit her that it was unfair some people were that naturally good-looking. Not the defined abs, which he definitely had, or the hard pecs, which hardly jiggled as his stomach clenched with each curl up to his bent knees before uncurling back. Those she knew he worked hard for. It was the whole package.

No one should be so perfect.

She was startled out of her thoughts when he said, "Come sit on my feet and I'll knock these out faster."

What?

First of all, how could he even talk while doing that? And second, did he say he could knock them out even faster?

She moved around to the bottom edge of the towel, then let her gaze slide up his shins, over his knees, to his flexing, bulging thighs... to the silky fabric that...

That...

Those were the shorts he worked out in? Was it the eighties? They looked as short as her PJ bottoms.

Though, he looked a lot better in his. Even at that angle. *Hell, especially* at that angle.

His arms were crossed over his slick bare chest like a mummy and his eyes caught hers as he lifted and fell.

No, if she was attempting to do sit-ups, she would be collapsing back down to the ground. He had that shit in perfect control.

"Knees on my feet." He didn't even sound out of breath!

"Can't I just use my hands?"

He rose, hesitated, said, "No," and went back down.

"I'm afraid I'm going to hurt you." It wasn't like she was the lightest woman she knew. She wasn't a petite gym bunny who wouldn't crush his toes.

He rose, hesitated, said, "You won't," and lowered back down, waiting.

Londyn shrugged and kneeled on his feet. Once she was settled, he began his sit ups again, almost knocking her off balance.

"Hold on to my knees."

When she did, she noticed his legs only had a light covering of hair, the skin on his knees was smooth and warm. And every time he lifted up, his face came only inches from hers.

He also hadn't lied; he did start to do them faster. The ripples of his stomach muscles and the ease in which he counted them off fascinated her more than it should.

"Seventy-four."

Seventy-four?

He wasn't even human.

Up. "Seventy-five," he whispered as his face once again came inches from hers. She sucked in a breath.

Down.

Up. "Seventy-six."

Down.

Londyn felt a bead of sweat break out on her forehead.

Anyone seeing it would think she was the one doing the sit-ups. In fact, her stomach clenched every time he came up.

Her fingers dug into his knees as she held on and her lips parted. Then she noticed something. Something other than the single tattoo she noticed on his ribs.

"I was wrong," she breathed.

"Eighty-two. About?"

"You're not perfect." She jerked her chin towards his crotch. "You've got a scar. Right there."

High up, a thin, white line marred his left inner thigh. Just visible below the silky fabric of his navy shorts.

Now that she noticed it, she couldn't draw her eyes from it. "From when you were a SEAL?"

"Eighty-six. No."

Before she gave it too much thought, she reached between his legs and traced her finger over the slightly raised line.

All the breath loudly rushed out of Brick as his back slammed onto the towel-covered concrete. "Londyn..."

Her fingers were so close to the radiating heat of the silk-covered mound. Now she wasn't only sweating, breathing was becoming difficult.

His hand grabbed hers, pulled it away from his thigh and squeezed her fingers tightly. "Are you always so impulsive?"

"It's a bad habit," she murmured, raising her gaze from their hands to his eyes.

"That's not keeping your hands to yourself," he reminded her, placing her hand back on his knee.

"It just... drew me. How did you get it?"

"Can I finish my sit-ups first?" With that, he whipped through the last of them, finishing when he counted to a hundred.

A hundred freaking sit-ups.

He was not a man; he was a machine.

Her name murmured in his low, deep voice got her attention.

"Yes?"

"You can get off my feet now."

She scrambled to get up, but before she could, he had curled his body up again and snagged both of her wrists, keeping her from moving away. Their gazes locked and neither said a word for a few seconds.

What the hell was happening? Why, with just a look, did her nipples pebble and her pussy clench?

She needed to break free of whatever his hold was. And not the physical hold he had on her wrists. "Does Mercy have a pair of those?"

He tilted his head and a smile spread across his face, and every time that happened, she had to catch her breath. "My guess? Yeah. We all do."

"I get it now. I'm going to high-five Parris the next time I see her."

His eyes held amusement for a second, then became serious, his smile disappearing.

He pulled her right hand back to his thigh where the scar was, sliding her fingertips lightly along the six-inch line. When he began to talk, a shudder swept through her. "I was seven and thought I was a daredevil. I raced through the woods on my bike and tried to jump a fallen tree."

"I take it you weren't successful," she whispered, mesmerized by the way he was moving her fingers back and forth over the scar.

How could a childhood story, not even a good one, turn so erotic?

"No, I crashed, and the pedal sliced into my thigh."

"You were lucky you didn't crack your skull open."

"It's pretty fucking thick."

"Your only scar is from childhood? You escaped your service without any?"

"It's not my only scar."

The way he said that drew her out of her daze. "Where are the rest?" He only wore tiny shorts and nothing else; it wasn't like he could hide much.

"Those are the ones you can't see."

Ghostly fingers slid down Londyn's spine and the hair at the back of her neck stood.

When Parris hooked up with Mercy, her sister had told her that his team at In the Shadows Security was made up of men who were all former special forces. She also mentioned that they all were broken in some way. Some more than others.

At the time, Londyn hadn't thought much of it because anyone—not just men or women who'd served in the military—could be broken. In fact, a lot of people were dealing with issues.

But the first time she met Mercy, she realized what Parris meant. His scar, his demeanor. He was not open and warm. The man was almost not even human unless he was looking at Londyn's sister.

However, the man still sitting on the towel in front of her, watching her closely, had been anything but that. He also had a sense of humor, totally opposite of Mercy.

Because of that, she wondered what invisible scars Brick was dealing with.

Not that it was her right to know. It wasn't. And, *hell*, they didn't even know each other well enough to ask. She had to fight the impulse to do just that.

However, they needed to get to know each other, and soon, since they were playing a married couple to fool another couple who could possibly be murderers.

That was some serious shit.

But whatever was in Brick's background, whatever had left a mark, couldn't be enough to worry that he'd hurt her. Otherwise, that would have been Parris's objection, not because he was a player, which was what her sister flat-out said.

She also reminded Londyn—as her concerned sister and not a sex therapist—that jumping into bed with anyone right now would just be on the rebound and could make dealing with her situation with Kevin worse.

However, as she stared at the man who stared back at her, she wondered if "only sex" would still be considered rebound. Going in with eyes wide open, no expectations of a relationship at all, simply using it as an outlet to help push her toward her fresh start... in a fun and satisfying way.

Again, she wasn't a gym bunny, not even close, so she wasn't even sure if a man like Brick would be interested in a woman like her.

"Plush," Kevin had called her once. As if she was a stuffed animal or something.

But, even so, Kevin had liked the way she was and so had plenty of other men in the past. Though, none of them had stuck. Most of her relationships had been short-lived. Kevin had been the longest, and, until she learned the truth, Londyn thought he'd be the last.

She stretched her fingers along the warm skin of Brick's inner thigh, halting the movement he was making. "We *said* we'd keep our hands to ourselves, but..."

He lifted a brow.

"But did we *sign* anything?"

Even his laughter was... orgasmic. Low and smooth as it lit up his face. Which made her wonder just how deeply held his "scars" were.

"I like the way you think." Brick released her hand at his thigh and surged to his feet, hauling her up with him using her other hand.

And when they stood face to face, he tipped his down to hers...

Her tongue swiped her bottom lip. Was he going to kiss her?

Should her "outlet" include kissing?

Kissing was so... intimate.

"Londyn..."

"Yes?"

"I can see your mind spinning like a fucking top."

"I'm wondering if this would be a bad idea."

"It'll be a bad idea," Brick confirmed with a grin. "But life is full of bad ideas."

That was certainly true. That was why she was now in Florida instead of New York.

With a man named Brick.

Who she was thinking all kinds of dirty thoughts about right now.

"I won't tell if you won't," she whispered.

"You can't say a word to Rissa."

Londyn made the hand movement at her lips of locking them by turning the key and tossing it away.

"Londyn, seriously, not even a hint."

"Not even a hint," she echoed.

His eyelids lowered and his expression became soft.

"Would you do me?" She tucked her bottom lip between her teeth and waited.

At her question, his face changed again, but this time his expression became hard. Maybe he misunderstood.

She quickly followed up with, "I mean, not 'would you do me?' as a request, but would you do me? As in, someone like me?"

His brow furrowed and his eyebrows pinned together. "Fuck yes."

"Because you'll do anybody?"

He stepped back, frowning. "Have you seen yourself?"

"Yes. And I've seen you. That's why I'm asking. I'm not sure why... I..."

He reached up and drew his thumb over her bottom lip. "Who fucked with your head? Was it Kevin?"

"Truthfully, it was society. I don't know any woman who is perfectly confident with her body. Even if she acts like it, deep down, she worries. Am I too fat? Am I too thin? Is my cellulite a turn-off? Are my muscles too masculine? Are my boobs too droopy?"

"There's nothing wrong with your body."

"You haven't seen me naked."

"Yet," he added. "I saw you in your wet bathing suit and that doesn't hide much."

She waved a hand in front of herself. "So, this doesn't turn you off?"

"Fuck no. If Mercy—" He quickly pinned his lips together, his jaw getting tight.

Londyn's mouth dropped open in surprise at his slip. "You would've dated my sister?"

His blue eyes slid to the side. "Not dated."

"Oh... I see. You would have 'tapped that.'"

They slid back. "Your sister is hot as fuck."

Londyn took that as reassurance since... "We look a lot alike."

"And that's what I'm saying."

"I take it if we weren't stuck in this house together for the next... who knows when... and you saw me... wherever... you'd hit on me?"

"If I saw your picture I'd swipe right so fast, I'd sprain my finger."

Her eyebrows pulled together. "Swipe right?"

He raised his in surprise. "I thought you met Kevin on the internet."

"I did. There was no swiping involved."

"Well, now that you'll be single, I'm sure you'll be swiping."

She shook her head. "I don't even know what that means."

One side of his very kissable mouth curled. "Welcome to the world of hookups. I have a lot to teach you, grasshopper."

"I'm not sure I want to learn. I need to be happy being single."

He jerked one shoulder up. "Being single doesn't mean you have to be alone."

Hmm... that could play into her sex as an outlet theory. "You're not helping."

Brick smiled, grabbed her hand and tugged her toward the door. "C'mon. I need some fuel and a shower first."

Were they doing this?

"Really? It surprises me that a man would put food before sex." Especially a man who was familiar with the "world of hookups."

"I'm sure you don't want me passing out when I'm in the middle of showing you how much I appreciate your body."

Hmm, food first might be a good idea, then. "I can't imagine some sit-ups would tax you much. Especially when you weren't even breathing hard."

"It wasn't just sit-ups. I went for a run—"

She yanked him to a stop just inside the house. "Wait. You went running *and* did a hundred sit-ups?"

He flashed his million-dollar smile at her. "You missed the hundred push-ups."

"Damn, I'll have to get up earlier," she whispered. She tilted her head. "I thought you said you were going to run past their house this morning. Did you?"

"I did. I didn't see them outside because it was early. So we need to get on that, too. We've got a busy day ahead of us."

Her lips twitched, as did her fingers in his. "Sex and spying?"

He dropped her hand, turned toward her and cupped her face, tipping it up. Once again that smile was gone. She mourned its loss.

"Are you sure you want to do this?"

She asked, "The sex or the spying?"

"The sex. You're stuck with spying."

"It's probably not the best idea," she answered, truthfully.

"We already covered that."

"But... what could it hurt?"

He didn't say anything for the longest time. And she didn't like how serious his expression became as he brushed a thumb back and forth along her cheek. "What happened with Kevin hit you hard last night. I watched you retreat. As much as I'd love to have sex with you, I'm not sure you're ready."

"It's just sex. We're not shacking up together."

"Aren't we?" He released her and stepped back, shaking his head. "I can't believe I'm turning down sex. What the fuck." He turned away from her and raked fingers through his hair.

In one way, she was thrilled he wanted to have sex with her. In another, she was disappointed he was turning her down.

She took a quick step back when he spun on her suddenly. "We need to spend the next two weeks, if not longer, together. If something goes wrong, it's going to make this job even more difficult. You do get that, right?"

"A lot of spouses don't like each other," she reminded him.

"I don't want you to hate me. Let's give it at least a few days before you do."

"You think us having sex will make me hate you?"

He took a visible breath and she watched every muscle in his body go solid, like he'd just stepped into a suit of armor. "You might not like me saying this and this might change your mind. I rarely have sex with the same woman more than once."

"Really?"

He shrugged slightly. "Yeah."

Parris wasn't exaggerating when she said Brick was a player. He just admitted it himself. "That's kind of gross. How many women have you had sex with?"

His jaw tightened and a muscle twitched in his cheek, which was not a good sign. "How many men have you had sex with?"

Londyn raised her hand and counted them off in her head and on her fingers. When she was done, she answered, "Seven," as she studied him. Why did he look surprised? Should it be more? Less? Then it hit her. Hot military man. King of "swipe right" hookups. Her gut twisted. "I bet that's just a typical week for you."

He showed zero shame when he admitted, "It depends on my schedule."

Damn. If he was trying to change her mind, to discourage her interest, he succeeded. "You're right. I don't want to have sex with you anymore. Thanks for the real talk."

"We're stuck in this house together, Londyn, for who knows how long. I can't have you leaving in the middle of this assignment because of something I did... or didn't do."

"You think I can't handle a random hookup with you."

"That's the problem. It wouldn't be random. You aren't just a face on a hookup app. I'd have to face you every morning. You're sleeping in my bed."

"*Your* bed?"

"*The* bed."

"Basically you're saying that once we have sex you'll no longer want to share the same bed."

"I'm saying it could get awkward and we're stuck with each other."

"You already convinced me not to sleep with you, so you don't need to keep trying."

"I'm trying to convince myself."

With pursed lips, Londyn stared at him. He probably wasn't used to turning down sex. Or even avoiding it. He was right, it was probably best they didn't take it there because it could get messy. Since that was now a dead horse, they needed to stop beating it. "As much as I'd like you to stay only wearing those," she waved a hand around in front of him, "*shorts*, why don't you go shower while I start breakfast, then we can plan our attack. Maybe while we eat, you can give me some pointers on what a good spy does." She moved away from him and went to grab a mug. She hoped he had brewed the coffee strong.

"That's easy. Act natural, blend in and ask questions in a way that doesn't raise suspicions."

"I doubt it's that easy."

"You build a persona that's believable. One that will give us access to their house and their life."

She huffed out a breath. "Again, sounds *soooo* easy."

"Just be yourself, Londyn."

"You mean the woman who was easily fooled, living a lie and too clueless to realize it?" She closed her eyes and sighed. Another dead horse she needed to stop beating. She'd decided she needed to move on, so she really needed to stick with that plan. *Hell*, she might end up being good with this undercover thing and have a whole new career ahead of her. It would probably pay a whole lot better than being a substance abuse counselor. She could see it now...

Londyn Gregory, International Discoverer of Lies and Deceit.

She only wished she discovered Kevin's lies and deceit a lot sooner.

Damn it.

She jumped when a soft "hey" was whispered nearby. She opened her eyes to see Brick standing in front of her, his face tipped down to hers. How could he move so damn quietly?

She lifted her eyes to his.

"Stop beating yourself up about it. The minute you found out, you took action." A little grin curled his lips. "By beaning him over the head with a lamp and shooting his ass."

"He deserved worse."

"He's lucky you didn't plug him between the eyes."

"I thought about it but realized he wasn't worth the prison time. And I don't think I'd look good in an orange jumper. Plus, as much as I want to give up men, I don't think I can join the other side."

"The other side?"

"Be a lesbian. I mean, I have some women crushes. Don't we all? But to actually follow through by—"

"Londyn," Brick groaned. "Stop. I'm struggling with my decision as it is. Don't put that vision of you being with another woman in my head."

"Are you a sex addict?"

"If I was a sex addict, we wouldn't be standing down here in the kitchen right now. I would've dragged you upstairs the second you made that offer and—"

His gaze dropped and he blew out a soft breath.

She knew exactly what he was looking at. At his words of him dragging her upstairs like a horny caveman, her nipples had decided that sounded hot as hell.

In fact, for a split second, her brain had forgotten he'd probably slept with 4.2 million women.

But only for a split second.

"I'm gonna go shower," he muttered and took a step back. He took one more good look at her, then turned and rushed from the room.

"I'll start breakfast," she yelled.

"Give me at least twenty," she heard yelled back. "No, thirty. Fuck!"

Londyn grinned.

Chapter Five

"WE NEVER TALKED about our background. Do we have jobs? Do we leave for work every day? Am I a housewife?"

Brick frowned at the foreign object on his left ring finger. It felt like a fucking noose. "Yeah, you're a housewife," he answered distractedly. "I'm an IT nerd who works from home."

"What kind of IT nerd?"

He pulled his attention back to Londyn, who was staring at him, hands planted on her curvy hips encased in tan shorts that stopped mid-thigh. His gaze lifted once more, taking in the hot pink polo top that hugged her tits and the open buttons that didn't leave much to the imagination when it came to her generous cleavage.

He had talked her out of having sex with him, which proved he truly was a stupid ass. "I don't know. What kind of IT nerd works from home?"

She turned her blue eyes up toward the ceiling and tapped her finger against her bottom lip as she contemplated his question. "Maybe a software engineer?"

"Fuck, he'd better not ask me for help with his computer. Because then we're sunk."

Londyn shrugged and Brick watched that cleavage jiggle. Just like a bowl full of Jell-O. *Damn*, he was suddenly craving Jell-O.

"If he does, then you tell him you can't do whatever he needs you to do at his house. You need to bring the computer over here or something. Then, bonus, you have access to his files."

"I doubt he put 'kill wife' on his Google Calendar."

Londyn rolled her eyes. "Who would've expected him to shack up with his lover so soon after killing his wife, either? We all do dumb things."

Brick glanced again at the wedding band on his finger. *Yes, they did.*

Luckily, it was only temporary. In fact, their plan to head over to the neighbors had to be postponed so they could run out to the nearest pawn shop to grab wedding rings. Instead of buying her a band—since they couldn't find one in her size—Londyn moved an antique diamond ring that had been her grandmother's from her right hand to her left. It would pass for her wedding ring.

But when slipping on his plain silver band in the parking lot of the pawn shop, his chest had gotten tight. Just like the noose on his finger.

Now that they were back from their errands, he was anxious to go two houses down to meet Mr. Christopher Kramer and, most likely, his female accomplice.

While they were out earlier, Londyn had made him stop at a thrift shop and buy some clothes that were not cargo pants, camo or jeans.

He tugged once more on the khaki shorts that felt like they lifted and separated his balls. It was not a feeling he liked and worried about chafing.

"Stop fussing," she said. "You look nice and like an IT nerd. Almost..."

She came up to him, snagged the chain at his neck and

pulled his dog tags out from the polo shirt he wore, not in matching hot pink, but navy blue. *Thank fuck.* Pretending or not, he did not want to be one of *those* couples.

As she began to slip his dog tags over his head, he grabbed her wrist, stopping her. "What are you doing?"

"You can see them under your shirt. You're supposed to be an IT nerd."

"There are IT nerds who have done time in the military."

"That look like you?"

He grinned. "Maybe not."

He gritted his teeth as she finished pulling his tags over his head. Not wearing them made him feel vulnerable. So, he snagged them from her and tucked them into his pocket. If he couldn't wear them around his neck, for now he'd keep them somewhere on his person.

She tilted her head and studied his face. "You need glasses yet. Too bad we didn't grab fake ones while we were out."

"I don't need fake ones. I have the real thing."

As she stared at him in surprise, her mouth opened and then shut before opening again to ask, "Where?"

"In my duffel. I wear contacts."

Londyn leaned in, close enough that he could pick up her scent, and locked her eyes with his. "Damn. You do. I hadn't noticed. I guess the rest of you was distracting me." She frowned. "I would think Navy SEAL snipers required perfect vision."

"They do."

"Then how do you wear contacts?"

"Shit changes the older you get, Londyn."

"On you? You could have fooled me."

"My eyesight when I enlisted at eighteen, or even when I entered SEAL training, is not the same as my eyesight now almost twenty years later."

"Did they kick you out when your eyesight began to go?"

"No. I left before it got bad enough for corrective lenses."

"And that's why you left?"

"No." And that was where he was shutting down this line of questioning.

"Then why—"

"We need to get going. Let's finish this conversation about being Mr. and Mrs. before we do."

Londyn quickly wiped away the disappointment on her face and got back to the important shit. *Thank fuck.* Because the last thing he wanted to do is have a conversation about why he left the Navy. When he said earlier that he didn't want her to hate him, he meant it. And his reason why he left might not give her the warm fuzzies.

She clapped her hands together once. "Okay, so I'm the little missus and you're the breadwinner as a software engineer for a company in which their software is proprietary and you can't talk about your work."

"Perfect," he murmured, studying her. At first glance, someone might think she was a bit dinghy along with being impulsive, but she was quickly proving otherwise. But it would be best if she acted that way with the neighbors. "I need you to act a bit spacy."

"Spacy?"

"Like an airhead. All looks, no brains."

"Why?"

"Because it will be easier to deflect questions asked of you or answer them with nonsense answers. Also, you can ask them questions and they'll probably excuse some of the more pointed ones thinking you don't know better."

"Am I supposed to be rude?'

"No. We're well-off and you're just my arm candy."

Londyn snorted. "I never would've thought I'd *ever* be arm candy."

"Londyn, you've got it going on." Why she had trouble seeing that, he didn't know.

She smiled and he blinked at how bright it was just from a simple compliment. *Damn*, why the fuck did he talk her out of having sex with him again?

"How long have we been married? Are we newlyweds and can't stand to be apart?"

"No, I think we should be more of a seasoned couple."

"Do we need to know each other's favorite color? Song? How about a habit we hate?"

"No one's going to ask you what my fucking favorite color is."

She shrugged. "You never know."

"Then pick one. Same with the habit. We need to head over there before it gets too late."

"Fine. Get your glasses."

With a nod, he turned and sprinted up the steps, not liking how his khaki shorts rode up his ass crack when he did so.

He removed his contacts, which he rarely ever did, and slapped on his glasses before heading back downstairs.

The glasses, the polo shirt, the shorts, the goofy-assed shoes...

As he hit the foyer, he heard a gasp. He turned to see Londyn staring at him. "Of course you'd make glasses look hot as hell."

He feigned a frown. "Do I?"

"You know you do. Don't play coy. But you still don't look like an IT nerd."

"It'll have to do."

"True. And you have to look good enough to warrant *me* as your arm candy."

He shook his head and laughed. "Right." He held out his hand to her. "Ready?"

Londyn slapped her hand in his and nodded. "Ready."

He squeezed her fingers and muttered, "Let's do this."

"*Hoorah!*"

"No. Just... fucking... no."

————

"Let me do the talking," Brick mumbled under his breath after pushing the doorbell. Her hand gripped his so hard, he was surprised she hadn't broken his fingers yet. "Let up."

"I'm nervous."

No shit.

"Don't be, just be yourself," he told her again and shook their clasped hands.

"Shit. We never decided how long we were married—"

Too late because one side of the double front doors swung inward and a tall man, in what looked like his early thirties, with dark brown hair, dark eyes and wearing a frown, filled the doorway.

Brick slapped on a friendly smile, but before he could greet the man, Londyn spurted out, "Hi! We just moved in a couple doors down."

Son of a bitch.

"I'm—"

He squeezed her hand hard enough to make her squeak. "This is my wife... Gertrude." She squeezed it back just as hard. "And I'm—"

"My husband Seamus."

Brick choked.

The man's dark eyebrows went low. "Can I help you with something?"

"We—"

Brick cut Londyn off. "Gertie here wanted to meet all the neighbors and you're our first stop. We hope we're not interrupting."

The man studied the two of them on the front stoop, his dark brown eyes lingering on Londyn longer than Brick liked.

While annoying, he might be able to use that interest later.

Christopher Kramer leaned out of the doorway and looked toward the house they had rented. He jerked his chin at it. "You bought that house?"

"Yes."

"I didn't see them move out the furniture."

"They didn't. We bought it furnished because we recently sold our last home which was much smaller and we—"

"We upgraded, since Seamus is doing so well now," Londyn finished with a smile. She slid one arm around Brick's waist and patted his polo-covered stomach. "I'm so proud of him. He's such a hard worker."

Brick dipped his head to give Londyn a kiss on the forehead. "Thank you, muffin."

She jerked against his side.

Again, Kramer's gaze landed on Londyn and stayed there when he said, "Welcome to the neighborhood. It's quiet and we'd like to keep it that way."

Damn.

"Oh, yes. Well, we don't have children, so you won't hear us... Unless Seamus here is feeling extra randy." She topped that off with an airhead giggle and another pat to his stomach. "But I promise to keep my enthusiasm to a low roar."

"I'll gag her if I have to." When that comment drew Kramer's attention to Brick, he gave the man a knowing wink. "How long have you lived here?"

"Less than a year."

"You're newcomers, too?" Londyn asked on a super-happy squeal and a slight bounce on her toes. Her eyes widened and she asked, "Have you met the rest of the neighbors?"

"No, everyone minds their own business."

"Oh, well, Seamus and I like to entertain. With having a pool now and a beautiful outside kitchen area, we plan on entertaining more often. We'd love for you and your... wife...?"

"Girlfriend," Kramer volunteered.

"Girlfriend to join us," she finished.

That a girl.

"In fact, I'd love to meet her. When we moved, I was sad to leave my friends behind, but I'm looking at this change as a chance to make new ones. Friends more at our," Londyn leaned in toward Kramer and dropped her voice low, "level, if you get what I'm saying." She gave him an exaggerated wink.

That wink, along with her smile, opened Kramer's expression a little more. "I understand. You always want to surround yourself with successful, like-minded people."

"What do you do?" Brick asked, pulling Londyn back into his side before she licked Kramer's arm.

"The stock market. I trade for a living."

Brick let out a low whistle. "You must do really well to have a place like this. You might have to give me some pointers. I've got money I need to invest. It's just stagnating in a low-interest bearing account."

Kramer arched a brow at Brick. "What do you do?"

"I'm a software engineer."

Kramer's gaze slid back to Londyn. "And you?"

Londyn dropped her head and then gazed up at him coyly through her eyelashes. "I stay home and take care of Seamus."

That lit up Kramer's eyes like a fireworks finale on the Fourth of July.

Brick dropped an arm around Londyn's shoulder and

squeezed her tight, pressing his lips to her temple, murmuring, "Muffin takes good care of me."

"And your girlfriend?" Londyn asked, patting Brick's stomach again.

"Barb works from home as an editor."

"Oooh!" Londyn cried out, bouncing on her toes again. "What kind of editor? For a magazine?"

"Fiction."

"I have to meet her!" Londyn exclaimed, pretending to be super excited. "I love to read. Maybe she edited some of my favorites."

"Maybe," Kramer mumbled.

"Is she home?" Londyn asked.

Brick's finger's dug into her shoulder. He didn't want her to push Kramer too hard. The man hadn't even invited them in and probably wouldn't, so they needed to move slowly.

"She's not."

Londyn's face dropped. "Oh, too bad." She twisted her head toward Brick. "Honey, maybe we can have them over for dinner this week. I'd love to make a new friend. Especially one I can talk books with."

Brick gave her a look, plastered on a smile and glanced at Kramer. "Absolutely. I love to grill. I didn't catch your name."

"Chris... Chris Kramer."

Brick dropped his arm from Londyn's shoulders and held his hand out to Kramer. "Seamus Ramsey."

Kramer shook his hand. "Interesting name, Seamus."

"It's an old family name. So, dinner? Tomorrow night?"

Kramer only hesitated for a few seconds before tipping his head and saying, "We'll swing by after the market closes. Should we bring anything?"

"Just yourselves," Londyn said again with a wink.

What was with the fucking winking?

"Sounds like a plan. Okay, muffin, time for us to let this man get back to his business. We've bothered him long enough and we have more neighbors to meet."

"Please tell Barb I look forward to meeting her," Londyn said and snagged Brick's hand.

Kramer nodded and shut the door.

"Seamus?" Brick whispered fiercely as he tugged Londyn from the stoop and began to drag her back to the house.

"Gertrude? Do I look like a Gertie? That's a cow's name!"

"It's better than Seamus."

"Why couldn't we just use our real names?"

"We're undercover! And Londyn isn't the most common of names."

"Then you should've warned me, and I would have picked a more appropriate name! And 'muffin?' Who uses that?"

Brick shrugged as he unlocked the front door and pushed her inside, slamming it behind him. "An IT nerd."

"I dated an IT nerd before, and he never once called me 'muffin.'"

Before she could walk deeper into the house and away from him, he snagged her wrist and pulled her until her back was pressed to the front door.

He stepped close enough their shirts lightly touched and tipped his face to hers. "You did good," he said softly.

She gave him a beaming smile. "Of course, I did. I'm a natural. I should be an actress."

One side of his mouth lifted. "What's natural is what ol' Kramer-boy was checking out."

"Which was?"

He jerked his chin toward her chest. "Your tits."

Her gaze dropped down to her cleavage and bounced back up. "Is that a good thing?"

"His very obvious interest may give us another angle if we need it."

Londyn scrunched up her face. Which Brick had to admit, it was pretty fucking cute. "He kills his wife, shacks up with his girlfriend and then is checking out other women all in a span of what? Not even two years? That's almost as gross as the 4.2 million women you slept with."

His head snapped back. "I didn't sleep with 4.2 million women."

"Okay then, how many?"

Jesus, this woman. "I didn't keep track."

"Yes, because if you had kept track with notches in your bedpost, it would look like a beaver ate your bed. But that also means you can't actually say with certainty it wasn't 4.2 million. Hopefully, you wrapped it tight when you did them all, stud."

"I always wrap it tight, muffin. And I get tested regularly."

She pursed her lips as she studied him. He had both palms planted on the door on either side of her head. Was she reconsidering sleeping with him? Because he sure as fuck hoped so.

"Did I tell you that you look hot in those glasses?"

He lowered his head until his lips were right above hers. "Not in those words."

She pressed a hand to his chest. "I haven't changed my mind, I..."

"You?" he prodded in a whisper.

Her fingers fisted in his polo shirt and she jerked him forward. Their lips crashed together and before she could take control of the kiss, he did. He swept his tongue through her mouth and they tangled and tasted.

Removing his hands from the door, he drove his fingers into her hair on both sides of her head, holding her still and taking the kiss even deeper.

A groan bubbled up between them. He was pretty sure it was from her and took that as a sign to continue.

With one hand she continued to grip his shirt while the fingers of her other hand dug at his waist. She wasn't pushing him away. No, she was pulling him closer. He also took that as a sign to proceed.

He gave her what she wanted and pressed his hips into hers.

And that's when she pulled her head back enough to end their kiss.

"It's a shame we're not going to have sex," she whispered on a shaky breath.

Yes, it was.

His cock was throbbing, and he did everything in his power not to thrust against her. She was warm and soft, her face flushed. Her blue eyes were hooded, her nipples unmistakably peaked under her shirt.

Fuck. Way too tempting.

He had no doubt she wanted to have sex.

For someone so impulsive, she was holding out.

But he was proven wrong when her hand wrapped around the back of his head, almost knocking off his glasses as she said, "Just one more."

She rose on her toes and kissed him again.

Instead of taking control this time, he let her have it. It was up to her whether she wanted to change her mind, not him.

All she had to do was say the word.

She swept her tongue through his mouth once more and then backed off, sighing softly.

All she had to do was say the word.

While he waited for that word, he ran his nose down her jawline and tucked his face into her neck. "You smell so fucking good."

And he waited for that word.

He ran his lips over her pounding pulse, more proof she wanted the same thing he did.

But she still remained silent.

In the end, she was going to fucking slay him.

By not giving in. By not pushing him away.

By remaining undecided.

He wouldn't push her, no matter what.

Did he want her? Fuck yes.

Did he want her running to Rissa afterward? Fuck no. That would create tension within his team.

She needed to be the one to say yes. To say it was what she wanted.

And like he said earlier, they would have to agree to keep it classified.

But right now, they simply stood there. Londyn, with her back to the door, staring at his throat. And him, still pressed against her, his erection wilting more with every passing moment.

It was weird, the feeling he got when Kramer showed interest in Londyn. It was only natural he'd want to protect her. Especially from a man who had most likely murdered his wife. But it was more than that.

From the second she burst through the door during their poker game, something about her pulled at him.

He'd been attracted to Rissa when Mercy brought her home to Shadow Valley a couple years back. And at first, he thought his attraction to Londyn was because she reminded him of Rissa. But since arriving in Florida yesterday, he realized, again, it was more than that.

The urge to kiss her once more overwhelmed him and was another unfamiliar feeling that surprised him. While he sometimes kissed the women he hooked up with, he never felt the *urge* to do it. A kiss hello, a kiss goodbye, a few kisses during their "date."

This was different. He wanted her to melt against him.

He wanted to hear those noises she made with those first two kisses. He wanted to feel her fingers digging into his flesh as she pulled him closer because she wanted the same thing.

And all those wants were strange to him, too.

The problem was, not much more than a month ago, she was in love with another man. One who betrayed her.

And he knew that hurt.

He didn't want to hurt her, either. Hooking up with her while on the rebound might do that. Which, again, could cause tension amongst their team. Mercy would be pissed and so would Rissa. Mercy took it personally if anyone pissed off his woman, so that needed to be avoided at all costs.

That meant he shouldn't kiss Londyn again.

So, he didn't. Instead, she kissed him one more time.

His fingers curled in her hair, gripping it tightly as hers gripped his face. And after a few seconds she did exactly what he had hoped... melted against him. He pinned her tighter to the door to keep her upright and by doing so, there was no doubt she knew how much he wanted her. Because his cock was once again hard for her.

She groaned into his mouth and, *fuck*, if he didn't want to pick her up, carry her upstairs and get her naked.

He wanted to see her without the bathing suit. Without the silky PJ's. Without the hot pink polo shirt and boring khaki shorts.

He wanted to explore and taste every inch of her. He wanted to sink into her wet heat. He wanted to hear her cry out when she orgasmed. And he wanted to feel her ripple around him when she did so.

And if he did all that?

He might be screwed.

He didn't find her on Tinder, or Fling, or any of the

other hookup apps he trolled. Where sex was just a transaction between two people looking for the same thing.

Hello. Fuck. Goodbye.

No ties to anyone he knew. No obligation to sit across the table and eat breakfast with that person. No explanations to people he knew.

Simple.

Londyn would not be simple.

His pocket vibrating was a good wake-up call. He reluctantly stepped back from Londyn, whose eyes were unfocused, lips swollen, and that flush in her cheeks even darker now.

It wouldn't take much convincing to take it further.

He pulled out his phone and glanced at the name of the caller.

Yep. His phone ringing was a damn good wake-up call.

Mercy was calling.

Thank fuck.

Chapter Six

LONDYN SIGHED SOFTLY. Her back was to Brick, and she was trying desperately to ignore the heat coursing through her veins. But her thoughts kept going back to their three kisses against the door earlier.

During those kisses, she went back and forth whether she should encourage him to take it further.

It was like tug-o-war in her head. Or like the devil on her right shoulder encouraging her to be bad, while the angel on her left shoulder was encouraging her to be good.

But then his phone rang, and he walked away to take the call in private. From there she had gone upstairs, got into her bathing suit and swam a few laps to cool off. It helped her get through dinner and the rest of the evening while she read and he played on his phone while watching TV.

Maybe he had been "swiping right" and looking for a local hookup. She couldn't imagine he went for very long without one.

She had gone to bed before him but was too restless to sleep. Once she heard his footsteps, she had turned over and gave him her back, hoping to not be tempted to continue what they had started earlier downstairs.

They both knew it was a bad idea.

But they both wanted it anyway.

She might never get a chance to sleep with someone who looked like Brick again. He might be her unicorn.

What if, for the rest of her life, she was stuck with only Kevins? Not that there was anything wrong with a Kevin—as long as he wasn't leading a double life—but he wasn't a Brick.

She guessed men dreamed about bagging a "ten" at least once in their life. Why couldn't women hope for the same?

This could be Londyn's only opportunity. One she couldn't pass up.

No one had to know.

No one but them.

They were two consenting adults, right?

This whole sexual indecision was stressing her out more than the idea of getting cozy with and spying on a murderer.

With another sigh, she rolled onto her back and turned her head to study Brick's broad, bare back, the way the covers draped over his hips and his long legs.

She rolled again, this time to her side, facing him. She tentatively reached out and ran her fingers lightly along the deep indentation of his spine.

Muscle. Everything about him was pure muscle. When she got to the small of his back, the two dimples above his ass, just barely visible above the covers, intrigued her.

She pressed the pad of her thumb softly against one, amazed how it fit in the little depression perfectly.

Brick shifted and tensed, and muttered a "No."

She couldn't see his face, so she wasn't sure if he was awake or asleep. But before Londyn could remove her hand, he began to repeat the word over and over, getting louder each time until he breathed a final ragged, "No, goddamn it," before becoming quiet.

She removed her hand from his back and turned to give him hers again. She wasn't sure if he was awake and telling her no, he didn't want her to touch him, or having a nightmare.

But either way, it was a splash of cold water and a good reminder once again that the two of them having sex was a bad idea.

She slipped from the bed and went to sleep in one of the spare bedrooms where temptation would be a lot less.

———

Brick hit the bottom step and instead of going straight outside for his run, he changed direction and headed toward the kitchen. When he woke up last night in a sweat, Londyn was no longer in bed with him. Since the light was off in the master bathroom, he had gotten up and headed down the hallway, wondering where she had gone.

He found her sleeping in one of the spare bedrooms. Another strange feeling overcame him. Disappointment. Disappointment she had abandoned his bed and he had no idea why. While he had wanted to carry her back where she belonged, he didn't.

Maybe he'd been snoring or too restless for her to sleep.

In the kitchen, he saw her leaning back against the counter, wearing that fucking silkie thing she wore to bed that he wanted to rip off her, with a steaming coffee mug raised to her lips.

Her blue eyes flicked to him, then back to whatever she'd been staring at previously.

"You moved out last night." He tried to keep his tone even, to pretend it hadn't bothered him.

She took a sip of coffee. "Mmm hmm."

That was Ms. Talkative's answer? Only a *mmm hmm?* "Why?"

"I figured it's for the best."

"It's? Not 'it was?' Does that mean it's permanent?"

"For as long as we're here."

"Londyn..."

"It's for the best."

Her tone indicated he should leave it at that. Well, fuck that. "You haven't told me why yet." He shouldn't give a shit why. He should be celebrating the fact he finally got the big master bedroom to himself.

But, *for fuck's sake*, he did give a shit.

"Do I need a reason to not want to sleep in the same bed with a man who is not my... who I'm not intimate with?"

Fuck. "No." He studied her for a few seconds and when she didn't say anything else or even look at him, he asked, "Why the change of heart? You wanted that room, that bathroom."

She took another sip of coffee and continued to stare over his shoulder as he moved closer. "I did."

"I'll make you a deal. You can have the room if you don't want to share it, and I'll move into the spare bedroom but only if you tell me why."

She dropped her gaze to her bare feet, her coffee mug clenched within her fingers.

He carefully pulled the mug from her and placed it on the counter, then lifted her chin with his index finger.

Was she blushing?

Her gaze slid to the side to avoid his.

"Hey, the room is yours. Just talk to me." This was not a way to start a marriage, fake or otherwise. "We need to be convincing, Londyn, and you not being honest or open with me—"

"You told me no."

He pulled his head back and stared down into her face. She was now meeting his eyes, her stubbornness returning in spades.

"I told you no," he repeated, running a hand over his chin.

"When I touched you last night."

"You touched me last night," he repeated, even more confused than before. "Uh... I'm pretty sure I'd remember you fucking touching me, Londyn. In fact, if you did, I sure as fuck wouldn't have said no."

"You not only said no, but you said it adamantly several times."

During the night he had woken up in a sweat after one of his nightmares. Had she touched him while he was reliving the time he wished he could forget?

"If I said no, baby, it wasn't to you. I swear. I was probably just having a dream."

"You didn't say no until I touched you."

"Coincidence."

"Was it?"

"Do you want proof? Touch me now that I'm wide awake."

"We said we'd keep our hands to ourselves," she reminded him with an arch of an eyebrow.

"Yeah, well, we keep failing at that promise."

She didn't say anything for the longest moment, but he could see her thoughts turning as she considered his suggestion. He was relieved when the tension seemed to leave her. "Do you know you have two dimples right above your ass?"

He grinned. "No, show me where." He didn't even bother to sound convincing in that lie.

She knew it was a lie, but she played along, anyway.

And, fuck him, she wanted to touch him, so he wasn't saying no. No fucking way.

He wished he would've woken up last night when she reached out to him. But they could make up for lost time, if she was willing.

"Turn around," she whispered, her eyes no longer vacant but heated.

He was wearing only his Ranger Panties, or Silkies, short athletic socks and running sneakers, so she'd have easy access to him. And in a second, he was going to be sporting an erection, too.

"Turn around." This time it was more of a whispered demand. And that made him lose his grin.

If he did this and she touched him, there was no going back. They were done playing the game of "they shouldn't."

Fuck that.

Brick knew the moment they got on that plane together it was inevitable.

He knew the moment she agreed to share that bedroom, it was inevitable.

The inevitable was here and now.

He wanted the opportunity to show her how beautiful she was and how perfect, too.

No more "they shouldn't."

He just needed to make sure she didn't hate him afterward. And if he had to get a taste of monogamy for the time they were there, he'd swallow it down. It would be temporary just like that wedding band on his finger.

He slowly turned, giving Londyn his bare back and he waited.

Except for their rapid breathing, the kitchen was completely quiet. The anticipation of her touching him was making both his heart beat a little faster along with that breathing.

The air shifted when she pushed away from the counter. His cock twitched in his shorts the second her fingers touched his skin. She drew her fingertips along his spine, starting from his shoulder blades and moving down...

Down...

Until the tips of all ten fingers swept from the center of his back outward to his hips and lower, skirting along the elastic of his waistband.

She was torturing him slowly, almost as slowly as she tugged down his shorts. Just low enough to expose the area above his ass where those dimples were. She spread her hands at his hips and then placed the pads of her thumbs in each indentation.

"You're perfect," she whispered, just like she had yesterday during his sit-ups, before seeing his scar.

No. "If that's what you think, then you'd be wrong."

"That scar doesn't mar how beautiful you are."

"I wasn't talking about that scar, Londyn."

"The scars that make you have nightmares?"

His cock swelled and got caught awkwardly in his shorts.

Her thumbs pressed harder into his dimples. "Will you tell me about them?"

His brow furrowed. "No."

Then the pressure was gone, and her warm hands slid up his back and down, skimming along the top of his shorts. He did his best not to turn around, put her on the counter and fuck her right there.

"Do you talk to anyone about them?"

"No." They always hovered at the surface. There was no point in bringing them to the light when all he wanted to do was bury them deeper. If at all possible, forget that fucking moment. That decision. That second that changed everything.

He wanted to enjoy her touch, not remember the past.

When he reached down to adjust himself, she stopped him by grabbing his elbow. "Let me."

Let me.

Fuck.

Releasing his elbow, she placed her hands on his ribcage and then slid them around to his gut. By doing so, it pressed her chest, braless and encased in that silky fabric, against his back. His muscles tensed beneath her exploring fingers and he held his breath, waiting for her to do what she was going to do next.

She took her time running her hands up his abs, over his pecs, lightly brushing her fingers over both of his nipples. When she trailed her fingers back down, his muscles flexed and rippled as she went lower... lower, brushing over his Ranger Panties.

Her breath beat a ragged rhythm against the skin of his back as she outlined his hard length. Closing his eyes, he dropped his head forward, wanting desperately to shove his shorts down, to feel his cock in her hands.

He wanted nothing between them.

"I was wrong," she whispered just loud enough for him to hear her.

"About me being perfect?" he whispered back, trying not to groan as she cupped his balls with one hand and stroked him over the silky fabric with her other.

"About you having a micro penis."

His eyes popped open. "What?"

"I'm sorry I ever doubted your manliness."

Was she kidding? He was hard as a rock, his cock was throbbing under her fingers, and leaking, too. This was not a time for making jokes.

He forgave her when her hot little tongue licked up his spine and she sucked on the back of his neck.

Unfortunately, his cock was still at an uncomfortable angle. When he again reached to adjust it, she smacked his hand away.

"I got it," she murmured against his skin.

Right, she's got it.

When he opened his mouth to argue, he quickly snapped it shut when his shorts were shoved further down. As his cock sprang free, she "got it."

Her hand slid along his length, stroking, squeezing, making his eyes close again and he thrust slightly forward, following her slow, steady rhythm.

"Londyn," came out on a croak.

Slow and steady could be great but he'd gone to bed with her for the past two nights and they hadn't had sex once. Which, for him, was a record. One he wasn't thrilled about earning. So, slow and steady right now was torturous.

His hips jerked as her thumb circled his swollen head, spreading the precum around, making him slick before she fisted him once more.

"Fuck," he groaned. "Londyn..."

Then she was gone. Nothing but air swirled around him. He deeply felt the loss of her heat, her skin, her hand...

Until she moved to stand in front of him. Again, her face was flushed, but not from embarrassment. The determined—or hungry, he couldn't decide which it was—look in her eyes made his cock bob. Her nipples were two hard beads pressing against the thin fabric of that loose, but clingy in just the right spots, PJ top.

And, *damn*, didn't that make his mouth water.

As he reached out to brush his thumbs against the tips, she moved out of reach by dropping to her knees.

Right there on the kitchen floor.

Dropped to her fucking knees.

He drove his fingers into her hair and tugged her face up to him. The hardest thing he ever said in his life was, "You don't have to do that."

"You're right," was her breathy answer. "But I want to."

As she gripped his cock tightly once more and her

warm, wet mouth surrounded him, he decided he wasn't going to argue.

His head dropped back as she licked the tip, then sucked it deep into her mouth with her tongue swirling around the crown and down his length.

His fingers dug into her scalp, he sucked in a breath and then shoved it all back out in his attempt not to hold her head and fuck her face.

Because that was what he was tempted to do.

His fingers twitched, his chest tightened as she sucked him hard and deep, as she circled the root of his cock like a vice within one hand, while the other gently kneaded his balls.

Jesus fuck, she was going to slay him.

Right here. In this fucking kitchen. In Florida.

This woman was going to slay him with a simple blow job.

The vibration of her moan had him dropping his head forward and opening his eyes. It was then he almost lost it.

His balls pulled tight and the pressure built deep within him at the sight of her fucking mouth stretched around him. She squeezed the root of his cock tighter and began to stroke his slick length with her fist as she concentrated on the tip with her mouth.

And, fuck him, did she concentrate on it.

He was so fucking close. *So* fucking close. When he pulled her hair away from her face so he could see all of her, she tipped her blue eyes up to him.

He was done.

Slayed.

By a woman he promised not to touch.

"Londyn," he warned in a low groan.

She needed to heed his warning, or she'd get a mouthful.

But instead of pulling away, she opened her mouth and

stuck out her tongue. As he came, his hips jerked forward, painting that pink tongue with his cum.

And when he was done, totally spent, she closed her mouth and smiled up at him.

Holy fuck.

Was she for real?

Fuck the promises. Fuck his conscience.

Fuck everything.

He hooked her by the underarms, hauled her to her feet, and backed her up until that delectable caboose of hers—which he was determined to eventually explore—hit the kitchen table.

"Get naked," he demanded as he finished dropping his own shorts to his feet.

"We don't have a condom."

"We don't need one. I'm about to eat breakfast."

She grinned. "It *is* the most important meal of the day."

Yes, it was.

"I just..."

He hesitated when she did. He quickly realized what her deal was. "Baby, get naked. I don't give a fuck what hang ups you have."

"I have cellulite and stretch marks..."

"You're fucking beautiful and I want to see you naked."

"Just like that, huh?"

"Fuck yes. Just like that." He didn't wait for her to pull off her top, instead doing it for her. "Now, that is fucking beautiful." He took in her large tits with proportionately large peaked, dusky nipples. And yes, as he tugged her little shorts over her soft thighs, thick enough to cushion his hips, he saw stretch marks and cellulite. And he didn't give a fuck, because she was so much more than that. "You need to stop picking yourself apart. I don't see those pieces of you, I see you as a whole. But even if I did, every piece of you makes you who you are."

"Because you just want one thing."

He straightened, letting his gaze rake over her as she sat at the edge of the table completely naked.

Was her stomach flat? Fuck no. Were her tits perky? Fuck no. Did she have a thigh gap? Fuck no.

And all of that made him want her even more. "You're right. I just want one thing. You."

Chapter Seven

SHE DIDN'T KNOW if she could trust his words, because if she could? *Woah.* She had not expected them to come out of a man who he himself claimed to be only into one-night stands.

He was probably good at knowing just what to say. But, honestly, his physical appearance alone would get most women dropping their panties. She was sure he didn't have to work hard at it.

Apparently, he didn't have to work so hard at it with her, either. Because here she was, sitting on the edge of the kitchen table as naked as the day she was born.

In the daylight. No mood lighting. Nothing.

All her. All Londyn. With nothing to hide.

She gasped when he wrapped his arms around her thighs and jerked her to the very edge of the table, spreading her thighs wider and planting her heels at the corners. Curling his fingers around the front of her neck, he pushed her gently until her back was flat to the table.

She felt like a turkey displayed on Thanksgiving Day. Especially when he stood at the end of the table, staring down at her, his blue eyes darker than normal as he took her all in.

He took his time doing so, too.

His thumb swept over the pounding pulse in her neck. Once, twice. She didn't realize how tightly he was holding her there until he released his grip and her breathing came easier.

His fingers trailed lightly from the hollow of her throat, between her breasts, over her belly and barely skimmed the top of her mound.

Then they were gone. He moved only far enough to yank out a chair from the side of the table and pull it up.

As if he was about to eat that turkey dinner.

Her thighs quivered and her breath quickened, her nipples pulled tight as he took his time settling into that chair and scooching it forward, all the while keeping their eyes locked.

His eyes slid from hers to what was displayed before him. She was open, already drenched and so ready for his touch. Even though she expected it, when it came, she still jerked anyway. One finger slid through her wetness, separating her for only a moment, then that, too, was gone.

She jumped again when his hands curled firmly around her ankles and he set her bare feet on his shoulders. "Keep them there."

Holy smokes, the light-hearted, humorous man was gone. The way he gave that order, she expected him to get out a ball-gag and handcuffs next.

At that imagery, the table shuddered when she did.

She was not into kinky play, but this man might be able to talk her into anything.

Which was stupid.

She squeezed her eyes shut. Kevin had talked her into moving across the country to be with him. And foolish her, she had.

Lips pressed to the top of her mound made any thoughts of that deceiving asshole disintegrate. Warm breath swept along her heated skin, then just the tip of his tongue touched her.

There. Right there. Lightly on her clit. Just a tease.

What the hell was he doing? Was he trying to kill her?

She groaned, tempted to grab his head and shove him against her to get his meal started.

Her head shot up and her eyes popped open when that very tongue slipped between her folds.

Then the man got serious at satisfying his hunger.

His fingers dug almost painfully into her thighs, keeping her spread open with his unspoken demand not to move. The barely-there beard along the line of his jaw scraped her inner thighs as his tongue delved deep within her, working her into a frenzy.

Holy smokes, he was good with his mouth. So freaking good. He knew when to suck, flick, nibble or lick. He varied the pressure. He...

Oh.

His name got caught in her throat as he gave her clit no mercy.

Her thighs began to shake as she got closer and closer, the swirl of heat building low in her belly, her core clenching.

And just when she thought she was close to coming, she whimpered when he stopped and took one of her folds into his hungry mouth, sucking it hard, before doing the same with the other.

Then he hit her center again, flicking her clit with only the tip of his tongue before scraping his teeth over the sensitive nub.

As much as she expected the orgasm which had been building, she wasn't expecting the intensity of the one that ripped through her, starting at her clit and moving outward.

Her palms slammed on the table as her hips shot up, dislodging his mouth. But he didn't move away. Even as she came back down, riding the waves to the very end, trying to catch her breath and her scattered thoughts...

He remained.

Warm breath swept over her swollen and sensitive flesh. He kissed one inner thigh and then the other before lifting his head.

Londyn tilted her own enough to see his lips shiny, his eyes focused on her. And when he rose to his feet, she couldn't miss that he was ready to do more.

So was she.

"How was breakfast?"

One side of his mouth pulled up. "Fucking delicious."

She jerked her chin toward his erection. "Are you still hungry?"

He wrapped his fingers around the base of it and squeezed, making the veins protrude even more than normal. "Fuck yes."

Her words caught in her throat and she cleared it to ask, "What are you going to do about it?"

He gave his cock one long stroke, then leaned over the table, between her thighs, until his face was right above hers.

As her lips parted, his dropped and he claimed her mouth. She tasted herself on his lips and tongue. A tongue which tangled with hers for a few seconds, before he moved away.

The disappointment from him ending the kiss so soon quickly disappeared when his lips slid along her jaw and down her throat to the hollow. Once his face was clear from her neck, his hand replaced it. His warm, long fingers wrapped snuggly around the front of her throat as he moved lower, no longer kissing or licking but biting instead.

Sharp nips began across both collarbones, down her chest, until each playful bite turned into him sinking his teeth into her flesh even harder. She couldn't be sure if he was leaving marks behind, because his head hid her view, but she could feel it. Just when she thought he'd get to the point where she'd have to tell him to stop, he'd let up and move to another spot along the curves of her breasts and do it again.

It wasn't just the biting which made her think Brick had a little bit of a freaky side, it was the pressure he put on her neck. Not quite cutting off her air, but his grip was tight enough for her to be super aware of what he was doing.

She wondered how far he would push it.

She wondered how far she would let him.

So far, she liked everything he was doing and what he had done.

His teeth scraping sharply over the tip of her nipple had her crying out and her back bowing off the table. When he sank his teeth around her areola and bit down even harder, she whimpered and grabbed his head.

She couldn't take any more.

But crazy enough, she wanted more anyway.

"The other," she managed to get out.

He lifted his head for only a split second, then did the same to her other nipple. The breath rushed out of her and she groaned. The man was bringing out the freak in her, too. And amazingly enough, she loved every second of it.

"Again," she urged, the word coming out a bit strained due to the pressure on her throat.

He willingly complied.

"Anything you want, say the word," he murmured against the curve of her breast, which stung from his bites.

Her nipples were so hard, they ached painfully.

Anything she wanted, he said she only needed to say the word. She was never one who liked to ask, she always assumed men knew what a woman wanted.

Maybe that was wrong.

"More."

His head lifted slightly, and his blue eyes hit hers. "More of what?"

"You."

With a serious face, he straightened between her thighs, pressing his fingers firmly into her knees and spreading them even wider. "Stay right where you are. Don't move. Don't cover yourself up. Don't hide from me."

Okay, then. She could only assume that meant she was getting more of him but in a different manner than how she'd already had him. And that was confirmed when he turned and walked away.

Totally freaking naked.

Damn. Those sexy lower back dimples did not even do the rest of his backside justice. A perfectly muscular ass sculpted by running, push-ups, sit-ups and who knew what else.

Had she won the man candy lottery? Won a stud jack-pot? Won badass bingo? She had to have won *something* for this to be happening.

She held her breath as she heard him run up the steps.

Run. Up. The. Steps.

Naked. With an erection.

That had to hurt.

She was also sorry she missed the show.

But she made sure not to miss him returning. Gloriously naked. His erection bobbing wildly with each long and determined stride back to her.

Within his fingers, he carried the reason he ran upstairs. A necessity to take this further.

As he stood tall at the end of the table, she cupped her breasts and ran her thumbs over the pointed tips. They ached once again for his touch, his mouth and his teeth. But the ache deep inside her was much stronger. She needed him there, too.

She hadn't wanted a man so badly since...

Never.

While she had loved Kevin, she had never gotten this wet for him. She had never desired him to the point of thinking she might die unless she had him.

Maybe it was because this morning they were taking their time getting to the main event. This wasn't a typical crawl into bed, have sex, and then go to sleep deal.

Or maybe it was because Brick knew what he was doing.

The sex with Kevin hadn't been bad. It had been comfortable.

Nothing Brick had done so far had been exactly comfortable. In fact, it had been the opposite. He had pushed her boundaries. Not a lot, but enough for her to realize there was so much more she could explore. More she could learn about herself. Even at thirty-three. Even after being with seven men.

And since she wouldn't get a chance to explore it all with Brick in the short amount of time they had together, she would do her damnedest to find the right man in the future to take that journey with her. No more rushing into relationships because she thought that was where she should be at this point in her life.

No more settling because she thought it was time to settle.

Brick was proof settling wasn't for everyone. He enjoyed a buffet instead of the same meal night after night.

Could the saying "variety is the spice of life" also be true when it came to sexual encounters? Maybe she'd have to consult with her sex therapist sister.

The tear of the condom wrapper brought her back to the moment. He slightly dipped his head for only a second before lifting it again and catching her eyes as he rolled the condom all the way to the thick root.

How could that simple action send heat surging through her?

Once he was done, she expected him to step forward. To stand at the end of the table. To take her on that table the same way he had while he "ate." But he surprised her by pulling the chair away and sitting in it instead.

"Londyn."

She rose to her forearms when he said her name. His voice, huskier than she was used to hearing, caused goosebumps along her heated skin.

Damn. He was so unbelievably handsome.

And, of course, he looked not only natural, but comfortable in his own skin, simply sitting naked in a kitchen chair. "Come here."

Those two words—two simple words and the way he said them—caused a gush of wetness.

She knew what he wanted. "You expect that chair to hold the two of us?"

Not only was his voice huskier than normal, but so was hers.

"Come here." Again a demand, not a suggestion.

But still... "The chair—"

"If you're worried, you're tall enough so you won't have to put all your weight on me."

True. "You'll cushion my fall if it breaks," she warned. "You could die."

"It's not going to break."

"But—"

"Prove me wrong."

Damn. His confidence was sexy as hell. She was sure her hesitation was not.

Why was she hesitating anyway? Screw it. If Brick was crushed to death, he knew the risk when he sat in the chair and invited her to join him.

"If you insist," she mumbled, pretending what she was about to do was a sacrifice when it was anything but.

When he held out his hand, she only considered it for a fleeting moment before placing hers in his. He helped pull her off the table until she stood in front of him.

It was the strangest feeling, just standing naked in a kitchen. Her whole life, she never flaunted her body. She was only naked when she needed to be. Showers, changing clothes, sex. And sometimes not even then.

She learned to hide or camouflage the parts of her she hated the most.

But the way he was looking at her right now... It chased away any instinct to cover herself.

"Fucking beautiful," he murmured, squeezing her hand and pulling her forward.

Those words, which sounded genuine, helped, too.

"Have you seen yourself?" she whispered.

He grinned and tipped his head toward his lap. "Yeah. I see how hard I am for you."

Okay, not quite romantic, but still very hot.

He placed the hand he was holding on his shoulder and waited.

She pulled a slow breath in through her nose and quietly released it between just barely open lips. And then she moved.

Straddling his thighs proved to be difficult at first because not only did he have thick ones, he had his knees apart and his feet planted on the floor.

His hands held her hips as she shifted enough to where she fit. *They* fit. Then his fingertips pressed into her, she assumed as encouragement. Or a way to tell her to hurry.

But she wasn't rushing this. She was going to savor every damn second.

Brick was her unicorn, and this would be a ride of her lifetime.

"Londyn... anytime now before you truly fucking kill me and not from the chair collapsing."

She swallowed down the apprehension of them taking this irreversible step. One they wouldn't be able to erase if things went wrong. "Are you sure this is a good idea?"

"Line me up." Again, a demand and not a suggestion.

Well, that answered that.

She closed her eyes for only a second before opening them and meeting his, which seemed hyper-focused on her. When she noticed a muscle tick in his jaw, she realized this had to be torture for him. She reached between them, wrapped a couple fingers around his hot, hard length and once she had the tip right where it needed to be, he pushed her down using her hips.

She made sure to plant her bare feet on the tile floor, giving her total control of the depth and speed, before taking her time lowering herself all the way down. Little by little he filled her, stretched her. And the more he did, the more she got the urge to wildly ride him. To just take what she wanted from him, using his cock to get herself off.

She struggled to remain still once he was fully seated. Her eyelids flickered shut as she savored that full feeling. Of being connected with another person. Something she missed and longed for.

A sharp smack to her ass cheek had her eyes popping open, as well as her mouth.

"If you're just going to sit there, you're going to end up back on that table and lose all the control I'm currently giving you."

Well, then.

He was *giving* her the control. That meant he normally liked to keep it himself. Which, after this morning, shouldn't surprise her. But what it did do was make her blood rush at the thought of totally letting go and letting him do anything he wanted with her.

Anything.

The thought should scare her, but it excited her instead.

This was all so crazy. So unexpected.

She assumed he was mild-mannered. Not intense like Mercy. But maybe she was *oh so* wrong.

Using her toes, she lifted herself slowly, feeling a rush with him sliding through her slickness until he was almost free. Then she took her time lowering herself again, appreciating every fraction of an inch until there was nowhere left to go. She settled on his lap, giving him a little more of her weight, and he couldn't get any deeper.

Pressing against her toes again, she began to rise and fall, increasing the pace, allowing herself to let go as much as she could with her being the one in control.

Her breathing became shallow and sped up as she rode him faster and faster until his fingers dug harshly into her hips, holding her still against his lap like it was too much.

So instead, she ground herself against him, then rocked back and forth, making sure he hit the right spots. A little noise escaped her, and her head fell back as she began to grind even harder.

This position made him so deep it was almost uncomfortable, but she couldn't get enough. She needed more.

"Ask me that again," he growled.

Her head dropped forward and she hesitated. "What?"

"Ask me again whether this is a good idea."

He got no argument from her. Whether they'd regret it later, she didn't know. But right now?

It was the best damn decision she ever made. Or at least, close to it.

"Fuck me until you come. Then I'm taking over."

The rough in his voice almost made her come right then. Almost. But what it did do was make her clench tightly around him which, in turn, caused a noise to come from him and his fingers to dig even harder into her hips to make sure she couldn't move.

After a few seconds, he released his grip and she was free to move again, her rhythm compounded by their rapid breathing. She had both hands planted on his shoulders, using them and her feet on the floor as leverage.

And then she was there. Her second orgasm this morning. She cried out as her toes curled against the tile and her core convulsed around him.

"Fuck, I can feel that," he groaned into her neck. "I can feel all of that. So fucking wet."

He pulled his face out of her neck and kissed her hard, holding her down on his lap and grinding against her sensitive clit. She gasped into his mouth and he said against her lips, "My turn."

His turn.

Without any kind of warning, he grabbed a handful of her hair at the back of her head and yanked it back, fireworks exploded along her skull. He again shoved his face into her neck but this time planting his mouth against her arched throat, sucking and scraping in what felt like a vulnerable spot. The line of her pulse which hadn't slowed one bit. And now with what he was doing, it wouldn't.

With one arm hooked around her ass, he wedged his hand between them, snagging her nipple and twisting it between his fingers, then he began to lift off the chair, driving his cock hard and deep into her.

If he wanted her to come again, he was going to succeed. This was not some gentle type of making love. This was skin-slapping, raw fucking. Each time he powered up, he grunted against her damp skin.

And it wasn't long before the build-up of another orgasm overtook her. As soon as it did, he settled back in the chair and released her hair.

Their eyes met and held, and he wore a slight grin.

Which was quickly lost when she squeezed his cock tight and grinned instead.

"You want to play? Let's play."

Holy smokes, if that didn't make her melt into a puddle of goo.

He released both her nipple and her ass and lifted his hand to his lips, his eyes never leaving hers.

He sucked the middle one—the longest of his fingers—all the way into his mouth, worked it around and when he slid it back out, it was wet.

She'd been rocking slightly back and forth on his lap after riding out that last orgasm, but her rhythm stuttered when both hands disappeared behind her and her breath caught as he smacked one side of her ass hard enough to sting. When he spread apart both of her cheeks, she felt the wet finger slide down along her crease, pausing, touching, then circling and pressing inward.

This should not shock her, either.

She loved ass play and only a couple of the men she'd been with in her past had been bold enough to do it, which surprised her.

The more he played with her there, the harder she ground against him, drawing a whimper from her. It had been a long time since anyone had paid attention to her there.

And she missed that, too.

But he wasn't giving her enough. He wasn't giving her what she wanted.

"Yes," she whispered. "Yes, please."

"More?"

"Yes."

"How much more?"

"Everything."

Pushing up on her toes, she pulled free of him, giving

him space to drag his finger through her wetness before putting the end of his finger at her rear entrance again.

"Keep it there. Give me everything." She reached between them, lined up his cock, held it in place, and when she lowered herself back down, she relaxed her anus enough to allow him to slip his finger inside.

God, he was now filling her up in both places.

She had missed this; she didn't realize how much until now. Kevin wouldn't entertain the idea and she had no idea why. So, she regretfully went without.

But now, Brick was willing to do things others might not.

"Londyn," he groaned against her throat. He moved to where her shoulder met her neck and sucked her skin hard enough to leave a mark.

"Brick, fuck me."

She drove herself down to meet every one of his upward thrusts, riding his finger and his cock at the same time.

But she still needed more. She needed everything.

Grabbing his face and pulling it from her neck, she took his mouth. They both groaned as he took control of that kiss, only ending it when both needed to catch their breath. She whispered against his lips, "Another one."

He pulled his head back and searched her face, his expression cautious. "Have you done this before?"

"I love anal."

His whole body jerked, and his blue eyes widened, which pulled a smile from her. "Holy fuck, woman, who are you?" he murmured. "It would be better with lube."

"Next time."

Their gazes locked and, after he schooled his face, he gave her a sharp nod. "Give me your mouth."

She did. And during the onslaught with his tongue, he worked a second finger inside of her.

She appreciated that he was gentle and did it carefully.

But the feeling was amazing as she rode him until they both came.

After that last grunt, the last twitch of his cock, the last ripple of her orgasm, she collapsed against his smooth, warm, but damp, bare chest. Putting her mouth to his ear, she whispered, "Best. Breakfast. Ever."

His chuckle vibrated through her as he gave her ass cheeks a final squeeze and planted a kiss on her temple. "I have a feeling brunch will be even better."

Chapter Eight

BRICK CAME around the corner and slid to a stop as he caught sight of Londyn bending over in front of the oven.

Fuck yes.

He had taken that ass earlier. And he couldn't wait to do so again. Her bending over like that and tempting him wasn't helping him be patient. But they couldn't spend the day in bed, as much as both of them had wanted to, because they had guests arriving soon.

Those guests were the reason they were in this house in Ft. Myers. The reason they were in Florida at all. The reason they were shacking up.

It wasn't for the sex, as good as it was. It wasn't to discover how high Londyn's freak flag few.

It was because they had a job to do.

And he needed that tacked onto his forehead. Or his balls.

Londyn straightened and placed a tray of what looked like cookies on a metal rack. She removed the oven mitt and threw it on the counter before glancing over her shoulder in his direction.

Her dark blonde hair was piled on top of her head, but it wasn't neat. It was a sexy mess with loose strands falling around her flushed face. He had to assume that flush was from the heat of the oven and not her uncontrollable desire to fuck him in the kitchen again.

His feet had a mind of their own as he crossed the kitchen.

She didn't move. She didn't turn around. But her blue eyes were locked on him as he approached, and a small smile curled the corner of her lips.

Lips he wanted to see wrapped around his cock again. And soon.

He stepped into her, pressing his chest against her back and enveloped her in his arms. He cupped both of her tits over the pink tee she was wearing, testing their weight in his hands while kissing the side of her neck before nibbling down its length.

"*Mmm.* You smell so fucking good."

Some strands of her hair tickled his cheek when she tilted her head to give him better access to the delicate line he was snacking on. "It's the vanilla. I always dab on a bit when I bake. I love the smell."

"Makes me hungry."

"We don't have time to satisfy your insatiable hunger."

"I didn't hear you say no earlier. 'Cause if you did, I missed it with all that groaning, moaning and your cries of 'Brick!'"

She tipped her head forward, her body shaking with silent laughter. "I need to stop telling you how perfect you are because you're full of yourself enough as it is."

"You were so full of me," he huffed. "Are you sore?"

She shook her head, then leaned it back into his shoulder. "No, it's been a while for me, but I'm fine."

He'd been with a lot of women over the years and

because most were just hookups, he didn't usually suggest anal. That took more time and prep than he wanted to spend with them. On the other hand, he also didn't turn it down when it was the woman who asked for it. The ones who did usually loved it and came with plenty of experience. He didn't have to go slow and be as careful with them.

After they had eaten a real breakfast this morning, they had moved upstairs to work on "brunch." Even though she claimed she loved it, Brick had taken his time with her.

And, *hell*, she not only loved anal, she could bake cookies. Was there a more perfect woman than that?

The woman standing in his arms kept surprising him.

He leaned his chin on her shoulder and peeked at the tray. "Please tell me those are chocolate chips and not raisins."

"Who in their right mind puts dead grapes in cookies?"

"Fuck, woman, you just stole my heart."

After turning in his arms, she slipped a hand between them to grab his cock over his jeans. "I don't want your heart. I just want this."

"And you call me insatiable."

She arched an eyebrow at him. "Are you complaining?"

He grinned. "Fuck no. I guess I better load up on carbs at dinner."

"Good idea, Navy boy, you're going to need it."

"Why did we waste two nights?" he muttered under his breath.

She shrugged one shoulder. "Because we were trying to be good."

"We were not only good, we were great," he announced before kissing the tip of her nose and letting her go.

If he kept standing there, he was going to shovel down a half dozen cookies and then fuck her right there on the floor in the crumbs.

He needed some distance. But, unfortunately, that distance made him more aware of what she was wearing.

Besides the pink V-necked tee that emphasized her curves, she wore soft cotton grey shorts which clung to her thighs. She was not short, and her legs were long and smooth. He needed to spend more time between them later tonight.

But now was not the time, since Kramer and his woman were coming over for dinner. Brick had to prepare the steaks and figure out whatever else they were going to serve the couple.

Reaching around Londyn, he grabbed one of the warm cookies off the tray before she could smack him away. He tucked it in between his teeth as he headed toward the fridge.

He quickly scarfed down the warm cookie and it was crazy good. Soft and chewy, the chocolate chips still hot and sweet on his tongue. Like Londyn.

He mentally groaned at that thought which reminded him of when he was a teen with raging hormones.

Grabbing the four remaining steaks from the refrigerator, he took them to the counter so he could season them.

"You'll probably spot it so I'm telling you first. I set up my rifle and scope in the spare bedroom at the end of the hall. It's on a tripod, so be careful. In fact, just stay out of that room. Rifle's loaded."

"For what?"

"That room has the best view of Kramer's backyard. I'll be able to do some surveillance from there. From what I could see, their backyard is set up like ours."

Ours.

Personal, not general. Like they were setting up a life together, not just playing a part.

Merely a slip of the tongue.

"I doubt they spend a lot of time out there."

He shrugged. "When they're out back, I can observe. And I can also see into one of their windows. Unfortunately, the house next door blocks the rest of them on that side."

"Wouldn't surveillance be easier by bugging their house?"

"It would be, if we had the equipment with us. But we don't and I'm not the expert on planting bugs."

"What are you the expert on?"

"Killing bugs."

"Like an exterminator."

She had no idea. "Something like that."

She glanced at the clock on the microwave above the stove. "I need to change before they get here."

"You look beautiful the way you are."

Her hand automatically went to the top of her head and it wasn't her mouth that smiled but her eyes. "I'm a mess."

"I know we're just sitting outside and grilling, but if you're going to change, then dress to kill. I'm not talking an expensive outfit, or pearls and heels. I'm talking *sexy*." As soon as he said that he regretted the words that turned her expression to suspicious.

"Why?"

He turned away from her to dig through one of the cabinets for spices. "Just do it. I want to keep Kramer on the hook."

"Wait. Am I the hook?"

"I'm thinking you will be. But we'll know better after tonight, if you cooperate."

"So, should I flirt with him? In front of Barb? That's kind of gross."

He finished shaking the salt on one side of the steaks and twisted his head to look at her. "No, not with him."

She squeaked out, "With Barb?"

He snorted and ground fresh black pepper over the platter of meat next. "With me."

"I'm supposed to flirt with you? My own husband?"

He put the grinder down and turned, leaning his hip against the counter. "Londyn, trust me. A wife flirting with her husband, showing everyone how happy and in love she is, how much she still wants to jump his bones after being together for years, makes the rest of us with functioning dicks want that. No, not 'that,' *her*. It's hot as fuck. We all want a woman who can't resist her man after ten years."

"Ten years?"

"Yeah, we've been married ten years."

"Glad we cleared that up."

He laughed. "Just trust me."

"You sure my fawning all over you won't just be for your benefit?"

"Oh, I'll benefit, too." But Londyn would be the cheese in the trap to help catch Kramer.

Unfortunately, he was feeling the snap of that trap himself. It was rare that he wanted to sleep with a woman more than once. Twice was usually his limit.

Three times? Never.

Three times makes it more than just a random hookup, it made it a "thing." And "things" tended to get messy.

Did that make him a dick? He mentally shrugged. He always made it clear he wasn't looking for long-term. Or even short-term. His bio on every app stated how he was only looking for "a good time." Minus the fun and friendship.

No deep conversations, no sharing of personal stories, no morning breath or awkward goodbyes.

None of that. He wasn't wired that way.

Though, his wires seemed to be a bit crossed, because tonight he would insist Londyn come back to their bed. His bed. *The* bed. *Damn it.*

He hoped after this morning's activities and discoveries, she wouldn't refuse.

She couldn't say no after that, could she?

Was she still talking? Her mouth was moving but he had no idea what she was saying because he was distracted. About earlier, about later. And especially with right now with what she was wearing. It wasn't even meant to be sexy. It was just basic cotton shorts and a tee.

But she probably had no idea how those little gray sweat-shorts hugged the curves of her ass and thighs.

He shook his head to clear it, struggled to pull his gaze from her and turned to face the steaks in an attempt to collect his scattered brain cells. Bracing his hands on the edge of the counter, he dropped his head and closed his eyes, unable to fight the memory. The one when he was deep in her ass and she was loudly encouraging him to take her harder.

He hadn't.

Not because of his concern of causing her discomfort, but because he didn't want to blow his load in thirty seconds flat.

So, using the excuse of not hurting her, he took his time, enjoying every fucking second, wishing it would never end. But all good things came to an end eventually.

Not "good," great. Because hearing and watching her reactions...

Fuck.

It was great. Better than great.

The best.

Between those shorts, the press of her nipples against the thin cotton of her shirt, and that hair he wanted to grab in his fist—all on top of the memory—blood surged to his dick. He set his jaw. "Londyn, go upstairs and do what you need to do. Otherwise, I'm going to season you instead of these steaks."

She gave him a warning, too, but hers came out a bit huskier than his. "Don't eat my cookies."

It was on the tip of his tongue to tell her he was going to eat her cookie later. Again reminding him of when he was a teen boy with out of control hormones.

He lifted his head once she left the kitchen, removing the temptation of everything that was her from within his reach. Just like those warm cookies sitting on the counter.

The cookies he could resist.

He wasn't so sure about Londyn.

———

BRICK SIZED up Kramer over the lip of his beer bottle as he lifted it to his mouth. He'd been nursing it for a while, and it was disgustingly warm, but he wanted to appear as if he was drinking as much as their new neighbor.

The more beer Kramer drank, the more likely he would loosen up. And while he was starting to, the man had a seriously long stick up his ass when it came to Brick. Not so much when it came to Londyn.

They had eaten, passed around the plate of cookies and, since the day's heat had waned a bit, now relaxed outside by the in-ground pool under the covered lanai which spanned the outdoor kitchen area where he had grilled the steaks.

The ungodly humidity had cemented his ball sac to his left thigh in the bullshit khaki shorts he'd put on before they'd arrived. He'd also removed his contacts and donned his glasses to once again play the part of IT nerd to the best of his ability.

Londyn had done as he suggested, *thank fuck*, and dressed in short, snug black shorts that made her ass look like a man's perfect playground and displayed a generous amount of her soft thighs. She also wore a sleeveless, red button-down blouse that left no doubt just how big her tits were. In fact, the buttons were straining a bit when she moved, which she did a lot of. If one of them popped off, it could take out an eye. Good thing he was wearing "safety" glasses.

She had muttered a couple times—when only he could hear it—how her "boob sweat" was out of control and she couldn't wait to take off her "damn" clothes.

He couldn't, either.

But right now, they were playing the friendly neighbor game. Londyn had also done a great job working on attracting Kramer's attention. Though, he was wondering if it was too good, since Kramer was ignoring his own woman. Brick worried if it was too obvious, Barb would get her panties in a bunch and drag Kramer home by his dick, cutting the night short.

In fact, when Brick would ask him questions to start some neighborly conversation, Kramer would answer distractedly since he was too busy eye fucking Londyn.

Unlike earlier, Brick's "wife" now wore makeup. It would be barely noticeable except for the bright red lipstick, which matched her blouse and also made him want her on her knees, sucking his cock. Or the smoky eyes, which made her look sultry as fuck.

While the attention Kramer gave Londyn bothered him slightly, it was all part of the game and he knew it would be his bed she landed in tonight.

He hid his grin behind the bottle as he swallowed a mouthful of warm beer.

The women sat nearby in lounge chairs, drinking wine and chatting it up like they'd known each other forever. Brick kept half an ear on them to make sure Londyn wasn't giving away any of their secrets since she was on glass number three.

He'd been counting.

But mostly, they were talking and giggling about books and other female bullshit, like shopping. In fact, he was relieved when Barb agreed to spend a day with Londyn showing her the area, getting lunch and doing some window shopping.

His and Kramer's conversation lacked the enthusiasm of the women's and most of the time it got uncomfortable. Brick did his best to find something he had in common with the bastard who'd killed his wife.

Allegedly.

Brick enjoyed sex, poker and shooting shit. Unlike Kramer, he preferred not to play with his balls on a golf course or tennis court.

One thing they both liked was football. Though Kramer-boy leaned toward college while Brick preferred the NFL.

When he began to run out of topics of conversation, he reminded the stock trader that he had money sitting around waiting to turn a profit, which once again perked up the man's ears and got him focused on something other than Londyn's tits.

It wasn't completely a lie. Brick was sitting on a nice chunk of change since he made obscene amounts of money being a Shadow and taking some of the specialty jobs that he did. Hiring him—who Diesel called a "target specialist" to blur the lines that Brick was a sniper-for-hire—wasn't cheap.

Brick fought a yawn since Kramer was now rambling about bull and bear markets, trends, IPO's, mutual funds and other boring shit.

His attention wandered back over to where the women had their heads close together and were talking softly.

Like they were best friends with secrets.

He was relieved that Londyn was pulling off her part easily. She was a natural at faking it.

Huh.

He frowned.

Had she faked any of her reactions with him earlier?

Fuck no. Impossible. He'd be able to tell.

When she reached for the bottle of wine to fill up her glass for the fourth time, he cleared his throat loudly. Then again to make it seem like he had something stuck in his throat instead of giving her a signal.

Londyn gave him the side-eye and lifted the bottle, offering to fill Barb's glass instead of her own.

"So, what do you think?" Kramer's question broke Brick's concentration.

Fuck.

"I'll have to think on it," Brick answered, wishing he'd been paying attention.

"I could see your eyes glaze over with the market talk. But investing wisely is important. Your money is stagnating in that savings account. I could help you."

Brick's eyes slid back to Kramer, who seemed a lot more relaxed and open now that he was talking about money.

"I appreciate the offer." Brick had no idea what the offer was.

"I can open an online trading account for you and once you deposit the funds, I can buy you some long-term stocks —a few that aren't too risky to start—that pay decent dividends. Then by having those dividends automatically reinvested, your money will grow faster than in that bank. From there you can branch out with more aggressive stocks."

Sure he could. That fucker was not getting his hands on Brick's money. Plus, even if he trusted the guy, he was not opening an account using the name Seamus Ramsey. Once this job was over, he never wanted to hear that name again.

"Well, I do want to make sure Gertie's taken care of, in case anything should ever happen to me."

Kramer actually cracked a smile. Brick was finally making some headway. "Solid investments are one way. But a good insurance policy is another. It's best to diversify your funds."

Brick saw his opening and wedged his toe in the door. "Insurance policy?"

"You know, life insurance. With the right policy, your wife would be set for life."

"As long as I lost mine," Brick semi-joked.

The man didn't even blink. "Of course, you'd have to die for her to collect."

Of course. That wasn't much of a sacrifice, right? "That would be a little inconvenient for me, don't you think?"

"It would make the grieving process a little easier for her."

Brick schooled his expression as he pushed his glasses up his nose with his middle finger like he'd seen nerds do. "Really."

Kramer leaned forward slightly. "It helped me when my wife died."

Bingo. His boot was now solidly planted inside the door. "Oh, I'm sorry for your loss. I didn't realize you were a widower."

Kramer waved a hand around like he was swishing away Brick's feigned sympathy. "It was rough, but the money helped make it easier to deal with all the expenses. You do have a life insurance policy, right?"

Kramer was not only opening the door, he was inviting Brick inside. Perfect. "Uh, sure. A small policy through my employer."

"What about Gertie?"

"No. She doesn't work." Brick pinned his eyebrows together, hoping he looked clueless. "Should she have one?"

"It can't hurt. Accidents happen all the time."

Yeah, why not benefit financially from your loved one's unfortunate "accident?"

Life insurance had its purpose, but a cushy windfall wasn't one of them.

"I'll have to look into it."

Chairs scraping across the brick patio caught both their attention. The women rose to their feet and Barb had fingers pressed to her temples while wearing a pained expression.

"Is everything okay?" Brick asked, sitting straighter, on high alert.

"She gets a lot of headaches," Kramer announced, not sounding concerned in the least.

As the women got closer, Londyn said, "I'm walking Barb home."

Barb tipped her head. "I'm sorry I have to leave early. It's one of my migraines. Maybe the wine set it off."

With the women standing next to each other, Brick saw how opposite the two of them were. Kramer's woman was petite with short dark hair. Even though she was pretty, she was a bit too thin for Brick's taste. She was not the type he would "swipe right" for. Even her clothes didn't compare. She wore denim pants that stopped mid-calf, a plain loose cotton tank top and pull-on white sneakers.

With the way Kramer was interested in Londyn, Brick was surprised the man had chosen her after losing his wife. Or even before. At this point, he was still considering Barb as Kramer's accomplice.

Maybe Kramer had a wider taste in women than Brick did.

"I'm sorry to hear that. That's unfortunate. We were in the middle of talking business," Brick said. "We can pick it up another time."

"Oh, he can stay. I'm going to climb into bed and hope this goes away before my date with your lovely wife," Barb said.

When the woman winced, Londyn curled an arm

around her shoulder, gave her a sympathetic smile, and said to Kramer, "I can take her home and make sure she's settled. You stay and finish your talk."

Yes, Londyn was a fucking natural at this. Brick was starting to think he couldn't have picked a better partner for this job himself.

Chapter Nine

BRICK DIDN'T TURN when he heard the glass door slide open. Instead he kept his eyes on Kramer. Who happened to be watching Londyn as she came back outside.

No surprise.

He finally turned his head to watch her approach. "She okay?"

Londyn nodded and released the plump bottom lip she had tucked between her teeth.

Sex kitten.

That's what she reminded him of.

A fucking sex kitten.

And it was something she didn't have to fake. It was obvious that she didn't know what kind of effect she had on men. Which surprised the fuck out of him, especially since she wasn't some naïve young woman.

But it could be that cluelessness made it even sexier.

She was far from conceited. Brick had plenty of those. Women who knew they were hot and tried to use it to their advantage. Hot or not, it was a complete turn-off for him. Most expected him to turn to putty in their hands so they could mold him to their wishes.

Fuck that.

That alone was another good reason why he kept "dates" limited to one night. And not even a whole night. A few hours were enough before he scraped them off.

As much as he had the need for these "dates," he always breathed easier once he saw the taillights of their car or cab disappearing into the night.

He was a pro at making excuses of why they had to leave in the middle of the night. He was a volunteer firefighter and got a call he needed to respond to. A sick family member. A friend needed bailed out of jail.

He was also good at faking emergency phone calls or texts.

There were even times he'd slipped the neighbor boy some money to make those middle of the night calls. But the kid was unreliable and apparently preferred sleep over ten bucks, so Brick always had a back-up plan.

Her blue eyes flicked to Kramer briefly before landing back on him and sticking. She plastered on a smile and practically bounced on her toes as she approached the two of them. Her eyes held some kind of mischief and he wondered what it was about.

Then he realized she'd hardly flirted with him all night. One of his requests. Now that Barb was out of the picture, apparently he was her next target.

He had to hand it to her, the fucking woman was good. Diesel might have to hire her whenever they needed a woman for a job.

And bonus! Mercy would fucking *love* it!

Brick smothered his snort as Londyn stopped next to his chair.

The smile she gave him now seemed genuine, even if it was over the top. She sounded extremely bubbly when she told him, "Honey, I'll have to borrow the credit card Friday. 'Kay? Thanks!"

As she bent over to kiss his cheek and give him a healthy view of her tits, he snagged her hand and yanked her off balance. She planted her other hand against his chest as she caught herself and twisted to land ass first in his lap.

Right where he wanted her.

He cupped a possessive hand over her bare knee and murmured, "Whatever you want, muffin."

That had her hooking her arms around his neck and settling against his chest. He wrapped one arm around her back so that his finger rested on the outer curve of her left tit and he let the other one wander from her knee down her *smooth-as-fuck* calf.

Her sandals had straps that not only wrapped around her red painted toes but circled her ankles and partially up her calves. It reminded him of what the gladiators wore—at least in the movies—but hers were much fucking sexier. He ran his finger slowly around the narrow strap of black leather that snaked around her lower calf. He didn't miss Kramer's eye following it like a hawk tracking a field mouse.

"You should've worn a skirt," he said softly, but loud enough for Kramer not to miss.

"Why?"

"Easier access." He slipped his fingers up into the bottom opening of her shorts and partially up her thigh, stroking her skin. Even though he was currently playing Kramer, if he wasn't careful, he'd be sporting an erection soon. "Friday, when you're out with Barb, I want you wearing a skirt with no panties."

Londyn's cheeks instantly went bright red and her arms tightened around his neck. "*Honeeeey*, I'm sure Chris doesn't want to hear this... conversation."

"Maybe he'll tell Barb to do the same. While I'm working hard to provide for you, I want to think of you like that when you're out and about." He twisted his head to glance at Kramer. "How hot would that be? Right, Chris? Knowing our women are out in public like that? Knowing, when they get home, all we have to do is bend them over and—"

Londyn slapped a hand over his mouth. Brick hid his smile before peeling her finger off his lips.

This was way too much fucking fun. But he wasn't done yet.

"Muffin, get Daddy a beer."

When Londyn opened her mouth to complain, she caught Brick's stern look. While she shut that mouth, he didn't miss the deadly glare in her eyes as she started, "Yes..." sucked in a breath, and finished with a tight, "Daddy."

Brick fought his smile again as he gave her a pointed eyebrow lift.

He gave her an encouraging squeeze that Kramer wouldn't notice, then released her. Using his shoulder for balance, she climbed off his lap and onto her feet. The sharp smack on her ass had her jerk forward before turning enough so Kramer didn't catch her answering eye roll.

It was no surprise that Brick wasn't the only one watching that caboose rocking and rolling on the tracks as she went inside.

Kramer had to give himself whiplash as he snapped his head back to Brick. "She calls you Daddy?"

Oh yeah, fucking with Kramer was fun. "When she's been a bad girl."

The man's dark brown eyes flared. "How was she a bad girl?"

Brick sat back in his chair, donning a serious expression. "I suggested she make brownies. She made cookies instead."

Kramer didn't bother to hide his surprise. "But the cookies were good. Best I've had in a long time. I wish Barb could bake like that."

Brick leaned forward and grabbed a cookie off the

nearby plate. He held it up and studied it. "But cookies are not brownies, Chris." Brick took a bite out of it and threw it back on the plate with a look of disgust.

"Maybe you should have told her what you wanted, instead of suggesting."

"Suggestions are a test, my friend. And this was one she failed. Because of that, she will get punished."

"Does she... like being punished?" The gleam in Kramer's eyes became brighter.

Hook. Line. And sinker.

A grin spread over Brick's face. "If she didn't, she would've made brownies."

Kramer sat back in his chair, scraped a hand through his dark hair and blew out a ragged breath.

Brick wasn't done fucking with him. "The secret to a happy marriage is using a firm hand, Chris. It not only keeps her obedient but keeps her happy. A woman needs that direction whether she realizes it or not."

"She seems pretty strong-willed to accept that."

Brick turned his head and met Kramer's eyes directly. "That's what makes it even better. She likes to challenge me."

Their conversation halted when the slider opened and Londyn stepped back out into the lanai, carrying not only his requested beer but a fresh one for Kramer.

When she handed Kramer his first, Brick was surprised the man didn't have to wipe drool off his mouth before thanking her. Then she approached him.

He accepted the beer and noticed it wasn't open. Another perfect opportunity. He tipped the top of the beer bottle toward her and she stared at it for a second, not understanding. He caught the slight flare of her nostrils when she got it and took it back from him, twisting the cap before offering it to him again.

"Good girl," he whispered just loud enough for Kramer to hear.

Londyn's mouth opened slightly and a puff of breath escaped.

Jesus fuck. Did she get off on what he had just said?

Brick's gaze dropped from her parted lips and landed on her pebbled nipples in that snug, red blouse. His cock twitched at the thought of their acting turning her on.

Time to wrap up the evening and send Kramer home, so he could start their night.

He caught her hand, lifted her palm to his mouth and kissed the center of it. "Now, go clean-up the kitchen and get ready for," he paused just long enough for Kramer to hang, "bed. I'll be up as soon as Chris and I finish talking."

She nodded obediently even though the look in her eyes was anything but.

Kramer called her strong-willed.

He had no fucking idea.

When he released her hand, she trailed her fingers over the short, wiry hairs along his jaw, tilted her head as she studied him for a moment, then turned to Kramer. "Goodnight, Chris. I hope Barb is feeling better. I look forward to spending time with her on Friday."

"Goodnight, Gertrude."

Brick saw Londyn's body jolt at the name before she nodded and went inside.

As soon as the sliding glass door shut behind Londyn, Kramer said, "You're a lucky man, Seamus."

Brick stared at the door where his "wife" disappeared, murmuring, "That I am."

―――――

LONDYN STARED INTO THE MIRROR, dragging the brush through her hair with more force than was necessary. She'd washed off the makeup, had brushed her teeth and was waiting for her "Daddy" to come up to bed.

It would serve him right if she went back to the spare bedroom she slept in last night. She was also surprised her tongue was still attached after as many times as she had bit it.

Daddy.

She shuddered. What other couples called each other was their business, not hers, but calling the man she was sleeping with "Daddy" was not and would never be her thing.

She dropped the brush to the counter. Other couples?

They weren't even a freaking couple.

This was all playacting.

A farce.

They hardly even knew each other.

They hardly even knew each other and here she was about to climb into bed with him again.

Even though the master bathroom was twice as large as her bathroom in New York, it suddenly felt cramped when Brick stepped through the open doorway.

She didn't hear him come upstairs or into the bedroom and wondered at what point he lost most of his clothes. Or put on a pair of long shorts that were loose enough at the waist to hang low, exposing the drool-worthy muscular V above his narrow hips.

She turned back to the mirror so it wasn't so obvious she was ogling him.

But, *oh*, she was ogling him. The thin silky fabric of those shorts clung in a way that made her wonder if he even wore underwear. Because he did not look contained at all.

At. All.

And while he wasn't totally ready for action, she couldn't help but notice he was semi-aroused.

Maybe it was the whole fucking Daddy thing. Maybe he

got off on that shit. But if he expected her to call him that when they were having sex, he was sadly mistaken.

Though... Seeing him the way he was dressed—or undressed—at that moment, she'd call him whatever the hell he wanted if it guaranteed getting a piece of his deliciousness. She just wasn't going to share that information with him.

"What was with all that?" she asked.

"All what?"

Oh, he was playing dumb. "You know what. Pretending you're some Dom."

He moved to stand behind her, grinned and lifted a brow, which she caught in the mirror. "Who said I'm not?"

She was tall. But even in bare feet, he was much taller. She liked that.

She also liked that even though she wasn't a smaller woman like Barb, him standing behind her made her feel petite. Almost delicate.

"You're a Dom?"

She watched in fascination when he chuckled, flashing his white teeth and drawing her attention to his lips which had done a lot of naughty, but spectacular, things to her earlier in the day.

"No. But it was fun to pretend I own your ass." With that, he smacked it again.

This time it didn't sting like it did when he did it in front of Kramer. It was more playful.

And, yes, *holy shit*, did she *like it*.

Her eyes met his in the mirror. And neither said a word for the longest moment.

He lost that panty-dropping grin of his. "He's got a hard-on over you, Londyn. That interest in you will keep him interested in *us*. Otherwise, we're just like every other boring couple in this neighborhood. *You* give him a reason to want to hang out with us. He wants a piece of your ass and we can use that to our advantage."

"He won't be getting a piece of my ass."

His fingers wrapped around the front of her neck and his thumb stroked the side of her throat. "No, he won't."

"You won't be either if you insist I call you Daddy."

He lifted his eyes from where they were focused on her neck, focused on where he was stroking her skin over her pounding pulse. "I don't want to be your Daddy."

"That's good," she murmured, her nipples pebbling at his warm, but firm, grip on her neck.

Stepping closer, he nuzzled her hair with his nose and sucked her earlobe into his mouth. His semi-aroused state was no more. His length was now hot and hard against the small of her back.

"You did good, Londyn," he murmured close to her ear.

"Did I?"

"I was impressed. I thought a couple times you might deck me, but you kept your impulses under control."

"Was I a 'good girl' like a well-trained dog?"

She not only felt him smile into her hair, but she saw a glimpse of that smile in the mirror.

The hand he had planted on her stomach slid up and grazed her aching nipples, then skated back down to where the top of her PJ's met the bottoms. This set was blue that matched the color of her eyes and was always her favorite. The satiny feel against her bare skin made her feel sexy, even if she was sleeping alone.

Tonight, she wouldn't be sleeping alone.

His fingers separated the bottom hem of her top and the elastic waistband of the shorts and his palm skimmed over the bare skin of her belly, making everything inside her clench. She lifted her gaze from where his hand was causing a fire inside her and saw he was watching her. His cheek was pressed to the side of her head and his eyes were intense as he shifted the fabric of her top higher, exposing not only her stomach but the bottom curves of her heavy breasts.

Her hand itched to stop him. Not only were they in the bathroom in the light, but she was directly in front of the mirror. There was no one harder on her than herself and she knew that.

Kevin had scoffed at her insecurities, but never did anything to help her get over them. When she'd mentioned her faults, he would simply shrug and ask her if she wanted him to turn off the lights.

She did. And he did. Problem solved.

But so far, Brick hadn't let her hide.

Not.

Once.

Chapter Ten

Brick didn't miss the second her breathing shallowed, or the moment she tensed.

He was ready when her mouth opened in protest. He used the hand planted just below her breasts to pin her against him and his other to cover her mouth. "Not one doubt, Londyn, not one. Unless you want me to spank your ass until it's red."

Her eyes, which went wide when he covered her mouth, became hooded at his threat. He dropped his hand at the sudden switch.

"Yes, please," she whispered.

His brow furrowed and his cock twitched since his brain was a sudden mass of confusion. "'Yes, please' what?"

"Spank me."

What?

"What?" It was supposed to be a warning. Not a reward. "You *want* me to spank you?" he asked carefully. While he was in the bathroom maybe he should clean out his ears. Because if he was hearing what he was hearing...

"Yes," she breathed, a flush rising from her chest into her cheeks.

Damn. She continued to surprise him.

Baking, anal, good at working undercover and now... spanking.

Though, he hadn't tested that last one yet. But if it was true...

He smiled.

She smiled.

If she had the same confidence about her body as what she did with that body, she would be...

His smile flattened.

Not moving across the country thirty days after meeting someone online.

No, she would hold out for the right time and the right man who would appreciate her for who she was, what she looked like and what she wanted.

Just like he did.

Just like he did.

Huh.

Or someone *like* him. Right.

He needed to get back to business here. If the woman wanted to be spanked, who was he to deny her?

But first...

Brick finished slipping her silky top over her head. He tossed it to the side then cupped both of her tits in his palms.

Full and beautiful.

He wanted his mouth on her beaded nipples, but he also wanted to watch her in the mirror.

He continued to knead her tits and brush his thumbs over hard points when he said, "Slip out of your shorts."

She only hesitated long enough to look at herself in the mirror, to look at the both of them sandwiched together, his chest to her back, then she gave a little nod—he assumed to herself—and tugged her shorts down over her hips. They only went so far before the fabric caught between her thighs and when she bent over to free them, he grabbed her hips and yanked her back.

She cried out in surprise and put her hands on the edge of the counter to catch herself so she wouldn't crack her forehead. As she was still bent over, he jerked her shorts down the rest of the way until they fell around her feet.

"Brace yourself," he warned quietly, seeing both surprise and heat in her face.

He moved to her side and with a last glance in the mirror, he turned his attention to her ass which was sticking out in the perfect position for her requested "spanking."

He wasn't into a lot of kink, but he did like to play and some things he liked more than others. He wasn't going to break out the rope and ball gag, nipple clamps and leather crop. But, in the past, he'd used neckties and scarves to tie up women upon their request.

He preferred to keep a woman's hands free, as well as her mouth. Mostly because he wanted to feel their nails digging into his back. He liked when teeth sank into his skin. He liked to be scratched, sucked, licked and kissed.

And he liked to do the same.

He also liked to spank. Normally, he did it when taking a woman from the rear, whether doggy-style or during anal. But he hadn't done it with Londyn earlier, because she had been on top this morning. He'd let her control the pace and the depth while he lay back and enjoyed the ride.

But now, it would be him controlling the power behind his palm meeting her flesh.

He didn't want to hurt her, he only wanted to drive her out of her mind. He wanted her wet and squirming. He wanted her to ride that sharp edge until she couldn't take anymore.

Precum leaked from his cock at just the thought of her begging him to fuck her and make her come.

Unfortunately, someone was going to be at that edge

sooner than later and it wasn't Londyn. He sucked air through his nostrils to tamp down his out of control thoughts.

He brushed his open hand lightly over one of her cheeks then the other, marveling at how soft and smooth her skin was there. And she had plenty of flesh to hang onto, whether she was on top or he was taking her from behind.

And, *fuck*, he liked that, too.

"Brick." His name trembled on her tongue and that same tremor swept through her.

"Are you changing your mind?" *Please fucking say no.*

"No. Just..."

"Just?"

"Please."

That "please" sliced through him like lightning, got caught in his gut and radiated out.

He stepped into her side, leaned over and licked down the line of her spine, finishing with a kiss at the top of her crease. "We've got all night," he murmured against her skin. "All fucking night."

Rising quickly, he swatted her ass and watched it ripple with the impact. She didn't even move. The only noise that escaped her was a rush of air.

He swatted her again on the other cheek. Again, not even the slightest movement beyond where his hand struck. But this time she groaned. It was low and long and pulled his balls tight.

Red began to bloom along her skin, and he turned his head to glance in the mirror. Her head was down, her face hidden between her extended arms.

"Londyn." Her name sounded gruff to his own ears.

She lifted her head slightly, her eyes meeting his. And he liked what he saw in them. Any doubts about herself were gone and only need remained.

"Watch me."

He lifted his hand and this time she did move, only slightly. Since she could now see his movements, she was anticipating it.

Expecting it.

Time to distract her. "Play with yourself."

He expected resistance or at least a snarky comment, but she said nothing. Instead she lifted her hand to her mouth, licked two fingers slowly and sensually as he watched in the mirror and then moved them to between her legs.

Fuck. She could very well slay him with those very two fingers. Just like a sword.

But now he regretted her being in the position she was in—bent over with her ass exposed—because he wanted to watch everything she was doing. Whatever she was doing to make her eyelids heavy, her mouth open and her body tremble. In fact, fuck the spanking, he wanted to watch Londyn make herself come. Not just the woman in the flesh before him, but the one in the mirror. It would be a three-sixty experience.

An experience burned into his brain forever.

But she wanted to be spanked and he should at least make an effort before she drove him to flipping her around and fucking her right there on the bathroom counter.

He swallowed hard and tried to concentrate on her ass, which was still showing a bit of pink, and give her a few more strikes with his hand so she'd feel it for a while afterward, especially when he propped her ass on the edge of the counter.

This time as she watched him, she didn't flinch or move when his palm cracked her ass so hard it even stung his own hand.

Damn.

Even though he was pushing his own limits, he would do it once more on the other cheek to make sure the flush of her skin was even. As he lifted his hand, hers moved faster between her legs and when he made contact with her rear, she cried out and jerked.

It wasn't from the spanking.

Fuck no. Her legs wobbled as she orgasmed, her eyes closed, and her head fell back.

Now that look of bliss was beautiful.

Everything about her was beautiful.

After a last glance at his handiwork, he grabbed a fistful of her hair, pulled her to a stand and twisted her around. "Ass on the counter, legs spread."

She didn't scramble to do his bidding. Hell no, she took her time, teasing him.

Before she could haul herself up, he had his hands on her waist and lifted her to right where he wanted her. "Spread yourself."

Her whisper was husky. "Where?"

"You know where."

Her knees went wide, and her fingers slid through her shiny, plump folds in a V as she offered herself to him.

He dropped to his knees, burying his face between her thighs. Not at all being gentle.

Her scent was all woman. Her taste addictive.

And he lost himself in her while bringing her to that peak once more. The room filled with whimpers and cries and, even better, whispers of his name. Her nails scraped along the sides of his scalp when she came again, bucking against his mouth, driving herself down on the fingers he had plunged deep inside her. He waited her out, sucking lightly on her clit and when every muscle went liquid, he stood, dropped his shorts to his feet and stepped between her thighs.

Because that was where he needed to be.

Between warm, soft thighs that hugged him, slick with her arousal.

His intent was only to kiss her. To share the same taste he now recognized as hers.

And as he did so, he slid his throbbing cock through her slickness, wanting to ditch the condom. Not wanting a damn thing between them.

And that made the hairs at the back of his neck prickle.

He never even considered taking a woman ungloved before. Not once.

He had no idea why now. Why with her?

It was stupid.

Reckless.

And he knew better.

But he still struggled with not wanting to just drive deep inside her. Feel that wet heat surrounding him, drawing him in.

Shutting the whole world out but her...

Her next words slapped some sense into him. *Thank fuck.*

"I got tested after finding out Kevin was cheating on me with his own wife. When's the last time you've been tested?"

While this was not a discussion he wanted to have at this very moment, it was an important one.

She was making him lose his mind, but she was also pulling him back to reality.

"A month ago."

"And you've..."

He dropped his head until they were making direct eye contact because he wasn't going to deny it. "Yeah."

It was there and gone in a flash. But he recognized it.

Disappointment.

Even though it was unrealistic.

Especially since he never denied who he was or how he was.

And if he did, she wouldn't believe him anyway. He never hid the fact that his life revolved around two things.

His team and hookups.

Like he accepted her as she came, she needed to accept him.

There had been plenty before her and there'd be plenty after, but right now it was just the two of them in that room. In the here and now.

Unfortunately, the room they were in didn't have any condoms. Fortunately, the room attached to it did. They would just have to shift their activity to the bed.

So, that was what he did.

———

SATED AND SPENT, Londyn laid across Brick's *hard-as-a-brick-wall* chest as it rose and fell quickly. Her cheek pressed over his heart, which still pounded a rapid beat. Her eyes were focused, not on him, but the dog tags sitting within reach on the nightstand.

The ones she'd removed from him. The ones he'd tucked into his pocket because she had a feeling he didn't like to be without them.

She reached out and, with one finger, drew them across the polished wood top of the stand. When they were at the edge, she flipped one of the tags over and read the stamped words.

Most of them were self-explanatory. The rest she could guess.

Her thumb swiped over his name.

Briggs

Ramsey W.

"Ramsey is your first name, not your last." Brick had introduced himself to Chris Kramer as Seamus Ramsey. She'd thought he'd pulled that last name out of thin air.

His rough voice rumbled through her cheek. "Yeah."

"Anyone call you Ramsey?" The name felt odd on her

tongue. But, in reality, it was no odder than calling him Brick.

"No."

She raised a brow. "No one?"

"My parents and grandparents when I got in trouble."

"What did they call you when you weren't in trouble?"

His deep chuckle shook her. "I was always in trouble."

Londyn smiled. "Where did Brick come from?"

"You mean where did I grow up?"

"No. The nickname."

"Got it during sniper school. I was told that I was as steady as a brick. And from there, Briggs somehow morphed into Brick. It stuck." He lazily combed his finger through her mess of hair spread over his chest. "There's also a quote by Lycurgus of Sparta. 'That city is well fortified which has a wall of men instead of brick.' One of my early spotters turned it around to: 'That city is well fortified which has a Brick instead of a wall of men.'"

She let that sink in for a moment. "Which meant you were good enough that an army wasn't needed to protect a city. They only needed you."

He jolted slightly beneath her. "Which is complete bullshit."

"There has to be some truth to it."

"I couldn't save everybody," he mumbled. He surged up, dislodging her from her comfortable position. "Gotta get rid of this." As soon as he was on his feet, he pulled off the condom. But before walking away, he snagged his dog tags from her fingers and fisted them tightly. "I feel naked without them. They've been a piece of me for so long."

"Your service was a big part of your life."

"It *was* my life. For a long fucking time." With that, he crossed the room and tucked the tags into the duffel bag which sat on the floor in a corner. When he straightened, he tossed an open box of condoms onto the bed. "For later."

"How much later?" she asked his back as he disappeared into the bathroom.

"You'll know as soon as I do."

She was still grinning when she heard the toilet flush and the sink run. She rolled to her side to make sure she had an unobstructed view of his nakedness as he prowled across the room back to the bed.

His eyes were on her and she didn't think there was an inch left on her untouched by the time he climbed back into bed.

Funny. For the first time, she hadn't felt the urge to cover herself up.

He said he liked her the way she was. She could believe him, or she could wonder if they were only hooking up because they were stuck together in this situation and she was convenient.

Either way, she liked the way he looked at her. It didn't seem forced or fake. His eyes always warmed when she was naked.

Even better, his cock always got hard. So maybe that was a sign it was all true.

As he settled onto his back, he tucked one arm behind his head and wrapped the other around her to pull her closer. But before he could plaster her to his side, she touched the tattoo on his left ribcage, which made him go solid.

The tattoo was hard to ignore, but she hadn't asked about it yet since she'd figured it was personal.

Still... They'd gotten intimate, so maybe he wouldn't mind sharing.

Or maybe she was just overthinking it and it was simply a tattoo. However, it was the only mark on his body besides the scar from his childhood injury.

She traced the outer edge once and on her second go-around she asked, "Are you religious?"

In the center of his solid tattoo were the letters and numbers: *Cor 9:27*.

While growing up, their parents had never once taken Parris and her to church, but even Londyn recognized what the combination was referring to.

"As a kid, my parents used to drag me to church every Sunday. Sometimes more, depending on how much trouble I got into during the week. But no, I lost my faith a long time ago."

"Then why do you have a bible passage on your ribs?"

He glanced down at it with feigned surprise. "Is that what it is?"

Londyn laughed and whacked his chest half-heartedly. "Even I recognize it."

"Then you know what it means."

"No, I don't know any bible passages. I mean, I recognize it's a specific passage but not what that passage says."

"It has to do with discipline. And, of course, being religious nuts, my parents knew how to dish it out. Once I 'found my way'—as my mother told me when I enlisted in the Navy—my life became all about a different type of discipline with both my dedication to serving my country, as well as my mind and body. Joining the Navy, becoming a SEAL, gave me all of that and then some."

The way he mentioned how his parents were religious nuts and how they knew how to dish out discipline made her wonder if he even had a relationship with them any longer. Or if his parents were long gone like her own.

"Are they still around?"

"Who?"

"Your parents."

"I guess so."

"You don't know?" That was strange. She couldn't imagine not knowing whether her parents were alive or dead. She only wished she could have had more time with them.

"Once I went into the Navy, I lost contact with them."

"On purpose?"

"Londyn..." He blew out a breath. She didn't think he would answer, but a few seconds later, he continued. "While they were happy I joined the Navy, they weren't happy that I actually had to... kill people. I'm not sure what they thought the military entailed. It's certainly not the fucking Peace Corps."

"You broke one of the commandments." *Thou shalt not kill.*

"I guess they thought I could serve our country without seeing active duty. I might have gotten away with it if I hadn't become a SEAL. It was that choice they disapproved of."

Now, it made more sense. While they liked the thought of him being a patriot and serving his country, when he'd become a SEAL and then a sniper, he'd taken it too far.

"I've seen on TV some of the training SEALs are put through. Seems intense and enough to break someone."

"Yeah," was all he breathed. "Some broke."

"But not you." When he didn't say anything, she added, "You were successful."

Again, he didn't respond. However, she was enjoying this post-coital conversation and wasn't ready for it to end. Plus, she really did want to know what his tattoo meant to him.

She traced the letters and numbers in the center of the tattoo. "What does the passage mean?"

He snagged her hand, stopping her movement and gave her fingers a squeeze. "There are many interpretations, but this one fits me the best: *But I discipline my body and keep it under control, lest after preaching to others I myself should be disqualified.*"

She boiled that down to, "Meaning you practice what you preach?"

He lifted one shoulder. "I can't judge you for being what and who you are without judging myself."

"That's what it means?"

"That's what it means to me." Then he just shut his mouth and stopped talking. Again.

Londyn wanted to scream. Maybe her asking about his tattoo took him somewhere he didn't want to go. A trigger of sorts.

On the surface Brick didn't seem bogged down. The man could joke, play around and be almost as chatty as her one moment, then shut down and retreat the next. Every so often, a glimpse of something deeper, darker appeared. Not often, but she'd caught it a few times.

Most likely due to those invisible scars he mentioned. Scars caused by something more complicated than falling off a bike. Scars that may never fade like that six-inch line on his thigh.

They'd only known each other a few days, so she didn't know all his moods and, for the most part, during that time he'd been open, warm and funny.

Did she want to scratch below the surface? Hell yes. While she wasn't a certified therapist like her sister, she always was curious about how people "ticked," which lead her to becoming a substance abuse counselor. Four years of college to become one had been more than enough for her. She had no desire to chase her master's degree like Parris.

She turned her face up toward him. He was staring at the ceiling. Was he reliving his time with what sounded like strict, religious parents? Or his time in the service? Or whatever caused him to retire from the Navy after working hard to become not only a SEAL but a sniper?

That decision to leave couldn't have come easy. You

couldn't just quit being a SEAL sniper like a kid working at a fast food restaurant at the end of summer break.

His blue eyes held something she couldn't read when they tipped down to her. He had taken off his glasses earlier and she didn't think he had replaced them with his contacts.

She wondered how bad his sight truly was. "Can you see me without your glasses or contacts?"

Instead of just his eyes, he dipped his head down toward her. "Yeah."

"Clearly?"

Did he roll those eyes of his at her?

"Londyn... You've got some shit you need to let go of."

He should talk. "I'm sure I'm not the only one in this bed who does."

His jaw flexed and he released her hand to draw the covers over them both.

"Wait. I need to get up and grab my PJ's in the bathroom." She sat up and began to swing her legs off the bed when he snagged her wrist in his tight grip and pulled her back down to his side.

"No. I want you to stay the way you are right now. I want to be able to roll over and wake you up properly."

Well, then...

"You're not going to wake up and go for a ten-mile run, do a thousand pushups and five hundred jumping jacks?"

"I don't do jumping jacks. I do mountain climbers."

It was Londyn's turn to roll her eyes. She snuggled under the covers next to him, absorbing his body heat. "You make me feel like a slacker."

"No judgment, right?"

She twisted her lips. "Right."

He brushed his lips over the top of her head, which she had planted once again on his chest. "Better sleep because oh-six-hundred comes early."

"Oh-six-hundred?"

"You'll be my warm-up for my run. I need to run early because of us being in Satan's sweaty armpit, remember?"

Right. "Maybe I should walk around the block while you run."

"Again, no judgement, Londyn. If you want to walk, you walk. You want to swim, you swim. You want to have breakfast waiting for me once I'm done, I'm okay with that, too. If you want to be that breakfast, even better."

He'd caused her to smile more in the last few days than she had in a long time.

Was he perfect? Definitely not. But damn well close enough.

———

BRICK SHIFTED and blew out a soft breath as he listened to Londyn's snoring. She had rolled away from him after falling asleep. Most likely his body temp was too hot for her. It was better she did, anyway. At home he sometimes awoke to sweaty, twisted sheets.

Which meant he had taken a trip back there again.

If he got too restless, he might hurt her by kicking or hitting her without knowing.

The last thing he wanted to do was hurt her.

But there was one person he did want to hurt.

A man only two doors down. Someone probably lying in his bed, fantasizing about doing the same things to Londyn that Brick did earlier.

His jaw tightened at the urge to smash Kramer's face in with the butt of his rifle.

He didn't like this feeling clawing at his gut, messing with his brain. He never felt it before, but he knew exactly what it was.

Because the more Kramer looked at Londyn, the stronger that feeling became.

His thumb spun the wedding band on his ring finger. Her being in his bed, him wearing that ring. Both of them being in Florida.

It was all temporary.

They were on a job. They were playing their parts. They were doing what needed to be done.

But, fuck him, if it wasn't going to fuck with his head to do it.

Chapter Eleven

LONDYN STUDIED the woman sitting across from her in the little café where they decided to grab lunch. She was trying not glance at the time, but Brick had given her the order to keep Barb occupied as long as possible.

In the few hours she spent with her, she couldn't see the woman harming a flea. She also couldn't imagine Barb having anything to do with helping Kramer commit murder.

But psychopaths could be very deceiving.

Now they had food in their belly, loads of charges on their credit cards, and too many bags in the trunk of Barb's car, it was time to start digging a little deeper, just like she'd wanted to do with Brick the other night.

"You and Chris seem so happy."

Barb sighed, sitting back on her side of the booth, and returned Londyn's smile. "We are."

"How long have you been together?"

"About a year and a half now, but I've known him a lot longer. We moved down here after his first wife died."

"Did you know his late wife?"

"We were friends."

Yikes! "Oh! I'm so sorry for your loss. I had no idea. I

don't think either of you had mentioned Chris was a widower."

Had she sunk her claws into Kramer before or after his wife died? Was it more than about the insurance settlement? Had Kramer wanted to be free of his wife to be with Barb? Were they having an affair before the murder?

Dun dun dun duuuuuun.

"We found consolation with each other after Teresa died."

Sure they did.

"And things developed from there."

No kidding.

"Well, at least you found solace within each other's arms. And love, too, right?"

"Oh yes." Barb's expression actually became...

Dreamy.

Now, admittedly, Kramer was a good-looking man, but he wasn't nearly as dreamy as Brick.

Londyn mentally rolled her eyes at herself.

"I'm sure her passing was hard on Chris. Did she suffer long?" *Holy smokes*, she normally hated asking those types of questions. But she was there to dig, right?

Though, even if she wasn't, she was nosy.

"It was quite tragic."

Londyn leaned forward with interest and waited for Barb to continue.

"It was a freak accident, really. Teresa had gone to take a bath, slipped in the tub and smacked her head. The impact must have knocked her out and she drowned."

A chill slithered down Londyn's spine. "I thought Chris worked from home. He didn't hear her fall or cry out?"

"He does, but he had gone out to run an errand when it happened. When he found her, she was already," Barb dropped her voice to a whisper, "gone."

Well, wasn't that convenient?

"He must have been devastated. And it had to be even tougher on him if he found her."

"Yes, he struggled with dealing with her loss for a while."

Until the life insurance payout came along. *Cha-ching.* After payday, move with your new girlfriend into a larger luxury home in another state.

"He was lucky you were there for him."

"I'm lucky to have him."

Until he kills you, too.

"You're the silver lining," Londyn mumbled, disturbed at her own line of thinking.

She should feel bad about already condemning Kramer with murder when they hadn't had a chance yet to dig around for proof. And there was no guarantee they'd even find it. But tonight Brick had a plan to at least get into the house. Londyn needed to continue to play her part to make sure the plan was successful.

If there *was* proof, the sooner Brick found it, the sooner they could head back to a cooler climate.

Not that Londyn had any idea where she'd go from there once that happened. It would be a good idea to start figuring that out before their job in Florida was over, even if she decided to stay in Pennsylvania near her sister.

Barb's next words drew her out of her thoughts. "Again, I'm sorry I had to leave early the other night. I feel awful for ditching that wonderful dinner."

"You felt awful, that's why you left. Was your headache a migraine?"

"Yes, I get them often."

Londyn picked up her invisible shovel and began to dig deeper. "Have you always had them?"

"They began about nine months ago, once we moved to Florida."

Londyn's skin prickled.

"Chris thinks it could be due to the heat and humidity.

But sometimes they are so bad, I can't even function for days and it causes me to... sorry... throw up. Unfortunately, it's hurting my editing business. If I can't edit, then I can't earn my fees."

"You never had any migraines before moving here?" And, more importantly, moving in with Kramer. "Did they start out bad?"

"No, like I said, I never got them before we moved here and they've gotten worse with time. I've mentioned moving back north to Chris, if they continue."

She guessed it would be a cold day in Satan's sweaty armpit before that happened. "And he says...?"

"We might have to wait awhile, since moving again so soon would financially cripple us."

Sure it would. Londyn wondered if Barb even knew what Teresa's life insurance payout was.

"What does your doctor say?"

"He put me on medication, but it hasn't helped."

Of course not.

Londyn reached across the table and patted Barb's hand. "I'm so sorry you have to deal with that." And she genuinely meant it. She hoped Brick was wrong and the woman wasn't involved in Teresa's death and she really hoped Kramer wasn't trying to "off" Barb, too. But Londyn had watched a lot of repeat episodes of Dateline NBC and she didn't put it past anyone to do some heinous shit out of greed.

People were whacked.

Barb squeezed Londyn's hand and gave her a bright smile. "Well, not today! Today I got to spend the day with a new friend without a hint of a headache so far. Even better, the day is still young. We have plenty of time for me to show you around some more."

Londyn pulled her hand away and gave her a wink. "And run up the balance on our men's credit cards."

"Exactly!" the other woman chirped.

Londyn had a feeling she'd be running around tomorrow returning everything she bought today. She certainly wasn't using Brick's AmEx, not that he offered, and since leaving New York, she didn't have a job. Her savings were slowly dwindling and would continue to do so until she sold her house up north. Even then, she didn't hold a lot of equity in that house.

And fuck Kevin if he asked for half of it. She'd slice off his balls and mail them to his wife.

Or maybe she'd introduce Kevin to Christopher Kramer.

She covered her face to smother her snort. Being in Satan's sweaty armpit was starting to make her think evil thoughts.

———

BRICK RANG the doorbell and took a step back. As he heard the heavy footsteps approaching, he scrubbed a hand down his face.

Show time.

He needed to play the concerned and controlling husband, but also make nice with Kramer. He never said he was an actor, but he'd do the best he could.

There was a pause at the door—probably Kramer looking through the peephole—before it swung open.

He plastered a concerned, but slightly annoyed, look on his face. "Hey, Chris. Sorry to bug you."

"What's up?"

"Is Gertrude here?"

"Uh, *nooo*," Kramer dragged out. "They haven't gotten back yet."

Brick scratched at the whiskers under his chin. "Huh.

I've been calling her and she's not answering. That's not like her and I'm getting a bit concerned."

"Maybe her battery died."

"No, that's not it."

Kramer shot him a frown. "How do you know?"

He tilted his head and gave Kramer a knowing look. "I just do." Londyn had texted him a warning that they were on their way back to Kramer's house and would arrive in fifteen, that was how he knew. "Do you mind if I wait? I want to make sure she doesn't hide any of her purchases."

There it was. Concern with just a hint of dominance. Hollywood would soon be knocking down his door.

"Uh, sure." Kramer opened the door wider and stepped back. "I'm done for the day and was planning on grabbing a beer and sitting out back for a while, if you want to join me."

Brick smiled big. "Would love a beer. Might cool down my temper a little bit."

He hadn't seen any evidence of it the other night at dinner, so he had no idea if Kramer was some abusive asshole with a bad temper and that's why he killed his wife, or if he was simply a greedy motherfucker, to whom money was more important than a life. Either way, it couldn't hurt to pretend he was capable of smacking Londyn around when she got out of line. It might open the man up if he commiserated.

It was a long shot, but he had to put out some more feelers to figure out if the man was capable of killing his wife. And if so, see if he could dig up any proof. Because without it, Diesel's client, Kramer's former father-in-law, was dead in the water with his claim of homicide.

Unless Kramer out and out admitted it, which he'd be a fool to do, trying to find proof was going to be about impossible. But the client had the cash, and he wanted something done, so Diesel agreed to at least give it a shot.

Brick could imagine a father's frustration thinking his son-in-law killed his daughter and was getting off scot-free. If it was his own daughter, Brick would do anything to change that. So, he understood the need at least try to uncover the truth.

He only hoped he found something. But it was like searching for the proverbial needle in the haystack. If law enforcement and the medical examiner couldn't prove it was homicide, then he wasn't sure he'd be able to, either.

Even so, he'd damn well give it a fucking shot.

Brick followed Kramer into the house, down a hallway and into a large, very neat kitchen, checking out some of the home's layout as they passed. Kramer grabbed two bottles of craft beer from the fridge and they headed out to the pool to wait.

They didn't have to wait long.

He was just starting to chat up Kramer when they heard female voices.

A few minutes later, the doors to the deck opened and the women stepped out, squawking with surprise to find the men together.

It might be a surprise to Barb, but Londyn knew the plan.

"Well, there you go. No worries. They're both back safe and sound," Kramer announced, like Brick couldn't see that with his own two eyes through the glasses he fucking hated.

"Where's your phone?" Brick asked Londyn sharply.

Her mouth dropped open but quickly snapped shut. "In my purse."

"And where's your purse?"

Londyn hesitated for a second, then slipped into perfect character by letting a tinge of fear cross her face before quickly hiding it. "By the front door with my bags."

"I was trying to call you."

She wiped hands down both sides of her thighs nervously. "Oh... I'm sorry, honey. I didn't hear my phone."

Kramer interrupted them in an effort to break the tension. "Hey, I can throw some burgers on the grill. It's not the steak you served us the other night, but..."

Brick forced a smile. "Burgers and beer are perfect. Right, muffin?"

Londyn also shot Kramer a blinding smile that was obviously fake. "Sure. That sounds wonderful."

"Barb," Kramer called out to the woman who had frozen in place during Brick and Londyn's tight, but perfectly executed, exchange. "I'll get the grill fired up, if you want to make a couple sides and then bring out the burgers and fixings?"

That got Barb moving. "I can do that." She quickly scurried back inside.

"Why don't you go in and help her, Gertie?" Brick suggested in a way that didn't sound like a suggestion at all.

She gave him a crooked smile. "I'd be glad to."

As she turned to follow Barb inside at a much slower pace, Brick stopped her by calling out, "Did you forget something?"

With one hand on the door handle, Londyn glanced over her shoulder. When Brick tipped his chin up and tapped his finger on his lips, she looked at him in confusion.

He could see her fighting not to roll her eyes as she changed her path and strode across the deck to him. But she failed to hide that eye roll as she leaned down to plant a kiss on his mouth. Before she rose, he snaked out his hand, drove his fingers roughly into her hair and fisted it tightly to keep her close.

"Good girl," he whispered against her lips, knowing Kramer's eyes were locked on them and his ears were probably straining to not miss a word. Brick held her in place a few seconds longer, then released her.

Her mouth opened and nothing but air came out until she gathered her wits and answered with a husky, "Thank you, honey."

Was she thanking him for calling her a "good girl?" *Damn*, she *was* good at this shit. "Daddy," he corrected on a growl.

Seriously, Golden Globe worthy.

"Thank you, *Daddy*."

As she turned to go inside, he slapped her ass hard enough to make her squeak and jump.

Brick watched her disappear into the house before turning his attention back to Kramer who was standing frozen by the grill, a spatula lifted in his hand and a look on his face Brick did not like but had to tolerate.

The man looked hungry, but not for hamburgers, when he asked, "What'd she do wrong today?"

She did nothing wrong, so far. She did everything right. But he couldn't say that to Kramer. "Spent too much money. She had an allowance and she went over it."

Kramer frowned. "How do you know?"

"I monitored the credit card while they were out."

"Why didn't you just tell her to stop buying when you noticed?"

Brick smiled and shook his head, acting like Kramer didn't "get it" at all. "What fun would that be, Chris?"

"I'm guessing for you, no fun at all."

"And you'd be correct." He rose from the Adirondack chair where he sat and moved closer to the grill, which Kramer was lighting. "Barb doesn't get an allowance?"

"She makes her own money. But, thankfully, she's pretty frugal."

Right, more money for him.

"Gertie loves to spend. Overspend, more like it. I have to remind her sometimes that I'm not made of money."

"You probably do all right being a software engineer."

Shit, he did not want the conversation turning toward a career he hardly knew anything about. "I do all right, but I'd like to do better. I'd appreciate some more of those stock tips, if you have them."

"Sure." Kramer grinned and echoed, "I do all right."

"I'm sure you do," Brick muttered. Especially using a couple million from his wife's "accidental" death.

But, luckily, the market was a topic Kramer liked to talk about, and like the other night he went on and on about it, with Brick encouraging him with an occasional question until he wanted to poke his fucking ear drums out.

That was exactly why he used a broker to invest his money, even though he told Kramer otherwise. All that stock market jargon made his brain hurt.

But he stood there listening with feigned interest, biting the inside of his cheek so he wouldn't scream, until finally the women coming back out with items to set the table in their hands distracted Kramer, causing him to switch topics when he asked the women about their day.

Thank fuck.

His relief was short-lived because then he had to hear about shopping, shoes, accessories and outfits for another ball-shriveling twenty minutes.

Fuck. How the fuck did people survive that "domestic bliss" shit?

His cheeks started to cramp from keeping a smile plastered on his face and faking his interest. He'd rather be treading water for thirty minutes in full gear and frigid, rough surf than take part in all the mindless chatter. But he needed an opportunity to get inside the house unescorted. That was the whole point of this fake friendship in the first place.

When Kramer began to put the grilled burgers on a platter, the women went back inside and the two men settled at the table in blessed, companionable silence, sipping the fresh beer Barb had brought them minutes earlier.

Brick sat where he could watch both the women coming out of the house and Kramer at the same time. As the two women carried out the dishes of food, out of the corner of his eyes, he noticed Kramer raking his gaze over Londyn, pausing on her feet, then giving Barb an innocent smile as she approached the table.

Fucker.

Brick hadn't paid much attention to what Londyn had been wearing when she left the house this morning, but he realized she wore those red heels she had worn when he first met her in Shadow Valley.

Those fucking heels.

He was going to make her keep those on tonight.

He was also going to make her get totally naked except for those, and then he would slip them off her feet one at a time, licking from her toes all the way up to her wet, slick pussy.

Brick shifted in his chair, his hand diving below the table to adjust his sudden semi-erection. Which quickly deflated when her heel got caught on the edge of a deck board and she almost fell forward.

Before Brick could scramble from his seat to catch her, Kramer's arm shot out and he caught Londyn, keeping her upright.

"That was a close one." Londyn laughed, still hanging onto the bowl of macaroni salad.

As her eyes tipped down to where Kramer's hand still held onto her tightly, her face changed and Brick dropped his gaze to where she was staring.

A bit of mayonnaise dotted Kramer's forearm.

"I'm so sorry!" she exclaimed, glancing around. "I don't have a napkin."

Their eyes lifted from the spot on Kramer's arm to each other. He seared her with a *don't-you-dare* glare.

She smiled. A real one this time.

Fuck me.

He narrowed his eyes even more and shot daggers at her.

"Not a problem. I have a napkin," Kramer announced quickly with a stilted chuckle, letting her go to grab it and clean off his arm.

Brick finally breathed. When Londyn settled in the chair next to him, he leaned over, pretending to give her a kiss at her temple, but instead whispered in her ear, "Those fucking heels will be the only thing you'll be wearing later."

Her lips twitched as she placed her mouth to his ear, pretending to return the kiss. "I can't wait."

Chapter Twelve

THE EVENING COULDN'T END SOON ENOUGH so they could get down to some real business. However, the whole plan tonight was to get a chance to explore some of the house to at least learn the layout.

His attention was pulled from the woman, whose lips had done some amazing things to him, to Barb when he caught the woman rubbing at her temples and wincing.

Fuck. That meant Barb was probably getting one of her migraines and would be heading inside soon. That also meant it might screw up Brick's plan.

He wasn't the only one who noticed.

"Are you okay, Barb?"

She gave Londyn an apologetic, but pained, look. "Seems like the day is catching up to me."

"Migraine?"

Barb squinted as if the light was causing her discomfort. "Yes, I'm sorry to cut the evening short again. I'm going to go upstairs, climb into bed and take a pill."

Londyn and Brick exchanged looks and he slightly tipped his head, hoping she would read into the gesture that the plan would continue. He'd just need to work around that hitch.

Kramer helped Barb from her chair, and she gave him a quick kiss before going inside with a last "goodnight," leaving just the three of them.

Hopefully, Barb would go directly upstairs and her migraine was debilitating enough she'd stay in bed and wouldn't catch Brick sneaking around their house.

He snuck a glance at his watch. It was getting late and he needed to do something soon. With Barb done for the night, there wasn't a good reason for the two of them to remain at their house. Especially if Kramer decided to bring the evening to an early end.

As soon as Kramer went inside to grab another round of beers, Brick leaned over to Londyn and whispered, "Keep him entertained while I go snoop. If he wants to go inside, stall as best as you can."

As soon as Kramer returned, Brick quickly rose from his seat by the pool, where they had migrated after dinner. He pressed a hand to his stomach with a frown. "Excuse me while I use your facilities. You don't mind keeping my muffin company, do you, Chris?"

The man gave Brick a predatory smile that he wanted to smack off his face. "Not at all."

Of course he didn't. It took everything Brick had to go inside and leave Londyn alone with him.

He moved quickly through the house, sticking to the first floor since it seemed Barb had done what she'd said and went upstairs. At the rear of the house, he found a room that appeared to be Kramer's office. Brick rifled carefully through the paperwork strewn across the large wooden desk and turned on the computer only to find it password protected.

If he got a chance he'd come back and get Walker on

the phone to see if they could hack into it. But for now, he didn't have the time. Tonight was simply for recon.

He pulled each desk drawer out, finding typical office-like things. Nothing suspicious. In fact, all very boring, normal stuff.

In one corner of the room, a large four-drawer file cabinet was unlocked and included normal files for a house-hold and someone who played the market, like utility bills along with tax returns and other business type papers. However, a smaller file cabinet sat next to that one. And, curiously, both drawers were locked.

He went to the closet next, hoping to come across a set of keys hidden inside. While he didn't find any, he did find a safe. Which meant important paperwork could be held in there. More than the typical birth certificates, car titles and property deeds.

Damn. He had no experience at cracking safes, nor did the rest of the Shadows.

Before closing the closet door, he spotted something propped in the back corner. It looked like a Mossberg 500, a shotgun used for home defense. He wouldn't be surprised if it was loaded, but there was no way he was checking and getting his fingerprints on it.

He closed the door and twisted his head to stare at the smaller locked file cabinet again. The keys had to be some-where in the office. He doubted Kramer carried them on his person and if he was like a typical homeowner, he'd hide them nearby out of convenience.

However, Brick really didn't want to spend too much time looking. While he had confidence Londyn was doing her best to keep him busy, he didn't want Kramer getting concerned with him being gone too long and have him come searching.

His eyes quickly scanned the room and landed on a cabinet with glass doors that held books. He checked a few of them and it didn't take long to find one of those hollow ones, good for stashing shit.

And, *thank fuck*, inside that book were a set of smaller keys that would fit a desk drawer or a file cabinet. He blew out a breath of relief when they fit the cabinet lock.

He yanked the top drawer open and stared at a compact handgun. He didn't recognize the manufacturer and he certainly wasn't touching that gun, either, but from the open box of ammo next to it, it appeared to be a forty caliber. There were also a couple boxes of double-aught buckshot for the Mossberg.

While it was good to be aware the man had a gun, owning one wasn't uncommon. And keeping it locked up—at least the handgun—was smart. However, that wasn't what he was looking for since Teresa wasn't killed by a bullet.

He quietly closed the top drawer and opened the one underneath it. More file folders. Only a few of them were marked. He thumbed through the ones that weren't.

And just as he suspected, Kramer had copies of Teresa's life insurance policies along with copies of the correspondence about the payout and more. However, having them didn't prove guilt.

In another folder, Brick found Kramer's current policy on himself which was for a measly—compared to Teresa's—two hundred grand in coverage. When he looked at the start date for the policy, he compared it to Teresa's. Same time. However, the beneficiary had been changed to Barb after his wife's death. In fact, not long after.

He lifted his head and listened for voices or footsteps. Nothing.

So far, so good.

He pulled out another folder and found something interesting but not unexpected. Two more policies, also taken out after Teresa's death, but these were on Barb. And fucking lo and behold, were they not for a million each, too.

What. The. Fuck.

Was the man crazy enough to try to pull the same stunt again? To murder his current woman just to cash in?

Nobody was stupid enough to take that risk, were they? Unless, again, money was more important than life. But how would Kramer spin it the second time?

It was time he and Londyn left, and now that he knew where Kramer's office was, he'd have to figure out another time to break in to search through paperwork much more slowly. Along with hacking into that computer.

He locked the cabinet back up, returned the key to its hiding spot and on his way past the guest bathroom, he quickly went in, flushed the toilet and ran the water, before heading back to join Kramer and Londyn outside.

But as he approached the kitchen, he heard low voices. Kramer must have come inside and Londyn followed to distract him.

Thank fuck.

But his head just about exploded when he heard Kramer practically purr, "I can't eat prime rib every night. But once in a while I like to sink my teeth into a nice fatty cut of meat."

What the fuck? Nobody was eating her meat except for him.

He waited to hear Kramer cry out when Londyn kneed him in the nuts for calling her a fatty cut of meat, but he only heard her giggle.

Giggle.

What angle was she playing?

A dangerous one, that was what.

It was one thing to have Kramer caught on her hook, it was another to encourage him for more.

He relaxed the muscles in his jaw, which had been popping, and stepped around the corner into the kitchen, where he paused.

Londyn, pressed against the sink, had her hands in soapy water and Kramer had her caged in.

His dick wasn't pushed into her back, but it was damn well close enough.

Son of a bitch.

She had her head turned to look at Kramer over her shoulder and she was *smiling*—not telling him to go pound sand—until she spotted Brick. "Oh, hey, honey! Chris is just giving me a hand."

Sure, he was giving her a fucking hand.

Kramer moved back quickly, his eyes becoming wary as he turned toward Brick. "Gertie was kind enough to help me clean up since Barb is down for the night."

Londyn nodded. "I didn't want her to come down in the morning and have to face this mess."

Right. Barb probably wouldn't want to face the "mess" of her man trapping Brick's wife against the counter, either.

Fuck. Seamus's wife.

Brick sucked oxygen through his nostrils and once he was capable of keeping his voice at an even level, he choked out, "That's my muffin. Always so helpful."

Kramer's gaze slid from Londyn to Brick. The fucker didn't even have the decency to act embarrassed for getting caught hitting on Brick's wife.

Seamus's wife.

Goddamn it.

"I'll head out to clean up the grill and grab more trash. Will you be all right?"

Would *she* be all right?

Maybe right now Kramer should be worried about if he would be all right.

Londyn patted Kramer's chest, giving him a small smile, and said, "I'll be fine."

With that, Kramer gave Brick a little nod and headed back out onto the deck. But from where he stood by the grill, he could see into the kitchen and Brick did not miss the fact Kramer was watching them with interest.

Whether the man was afraid of Brick punishing Londyn or whether he was excited about that prospect and wanted to watch, Brick didn't give a shit.

What he did give a shit about was Kramer putting his hands on Londyn.

Instead of approaching her, he said, "Muffin, I think you need to go to the bathroom." Londyn went stock still for a moment and when she lifted her eyebrows, he said under his breath, "He's watching."

Shaking her head, she slowly wiped her hands off with a dishtowel and whispered back, "Then you better come get me."

He took long, determined strides across the kitchen, his jaw tight, his nostrils flared, playing the part of a pissed off husband.

The only problem was, it wasn't all acting.

Snagging her wrist, he dragged her out of the kitchen into the hallway and pinned her against the wall, his chest to hers, holding her wrists restrained within his hands.

"You wanted me to distract him so that you could do what you needed to do. You were taking forever."

A growl rose up Brick's throat and he got in her face. "He can look. He can hope. He can even fantasize. But what he *cannot do* is fucking touch."

Her blue eyes widened and then her eyelids got heavy and a smile curled her parted lips. Her warm breath mingled with his when she breathed, "You just made me wet."

"Was it me or Kramer?"

"It was you going all growly. All 'Me, caveman,' 'you, woman.' That was so hot."

The anger rushed out and the desire to fuck her against

that wall, right there in Kramer's house with the risk of the man catching them, rushed in.

"How wet?" he murmured against her lips. Taking both of her wrists into one hand, he pressed them against the wall above her head and skimmed his knuckles over one, then the other, of her peaked nipples before going lower.

Keeping their gazes locked, he thumbed open the button on her skirt and slid the zipper down enough to slip his hand inside. She had not only worn the skirt he'd insisted on, but she hadn't worn any panties.

Just. Like. He. Had. Told. Her.

He never expected her to go all day without them, never expected for her to listen to that demand since it had been part of their acting.

But she did.

And now, her breathing became ragged as the tip of his finger found her clit and circled it. Then he took her mouth to capture her groan as he slid his middle finger inside of her.

Fuck yes, she wasn't lying. She was wet as fuck.

Their kissing became frantic as Londyn began to buck against the wall, riding his finger as he pressed his thumb against her clit.

It didn't take minutes. It took seconds. For her to explode. For him to feel her heat pulsing around him. For him to muffle her cry within his mouth.

When she settled back against the wall, he cautiously broke the seal of their lips and slowly slipped his hand from her skirt. Before he released her wrists, he raised his hand and slid his middle finger into his mouth, sucking it clean.

When he was done, he leaned close, growling against her ear, "He can never have that. That's mine."

Her body twitched against him and he released her before he took it further.

"We'll say our goodbyes and then we're heading home.

No delays, no excuses. And when we hit that door, you go right upstairs, and take everything off except for those heels, get on the bed and you wait for me."

When her legs wobbled, he curled his fingers around the back of her neck and pulled her to him. "Need me to help you?"

She nodded and breathed a shaky, "Yes."

Brick let his grin grow as he helped her fasten her skirt and escorted Londyn back out to the deck to let Kramer know they were leaving.

With one arm wrapped around Londyn's waist, he extended his hand and Kramer shook it.

Then he took his woman home.

———

BRICK WAS BEING the big spoon as he curled around her, his heat warming her from the outside in.

The sex, after they'd returned from the neighbor's, had been explosive and she might have even blacked out a couple of times with some of the things he did with his tongue and other digits.

He had demanded that she keep her heels on. She had.

After fucking her the first time rough and fast, when he *slowly* slid them off one at a time, she just about orgasmed when his mouth did all kinds of things to her feet, her ankles, her calves, behind her knees...

Everything clenched on her again from the memory.

She turned in his arms to find his eyes closed, his lips parted slightly, and him breathing evenly like he was asleep.

She wasn't sure if he was or wasn't since usually after she fell asleep, he moved away from her to give himself some space.

She traced her fingertips over his relaxed features. Across his forehead, down his nose, across both cheekbones, and along the short wiry hairs that covered his upper lip and sharp, strong jawline.

She was lightly outlining his lips when his tongue came out and touched her finger, but his eyes remained closed.

She felt sorry for all the women he'd had throughout the years, who only got to enjoy him for a sliver in time, who didn't get to experience all of him. They only got a small piece, even though, in truth, the "piece" they got wasn't that small.

But she had gotten so much more.

They'd never know he was much more than just a one-night stand, because he didn't give it freely.

When this job was done, she would miss this. This intimacy with a man who had never shared it with anyone else before. She wondered if he only did with her because they were stuck living together. Or, if outside of this assignment, they would have ever connected otherwise.

She'd never know.

"You're so pretty," she teased softly. "You should've been a model."

His eyes popped open and he glowered at her. "Pretty? You don't call a fucking man pretty. You tell him he has a big cock. A skilled tongue. A way with words. But not that he's pretty. Holy fuck."

She fought her grin at his fake outrage. "Okay, you have a big, pretty cock. Your tongue isn't half-bad, either. And what you did in the hallway at their house earlier..." Londyn blew out a long, soft whistle.

"You liked that, huh?"

She lifted an eyebrow at him. "You couldn't tell?"

He grinned.

The hallway episode made her realize... "You didn't wash that hand before you shook Kramer's."

"Must've forgotten."

Bullshit. His eyes said it all. He had been marking his territory like a dog.

"Did you forget that we're not really married?"

Something flashed behind his eyes, and she heard his growled words again in her head, *"That's mine."*

That. Not *you're.*

"Or that you don't own me?"

"He needs to believe I do."

"Does he? Or do you?"

"Londyn... This is a job and we're playing our parts."

"In this bed, too? This wasn't part of the assignment."

"This is real."

"What's real? Certainly not Seamus and Gertrude."

"What happens in this bed. Your orgasms. All real."

"So, what happens between Brick and Londyn is real." She wondered if he realized what he just said. It didn't matter. He was right, they were on assignment, playing parts. "What you're saying is, Seamus owns Gertie."

"Right. He owns her ass."

"That also means you don't 'own' my ass."

His eyes narrowed and his expression went blank. "Right."

Right.

Bullshit.

"Have you ever been possessive of any woman before?"

A muscle ticked in his jaw. "Why are we discussing this?"

"Just answer the question."

"No, but then I don't keep them around long enough for that to even be a risk."

A risk.

"Was there ever any woman you thought about inviting back, maybe inviting her to spend a little time in your life?"

"No."

"Why?"

"It's not what I'm looking for."

"What are you looking for?"

"Londyn..."

"What are you looking for?" she prodded.

"Why do you fucking care?"

She shouldn't, but she did. "Do you even know?"

He flipped to his back, avoiding her searching gaze. "I'm not looking for anything. Now let's fucking drop this shit and get some sleep."

"If I could sleep, we wouldn't be having a conversation."

"I fucked you twice, that should've made you tired enough to sleep."

"*You* fucked *me* twice. Did you ever notice how you word things? *You* fucked *me*. Not we fucked each other. *That's mine*. A claim."

"Are you seriously pulling some feminist bullshit right now? You told me earlier that the caveman shit got you wet. Were you lying?"

Damn, that was true. "No." None of this mattered anyway. For the thousandth time, she reminded herself that they were in that house for a reason and once that reason was over, they would go their separate ways. Brick back to "swiping right" and banging everything with two breasts, and she'd go...

Wherever.

She still had no idea where. Just not back to New York.

There was no point in riding him about something that soon wouldn't matter, so she needed to drop it. She needed to just concentrate on why they were there in that house in the first place.

"It's a shame."

Brick's body went solid next to her. Probably expecting her to bust his balls some more.

She put him out of his misery. "I kind of like her."

He relaxed. "Barb may be an accessory to murder."

"I could see us being friends if it wasn't for this whole

situation." She had rolled to her back when he did, now she turned to study his profile in the dark. "You were a sniper. Snipers don't plink at cans. And I'm sleeping with you."

"I never killed anyone simply for profit."

"War isn't for profit?"

He sighed. "None of that shit went into my pocket. We were just the suckers who did the dirty work to put the money in someone else's."

"And bore the scars."

"And bore the scars," Brick repeated under his breath. "What I did during my service wasn't considered murder."

"Only on paper. But you still took lives."

"It was my job."

"Not an easy one, I'm sure. What about now?"

Once again, he went solid next to her. "Now?"

She waved a hand around in the air. "These *paid* assignments. You never kill anyone?"

"Londyn..."

"What? You think I can't figure out what you all do? Tell me, have you ever killed someone who didn't deserve to die?"

"It's fucking midnight. If you're feeling chatty, go downstairs and call your sister."

She ignored his griping because she needed to discuss her concerns. "I'm really not sure she's an accessory, Brick. I just can't see it. And these migraines of hers have me suspicious. She said they didn't start until Kramer and her began to live together. She never had them before in her life. It could be coincidence, but what if it's not?"

"A lot of people get migraines."

"It's a gut feeling."

He groaned. "I hate to say it, but your gut feeling may be right. Not only did I find the policies Kramer had on his late wife, but I found two on Barb in a locked file cabinet."

Londyn sucked in a breath. "For how much?"

"Do you need to ask?"

"Damn. My feeling is right."

"Possibly. And if you're right, I can't imagine Kramer would off Barb the same way he did his wife. It would have to be a different type of accident or some sort of sickness. Otherwise, it would throw a red flag."

"Wouldn't two women you're involved with, dying within a few years of each other, be enough of a red flag?"

"Or it could be chocked up to him being an unlucky bastard." He rolled onto her and pinned her to the mattress with his crushing weight. "Now, since you won't let me sleep and your mouth keeps running, I have something better you can do with it."

"What's that?" she teased.

Instead of answering, he jackknifed up and moved until he was straddling her waist. After grabbing a couple pillows, he shoved them under her head. As he did this, she watched his cock grow. He moved forward until it was bobbing inches from her lips.

"Should I take a guess?" she asked.

"You get one."

"Karaoke?"

"Close enough." His thumb tugged her bottom lip down, opening her mouth. "Tongue out." He gathered the precum from the tip of his cock onto the pad of his thumb and wiped it down her tongue. "Close your mouth and tell me what that tastes like."

"You."

"Do you want more?"

"I want all of it."

And he gave it to her, too.

Chapter Thirteen

A BEAD of sweat slid down his forehead and stuck in his eyebrow for a second before rolling into his eye, causing a sting.

Then another.

And another.

He blinked to clear his vision, but other than that, he did not move.

He did not look away.

He kept focus.

On the dark doorway of the mud house.

Until the shadows seemed to shift.

But he could be mistaken. He could be imagining it.

It turned out he wasn't.

From the shadows appeared a boy.

Five.

If that.

A five-year-old who should be sent outside to play with Matchbox cars, not explosives. A five-year-old who should be hugged by his father, not by a suicide vest.

What father—Brick hoped to fuck he was wrong—could sacrifice his child like that? For what?

The father kissed the boy's forehead, then ruffled his hair. The explosive vest had to weigh almost as much as the kid.

A fucking child. A tool in the ugly face of war.

A child. Soon a memory.

Possibly a memory to a family who used their child as a pawn. But definitely an unshakable memory to Brick.

His spotter urged, "You've got a clear shot. Send it!"

And again. "Briggs, you need to take the shot. Now."

And again. "You'll never be able to live with yourself if you don't."

I'll never be able to live with myself if I do.

Brick exhaled every last molecule of air from his lungs. He had a clear shot. A clean one. But not for his soul.

Sacrifice one to save many.

Sacrifice one to save many.

Sacrifice one to save many.

But a child shouldn't be that one.

A child who was no longer a baby, an innocent but a killer. Not by his own choice, but by the adults the child loved and trusted.

He emptied his lungs again as another drop of sweat rolled down his temple. His finger lightly caressed the trigger.

It was now or never.

He had no choice.

Sacrifice one to save many.

He smoothly squeezed the trigger. Then squeezed his eyes shut.

He didn't have to look to know if he hit his target. He knew. The explosion told him so. The suicide bomber had activated the detonator when he fell to the ground. The only difference in the outcome was where the blast occurred. Brick took out the bomber before he could take out a bunch of his fellow troops.

He saved a few lives that day. But he destroyed one he'd never forget. That memory would sear his soul forever.

Not because he took out a threat. But because that threat was an innocent boy.

After ignoring the chatter in his ear and what felt like a lifetime later, he finally opened his eyes.

The father, the son, the home. All gone. Bits of nothing left.

Almost as if they never existed at all.

––––––

HE COULDN'T BREAK free of the grip on his uniform. He was being pushed somewhere he didn't want to go.

Which was underwater.

In full gear, he was heavily weighted and already struggling to keep his head above it. Every time he fought to the surface, he was pushed back down.

Saltwater filled his nose and lungs, stung his eyes.

He couldn't see. He couldn't scream. He couldn't breathe.

He was drowning.

He needed to fight. To break free.

So, he fought, he struggled.

He could see the surface, it was right there. A few more kicks with his heavy, water-logged boots and he'd be able to suck in fresh air.

Just a few more kicks.

And he'd be able to breathe.

––––––

BRICK GASPED for breath as his eyes popped open. It was dark. And a noise next to him had him jackknifing straight up into a sitting position. It took him a few seconds to realize where the fuck he was and once he did, he switched on the lamp beside the bed.

Fuck. Fuck. Fuck.

He lunged to Londyn's side of the bed where she sat up, her hand to her cheek, her face wrinkled in pain.

"What the fuck happened?" he bellowed, grabbing her hand and pulling it away.

"You elbowed me hard in the face."

Jesus fuck.

He squeezed her hand gently and searched her face for blood. None. But she did have a large red mark on her left cheek. An impact hard enough it would eventually turn into a bruise.

"You were talking in your sleep."

"What was I saying?"

He should've known this could be an issue. He knew he had nightmares; he just didn't realize what damage they'd cause.

"You were yelling, 'I don't want to fucking do this! I can't do this!'"

Jesus fuck.

"And as soon as I touched you to wake you up, you freaked out."

"I'm so fucking sorry. I'd never fucking hurt you. You know that, right?"

"You didn't do it on purpose."

"I shouldn't have fucking done it at all!" he yelled, getting out of bed. He dropped his head, took a breath, then lifted it to look at her, appearing small in that big bed. The red area was already turning darker.

Fucking motherfucker.

"I'm getting you ice."

He didn't even pause to pull on shorts. He ran down the stairs, grabbed a bag of frozen corn he found in the freezer and took the steps two at a time to get back to her.

When he returned, she was leaning back against the headboard, wincing as she touched the injury.

"Don't touch it, it'll just make it worse."

He climbed back into bed, settled against the headboard and pulled her into his lap. She took the bag from him and pressed it to her cheek with a hiss.

"It hurt?"

"It's cold."

"It's supposed to be cold, baby. It's frozen." Pulling her against his chest, he stroked her hair as they sat there for a while with the frozen corn against her face. "Maybe we shouldn't sleep together."

"At all?"

"I meant the actual sleeping part. I didn't realize I talked in my sleep until you." Because he never slept with anyone. Sex, yes. Sleeping, no.

"Because you don't let anyone in."

Brick stiffened. "What do you mean?"

"I mean you let people see you at surface value. You don't let anyone get deeper than that. That's why you like hookups. No one gets a chance to see anyone but who you allow them to see."

"Are you psychoanalyzing me?"

She pressed her hand against his chest. "No. I'm just telling you what I've observed since I met you and I'm piecing that together with what you yourself have told me."

Christ. The answer wasn't "no," it was obviously "yes."

"You figure if you don't let anyone close, no one will see what you're hiding."

Fuck him, analyzing or not, she was right. No one would ever expect what haunted him because he hid it so well. Hidden or not, ghosts like his were hard to kill.

They lingered like a bad odor.

"I've got ears, I'm here if you want to talk about it."

He played dumb. "About what?"

"Whatever you have nightmares about."

"Why would I want to talk about it?" He wouldn't.

"Maybe it'll help?"

"I never talk about this. And the reason is, talking about it brings the ghosts closer to the surface. Then they're harder for me to fight." He shouldn't have even said that much.

"Maybe if you bring them to the surface, you can break free of them."

A shiver shot up his spine. What she just said was eerily similar to the part of his nightmare right before he woke up. The part where he was no longer in the desert but was drowning instead.

He pressed a kiss to her temple, careful of the injury. "I'm sorry I hurt you."

"But you don't want to talk about it."

"But I don't want to talk about it." *I can't. If I do, you may never look at me the same again. And that will fucking slay me.*

"Can I ask you something?"

He didn't even need to answer, because no matter how he did, she would ask the question anyway.

That was just Londyn.

"Does taking a human life eat at you?"

Fuuuuck, he wasn't expecting that one. It made his chest tighten and his stomach churn. "It's just a target. Nothing more."

"Never?"

"It can't be anything else."

And that was the biggest lie he'd ever told.

Chapter Fourteen

HE MADE no noise as he approached but she could feel his presence. It was a little unnerving how quietly he could move when he wanted to.

For some reason this afternoon, he wanted to sneak up on her.

But whenever he got close, her blood began to hum, so, for the most part, he'd never be able to surprise her. That didn't mean she couldn't play along.

She gave the brownie batter one last stir and waited. As she did, a tingle ran down her spine which made goosebumps break out along her skin. Of course, her nipples became two big goosebumps that began to ache for his mouth.

Unfortunately, that would have to wait. She had brownies to make. And they had a job to do and they weren't going to get that job done by staying in bed all day.

Not that she'd complain if they did.

Last night, after the frozen corn had turned to mush, he had moved into the spare bedroom for the rest of the night and Londyn hated every second of it. Everything about it felt wrong.

It *was* wrong.

She wouldn't allow that again tonight. She'd promise not to wake him again during a nightmare. Hopefully that would be enough so he'd agree to come back to the master bedroom.

The only good thing about him moving out was he hadn't woken her up when he got up at the butt crack of dawn to go running. But that meant it wasn't long past the butt crack when he returned all sweaty and climbed into bed with her.

Then he did his best to make them both sweaty. He succeeded. That meant they had to shower. Which they did together before breakfast and loads of coffee.

Londyn never had so much sex in her whole life. And there was no freaking way she was turning him down.

She wasn't insane.

Soon enough, this assignment would be over and Londyn would be once again "single." So, she needed to get it while she could.

She had her hair thrown into a messy knot on the top of her head to keep it out of her face while she baked, leaving her neck exposed, as well as her shoulders. She once again shivered as, without saying a word, he whispered his lips across them and up to her hairline.

Even though they didn't quite make contact with her skin, the short wiry hairs of his tightly trimmed beard did briefly here and there. The result was an even stronger shudder as everything on and inside her tightened and squeezed.

If he wasn't careful, she'd tackle him right there on the kitchen floor.

He pressed his lips to her neck and murmured, "What are you making?"

She glanced down at the dark brown batter, wondering why it wasn't obvious. "Brownies."

His lips twitched against her. "Then Gertie learned her lesson." He stepped back.

She had no idea what that meant, but it didn't matter since she was too busy lamenting the loss of his touch. "I figured they'd be a good excuse to go over to Kramer's. I can check on Barb and see how she's feeling, plus thank her for the great day we had together on Friday."

"Good thinking. How's your face?"

When she turned to face him, he stumbled back, wore an expression of horror and yelled, "*Daaaaaaaamn.*"

Londyn rolled her eyes. "Like you didn't see it this morning when you joined me in bed. Or in the shower."

"I wasn't looking at your face." His shoulder brushed hers as he leaned past her and dipped his finger into the bowl of batter.

"Hey!"

Instead of eating it, he dotted the end of her nose with it, *then* licked his finger. "And anyway, I know what it looks like, I was asking how it feels."

"Did you just put batter on my nose?"

He shrugged and smiled. "Did I?"

She planted her hands on her hips. "Now you need to clean it off."

He was wearing his contacts, so his blue eyes twinkled. "Do I?"

"Yes."

"Or what?"

"Or else."

His brows shot up and his eyes went wide as he yelled, "*Or else?* That's fucking frightening!"

"It should be," she huffed. She yanked up the bottom of his T-shirt, struggled to ignore his chiseled abs and wiped off the chocolate.

"Hey! That was a clean shirt!"

"Was it?" Two could play at that game.

"You are such a fucking smart ass."

"Am I?"

His mouth made an *O* of fake outrage, then he exclaimed, "Wow. You're just asking for it."

"What am I asking for? A spanking?"

His nostrils flared and his eyelids got heavy. "Is that what you want?"

"No."

"Liar," he whispered.

He lunged toward the bowl again. When she tried to block him, her arm knocked into it, spilling the whole bowl of batter. "Brick!"

"You did it!"

"Because of you!"

He laughed as he swiped his finger through the batter spreading like lava over the counter, dripping off the edge and landing in thick plops onto the floor.

"Don't do that! Grab a towel." As she scrambled to the drawer that held the dish towels, he snagged her arm, spun her around and swiped a line of chocolate down her nose.

"Hey!" She tried to pull away. "I already showered."

"I don't care."

"You should."

"Why?"

Her eyes followed his finger sliding through the mess again. Her heart began to race. This was not going to be good. "Because you're going to need one, too."

He laughed again and that sound, especially after last night's nightmare, was music to her ears.

He had the best laugh. The deepness of it encompassed the whole room. She couldn't help but laugh with him as he flicked the batter clinging to the tip of his finger in her direction. And, of course, because he held her with one hand, she couldn't escape.

The batter splattered her face and chest and landed on

the light pink camisole she was wearing. "Oh, you asshole! This is war!"

"One you can't win."

"Oh yeah?"

He spread his feet and pulled his shoulders back. "Fight me."

Her mouth dropped open, her eyes bugged out and when he released her wrist, she lunged toward the spilled batter. She gathered two handfuls, which seeped through her fingers and whipped it at him with all her might.

He ducked but most of it landed on his head and upper back, along with it splattering on the floor and cabinets. She hurried to reload her weapons and when she had two more palms' full, she rushed him, planning on wiping it down his face and chest. Except her bare feet slipped in the slick batter and she just about did a split. Her arms wind-milled to catch her balance and she not only coated him with some of the brownie batter but also herself.

Chunks of his hair were sticking together, his shirt was a mess, his face had what looked like chocolate tears streaked down it and he was...

Smiling.

It was the most beautiful thing ever.

"Look at this mess! You're in so much fucking trouble," she warned him with narrowed eyes.

"You are. You started it." He slipped past her, scooped a wad of batter and plopped it on top of her hair.

"Hey!" she squealed as the wad slid off her head and landed onto her shoulder. It felt like cold mud.

"Now you can say your hair looks like shit."

She grabbed another handful and shoved it point blank into his face. "I think you're due for a facial, pretty boy."

He scraped the excess batter off his cheeks and from around his eyes, and it landed with a wet splat onto the floor. He grabbed her wrists and as he jerked her toward him, he slipped. Before he could catch his balance, he went down hard, unfortunately taking her with him. She gasped as he twisted enough to help cushion her fall. When they hit the tile, the air rushed from them both.

"Happy now? We not only made a mess but now we're both lying in it."

"*I'm* lying in it," he corrected her.

She squealed as he rolled them over so her back, and everything else, squished into the cold batter on the floor.

"*Now* you're lying in it."

She blinked up at him. "Who's going to clean up this mess?"

"You."

"Mmm hmm. With your help. How come you still look good, even when you're filthy?"

He wiggled his eyebrows and tapped a finger to his temple. "I'm always filthy. And you look fucking edible right now."

He cupped her face with his batter covered fingers and stared down into it only for a second before licking the end of her nose, the corners of her mouth, and then kissing the batter off her cheek. Okay, more like smearing it across her cheek with his lips. He was not helping. But she doubted he cared.

"The batter has raw eggs in it. You could die of salmonella," she murmured, but not wanting him to stop.

"It's a risk I'm willing to take since I'll die happy."

Her heart squeezed. Did he even realize what he said?

"But hopefully a little brownie batter won't take me out."

"It might not take you out, but it might clean you out," she warned him.

He barked out a laugh. "Londyn..."

"What?" she whispered as his erection pressed into her thigh. She had a feeling she knew where this was going.

"You slay me."

There he went again saying that. "I'm going to take that as a compliment."

"It is," he murmured, lowering his head until his chocolate-covered lips brushed over hers. "Brownies are my favorite."

"Cake-like or gooey?"

"Oh, they need to be gooey. Soft and warm in the center. Like you."

"Then you better test the center," she whispered. "To make sure I'm just right."

"I will, but it won't be with a toothpick."

She laughed, but quickly got serious with the way his eyes held a fire. She now recognized that look since he got it whenever she was naked and when he was determined to make her orgasm to the point she turned into a puddle of goo. Or brownie batter, in this case.

"You don't happen to have a condom in those cargo shorts of yours, do you?" *Please say yes.*

"I'm like a Boy Scout, I'm always prepared."

His lips crushed hers and she groaned into it. Partially from his comment, the rest from the way he took her mouth, taking control, digging his fingers into her hair and gripping it tightly.

Holy smokes, she loved that he was a "take charge" type of man.

She pulled at the back of his shirt and they broke the kiss long enough for her to rip it over his head and toss the damp, batter-stained shirt somewhere in the kitchen. He tugged her cami up over her belly, following it with his mouth, smearing more brownie mix where she previously had none.

But she didn't care one iota.

He freed her breasts and lifted her just enough to jerk

the camisole over her head before tossing it in the same direction as his T-shirt.

Going to his knees, he shoved his shorts down his thighs then worked the button on hers before demanding she do the rest with a growly, "Get them off."

While she was shucking her shorts, he slipped out of his and, after digging a condom out of his wallet, both pairs disappeared somewhere over his shoulder.

There she was, laying naked on a tile floor covered in raw brownie batter, in a kitchen in a house in Florida with a man she never would have guessed would look at her the way he did.

Like he was going to die if he didn't have her that very second.

But he didn't rush, as much as she wanted him to. No, he took his time and once again surprised her with how soft and tender he could be. And she liked it. As much as when he was rough and demanding at other times.

It all depended on his mood or what she asked from him. Because she could ask him for whatever she wanted at that very moment and he would give it to her.

She had no doubt about that.

That realization, that exact moment, was when her heart melted.

Right there in that kitchen, outside of Ft. Myers, she fell in love with the gorgeous man who could have any woman he wanted but was kneeling in raw brownie batter to be with her.

And when he began to kiss every stretch mark on her hips, her stomach, her thighs. As he used his tongue to trace them along her breasts. As he whispered how much he wanted her and how beautiful she was. As he showed her the same...

That tenderness, that genuine caring, the way he worshiped

her, caused a rogue tear to slide from the corner of her eye. She didn't bother to wipe it away since she was afraid of smearing the mess on her face even worse. And, anyway, if he asked, she could say a little bit of batter got caught in her eye.

So, she let that tear run, along with a few more, before he took her breath away by scraping his teeth over the tip of her nipple, before sucking it deep within his mouth. At the same time, his fingers played along her pussy, she was sure finding her wet and ready.

He continued to tease her by stroking her lightly, brushing his thumb over her clit, but only for a second before sliding a finger through her wetness and even lower. He nibbled his way from one breast to the other and nipped it, making her back arch off the floor.

He lifted his head. "Give me your mouth." He wasn't asking or suggesting, he was demanding it, causing heat to rush through her veins.

"Come take it."

His eyes narrowed and his grin widened, and he did just that... took it. No longer tender. No longer worshipping. But hungry. Needy. Demanding.

As their tongues tangled and wrestled, he drew his finger through her wetness again and circled her anus.

He loved ass play as much as she did. How the hell did she get to be so lucky?

She might have to rethink hating Kevin and send him a thank you card instead. Because if Kevin hadn't been such a dick, Londyn wouldn't be getting Brick's.

Every second of her heartbreak was now worth it.

Brick sucked on her tongue, then kissed her even deeper as he slipped his middle finger inside of her. When he broke the kiss, he slid down her body and sucked her clit into his mouth.

Her hips surged off the floor as he sucked hard and

relentlessly. Until everything on her was pulsing. Her pulse, her clit, her core, every cell in her body.

He didn't want to coax an orgasm from her, he wanted to rip it out of her.

He achieved that when everything on her seized and, a second later, exploded. Her fingers gripped his head, holding him between her thighs, as she rode out the waves crashing through her.

However, before she came down off her high, he was gone, but for only a moment.

Their gazes locked as he tore open the condom wrapper and rolled it down his length. They remained locked as he settled between her thighs, sliding his cock through her slick, throbbing pussy until he was there.

Right where he needed to be.

Audible sighs escaped them both as he entered her slowly, taking his time filling her. Another sigh slipped from her as he began to move.

Digging her heels into the back of his thighs, she wrapped her hands around his head and pulled him down to her. But she avoided his mouth and instead buried her face against his throat, feeling the vibration against her lips of his deep grunt that accompanied each thrust.

She licked along his pulse line and the corded muscles that were straining. But she had to stop when he rose, planted one hand on the floor next to her head and began to drive into her hard and deep. His grunts become louder, and each thrust powered by his muscular thighs slammed the air out of her lungs.

She loved when he was gentle. She loved when he wasn't. She loved it all. How ever he wanted to give it to her, she would take it.

The last few times they'd had sex, he had fucked her until she came, then finished in her ass. And, *holy smokes*, she loved that, too.

But at the current pace he was going that wasn't going to happen.

No, because his blue eyes were hitting hers and they weren't letting go.

They were holding her captive. Trapping her forever.

Something ghosted behind his but was quickly hidden as his nostrils flared and, with a grimace, he hammered her even harder. Hard enough to push her through the spilled batter. But he didn't stop. He gave her everything he had.

She dug her nails into his back and arched her head back, but he quickly grabbed her chin and made her look at him.

"I want you to come again," he rumbled.

"Make me."

It was a challenge he wouldn't resist. "I make you, I finish in your mouth."

Was that supposed to be a deterrent?

"Clit or tit?" he demanded, since he only had one hand free, the other still planted on the floor so he wouldn't crush her with his weight.

Like she was going to help him... "You figure it out."

"Both," rumbled from him as he dropped his head and captured her nipple between his teeth. At the same time, he shoved his hand between them, finding her clit and pinching it.

She bucked against him and whimpered as sparks shot from both her breasts and pussy and met in the middle, exploding in her center and shooting bolts of lightning back down.

His cocky smile of achievement turned into a grimace as she cried out his name, sank her nails into his back and tightened around him as an orgasm once again was torn from her.

Before she could even come down from her climax, he pulled out, ripped the condom off, yanked her head up by her hair and shoved his cock into her gaping mouth. He was not gentle with any of that, either.

A tear slipped from her eye at the force of his quick thrusts and how deep he went. She was afraid she might have to tap out.

But, luckily, it was only seconds before he closed his eyes, threw back his head, pumped his hips forward one more time, then with a loud, long grunt-groan combo, shot his cum down the back of her throat.

She accepted all of him and was surprised when he didn't pull out right away. Instead he kept his cock buried in her mouth as his head fell forward and his eyes opened.

"Holy fuck," he breathed. He loosened his grip on her hair just enough so the pull didn't sting her scalp but not enough where she could move away. "I don't know what I like better. Finishing in your mouth, your pussy or your ass."

His thumb wiped away another tear that had escaped because of the deepness of his thrusts. Then he slid that thumb over her stretched lips. "So goddamn beautiful." He slipped from her mouth, but before he let go of her hair, he leaned down and touched his lips briefly to hers. "That was so fucking hot."

Yes, it was.

As he carefully stood and she accepted the hand he extended to her, he helped her to her feet so she wouldn't slip.

"While I agree that was hot and I'm all for a repeat performance, I now have no brownies to bring along with me when I see Barb." Though, it was worth the sacrifice.

"You go shower while I clean up the kitchen. Then make two batches. One for them and one for me. I'll enjoy eating a brownie later and thinking about what we just did."

He wouldn't be the only one. "You're going to clean up the whole kitchen yourself?"

He captured her face and said, "Baby, that was so

fucking worth it," before pressing another chocolate flavored kiss to her lips.

She wasn't going to argue if he was volunteering for clean-up duty. And she definitely wasn't going to argue whenever he called her "baby." It was a million times better than "muffin."

"I don't know what I like you wearing more. Those fucking red heels or brownie batter."

She had to look like she'd been dipped in a chocolate fountain. She hoped the wasted raw eggs and vegetable oil in the brown batter would at least condition her hair. "The heels are easier to deal with."

Brick glanced around the disaster they created in the kitchen and blew out a breath. "Yeah. Fuck me. I might be awhile."

"I can help."

He shook his head. "Baby, go shower so you can bake brownies and we can head over there before dinner."

The "we" part unfortunately distracted her from the endearment part. "We?"

"I'm going with you."

"Why?"

"I'm not leaving you alone over there with him."

"Because he wants to get down my pants?"

"How about because he probably killed his wife and may be plotting to kill his current girlfriend."

She couldn't argue that so she sighed instead. "Fine, you can go."

"I didn't need your permission, muffin," he told her as he grabbed a roll of paper towels.

"Well, Seamus, you're going to need more than paper towels. There's a bucket and a mop in the laundry room. But if you're going to tackle this while you're naked, I might have to stick around."

He grinned and slapped her bare, brownie batter

covered ass. "I'll still be naked when you come back down, because like I said, this is going to take a while."

She grabbed a clean dish towel from the drawer and carefully made her way out of the mess to where she could wipe off the bottom of her feet. "The thought of you scrubbing a kitchen down while naked will have me taking the fastest shower of my life."

He paused as he pulled a bunch of paper towels off the roll and narrowed his eyes on her. "Don't ever fucking breathe a word of this to anyone. Not even Rissa."

"I won't say a word. I'll just show her all the pictures I plan on taking."

Londyn squealed and ran out of the kitchen as he began to chase her. She smothered her laugh as she heard him curse and crash to the floor.

Chapter Fifteen

SHE HAD COVERED the bruise from him elbowing her with makeup but unfortunately not enough to where Barb couldn't figure out what she was trying to hide.

Which was evident when the woman leaned toward her and with a low voice asked, "Are you okay?"

As soon as she and Brick had arrived at Kramer's, Barb had taken one look at her face and had pulled Londyn upstairs to her second-floor office. The excuse she made to the men was to show Londyn her collection of signed books she had received from the authors she edited for.

It was impressive.

After she read the hand-written inscription on the title page of one of those paperbacks, Londyn lifted her head and frowned. "Yes, why?"

"He seems really bossy. And controlling. You tried to hide that bruise with makeup, but I can see it."

Her fingers went up to her cheek. *Damn it.* "Oh, this? I... uh... ran into the door. I'm pretty clumsy." Telling Barb that Brick had night terrors from being a Navy SEAL sniper *just* might blow their cover.

Barb gave her a doubtful look. *Holy shit.* The woman

thought Brick had backhanded her or something. "Seriously, Barb, it was just an accident. My middle name isn't Grace for nothing."

Barb ignored her lame attempt at a joke. "If you need help, all you have to do is ask."

Londyn chewed on her bottom lip as she returned the paperback to the shelf and grabbed another one from an author whose name she recognized. She paged through it as she ran the current situation through her mind.

Should she play up the battered wife? Would that help them in any way?

Since she wasn't sure, she figured she'd deny it for now and run it past Brick later.

She had one goal for this visit, besides the obvious one of checking on Barb's well-being, and that was to see if Barb knew Kramer had two humongous life insurance policies on her. That would give them an idea if Kramer had Barb in his sights as his next target.

Londyn hoped to hell he didn't. Barb truly seemed to be a sweetheart even if her boyfriend was a murdering, cheating, greedy douchebag.

And the woman was worried about her. *Ha.* If she only knew the truth.

During their short walk to Kramer's with a whole tray of warm brownies, Brick had told her, "Ask her about her policies. If she has no idea how much hers is or thinks it's a lot lower, that could mean he's trying something. If she's aware of the amount, it could be that she just gets headaches from living in Satan's sweaty armpit."

Londyn needed to get them off the subject of her being abused and onto the policies before heading back down to where the men were. Brick was relying on her stellar acting abilities.

"I appreciate your concern, Barb, I do. But I swear I'm just a klutz. I spilled brownie mix on the floor," sort of, "and slipped in it," sort of, "which caused me to face plant into the pantry door which I had left open." Which was a lie. "It was all my fault." Another lie. "Seamus was super sweet to clean up the mess I made on the floor." She omitted the most important fact that he'd been naked while he'd done so.

Londyn had photo proof of Brick, still only wearing brownie batter, with a mop in hand and a bucket at his feet. He had mugged it up for the camera as she took a couple but then told her, in no uncertain terms, she'd die a slow, torturous death by being coated in honey and staked over a fire ant hill if she ever showed them to anybody. They were solely for her own "spank bank."

That's exactly what he said.

Since she didn't think that would be a pleasant or peaceful death, she created a folder on her phone, named it "spank bank" and filled it with material for her use later. Once this assignment was over and it was once again only her and her battery-operated boyfriend, which she was now dubbing Brick Jr, she'd probably need them.

Though, her memories of all their sexy times might work just as well.

Concentrate on the task at hand, Gertie girl.

She put the second book back and shot Barb a smile. "If you ever need help with proofreading, I used to be the editor for my high school paper." Like a million years ago.

Barb's smile started to slip. "Oh... Thanks. I'll let you know."

Londyn sighed and moved to the window. Even though it overlooked their backyard, she couldn't see the guys. They were probably under the covered portion of the deck, drinking a beer in the shade and yucking it up.

"I just get so bored sometimes not having a job." Londyn added a little whine to make her acting more award-worthy.

"Why don't you get one?"

"Seamus..." She took a long dramatic pause. "He needs to be the provider, since he's the *man* of the house. You know how that is, right? I'm sure Chris likes to provide for you."

"He—"

"You know, like buy you nice things? Shoes, jewelry, purses when you're a good girl?"

"I—"

"Seamus feels like it's his job to take care of me financially since I take care of him in other ways." *Hint, hint.*

It was a shame she was wasting all this acting ability on one person. She needed a bigger audience who could truly appreciate her skills.

"That's sweet," Barb choked out behind her.

"Isn't it, though? I feel so *loved.* There can't be a luckier woman than me. He's even talking about upping our insurance policies from two hundred thousand to a million each. He wants to make sure I'll be taken care of if anything happens to him."

"If he wants to make sure you're covered if, God forbid, anything happens to him, why would he need the same policy on you?"

Londyn took a deep breath, bugged out her eyes and spun to face Barb. "Good question. Do you think that's excessive? What do you two have?"

Barb's mouth opened and closed and after a few seconds said, "After we moved in together, we each got one for two hundred and fifty thousand."

Londyn pursed her lips and made a show of considering her answer, though she really wanted to scream, "Bingo!" and sprint downstairs to tell Brick. Okay, maybe not sprint, because she'd probably tumble down the steps and break her neck, but it took everything she had to remain standing there with a woman who might be slated to be Kramer's next victim.

Her heart beat furiously in her throat and her blood rushed in her ears. "That's probably a reasonable amount. I'm not sure why he needs a whole million dollars if I die. I only want to be cremated and I can't imagine that costs more than a couple hundred bucks, right?" She waggled her eyebrows and joked, "With that large payoff, I'd be worried about him trying to kill me and run off with some younger woman, you know?" She added a "just kidding but am I *really*?" laugh to make it sound more convincing.

"I'm sure he wouldn't do that."

"We've been together a long time. But when you think about it, just how long does it take to really get to know someone? I mean, sometimes Seamus does stuff and I wonder who the hell he is." Again, she added a stilted laugh. "Like, do I really know who I'm married to?"

Barb's expression turned concerned again. "What type of stuff?"

"Oh, you know, leaving the lights on and the toilet seat up. Things like that."

Londyn got a look from Barb like the woman didn't believe her.

Good. Leave her guessing. The abused spouse angle might work in their favor.

"Is Seamus always bossy with you?"

"When we were first married, he limited it to the bedroom. And, I have to admit, I loved it, so I didn't discourage it. Then it moved out of the bedroom. But I'm used to it and he does take good care of me." Barb's face had turned pink when Londyn mentioned the bossy in the bedroom part. "Chris isn't like that?"

"No, he's always sweet, but protective, with me. He's always asking me if I need anything and bringing me tea or soda. Sometimes he even brings me breakfast in bed."

Hmm. And poisons that food and drink?

She wanted to ask Barb a million and one questions, but

she also didn't want her to get suspicious. Or think Londyn was a total loon.

"That's really nice. Seamus helped me make the brownies after he cleaned up my mess today."

Barb's smile grew.

"He probably just wanted to make sure I didn't make another mistake."

That smile faltered. "What would've happened if you did?"

"I'm just glad I didn't have to find out." Londyn grimaced at that on purpose "accidental" slip. She grabbed Barb's arm and tugged. "Come on, let's go see what the men are up to. It's getting late and Seamus likes his dinner on the table at six and I don't have anything planned yet."

———

BRICK TOOK a chug of beer and glanced at Kramer over the lip of the bottle.

The man had been skirting around the topic of Londyn's bruise, but Brick could see he was chomping at the bit to ask about it.

"Best brownies I ever had," Kramer finally said, eyeing Brick carefully. "But the chocolate chip cookies were just as good."

There it was. An opening for Kramer to ask about the bruise.

"She can make them for me anytime."

Brick cocked an eyebrow at Kramer. "For you?"

"For us," he corrected quickly. "Was that a test, too?"

Brick took another long pull on his beer. "Everything's a test, Chris."

"Well, then she passed if she made brownies, right?"

"Maybe I didn't want brownies today."

The look on Kramer's face was priceless. "Did you tell her what you wanted?"

"Again, Chris, what fun would that be?"

Kramer leaned forward, planted his elbows on the arms of his Adirondack chair and asked, "You hit her?"

"It's discipline." Brick tilted his head and made a show of studying Kramer before saying, "You going to call the cops?"

Kramer lifted his hands, palms out. "I'm not judging the way you run your household."

Asshole. You just showed your hand.

"You know how it is. You can't live with them; you can't kill them." Brick barked out a laugh, while watching the man's expression carefully.

Kramer lifted his beer in the air. "Isn't that the damn truth." His brown eyes hit Brick's.

"So, you discipline them instead."

"Does she like it?"

Brick forced a chuckle. When really, he wanted to beat the smirk right off Kramer's face. "We had that discussion the other night, Chris. Why do you keep asking?"

Kramer sat back in his chair and blew out a breath before lifting his half-kicked beer to his lips. "I like the idea of keeping a woman in her place. I doubt Barb would like it, though. Not like Gertie."

Brick lifted a shoulder in a casual half-shrug. "Find a woman who would."

"Yeah," Kramer said softly. "I might have to do that."

Now there was a hand Brick needed to play. "Nothing like having all that power in your hands, Chris. It's a feeling like no other. She loves to be choked when I'm fucking her, and I've come close to not stopping. Sometimes I wonder what it would be like to take someone's life like that. Like a god. You choose whether that person lives or dies. It's a heady feeling knowing she only breathes because I allow her to."

Kramer's eyes burned with excitement. "What stops you from taking it to that next step?"

"Prison, my friend."

Kramer said nothing as Brick put his beer down. His stomach was turning sour at this conversation. It was one thing to kill to save your own life or others, or because the target deserved it, it was another to kill someone you professed to love.

"Plus, I'd miss her. No matter what she does wrong, I still love her. And the sex is..." He focused his gaze on the pool and let his words drift off before shaking his head. "Hottest fucking sex of my life. That's why I married her."

"And she can bake."

Brick forced out a chuckle. "Yeah, she can bake."

The sliding glass door opened and the women joined them.

"Honey, we should head home if you want me to have dinner ready at six."

"If?" Brick asked, climbing to his feet, eyes narrowed.

Kramer also stood, his gaze sliding right past Barb and getting caught on Londyn. And her cleavage. Before raising his eyes to check out her bruise again. "Shame you have to run off."

"We just wanted to drop off the brownies and I wanted to make sure Barb was okay. But we really need to get back now," Londyn insisted.

Brick extended his hand and Londyn stared at it for a second, then put hers in his. He pulled her into his side. "What's on the menu?"

"I... I don't know," she finished off in a shaky whisper.

"You don't know?" he asked sharply.

"That's why we need to get back. Or, if you prefer, you

can stay and continue your visit with Chris and I can head back, honey."

He slid his hand over Londyn's ass and squeezed. "No, I'll go with you, muffin."

They said their goodbyes and Brick didn't drop her hand once they hit the sidewalk. Because of that, he could tell she was jumping out of her skin.

He had to walk faster to keep up with her.

As soon as they were on the other side of the front door, she practically squealed, "She thinks you're abusing me." Like that should be something to celebrate. "She asked if I need help."

"Crazy that she's more worried about you than her man trying to get down your pants."

Londyn ignored that. "Can we use this?"

"I don't know. Hopefully. He asked if I hit you."

"And you denied it?"

"No, I didn't deny it. I played it up."

"That means you do think we can use this angle."

"It can't hurt unless Barb calls the fucking cops on me. That'll fuck everything up." He removed his glasses and rubbed his eyes. "Let me think on how we can use this."

"Maybe I can ask Kramer for help."

Say what? "No. The help he wants to give you will not help me find any evidence. If anything, he'll get handsy with you and then I'll have to kill him."

She moved into him and fisted his shirt. "Really?"

He dropped his head and stared into her wide blue eyes. "Yeah, really. You don't touch another man's wife."

"I'm not your wife," she reminded him in a whisper.

"Right." *Right.* He needed to remember that. But she was still in his bed. Same shit.

"Anyway, Barb thinking you beat my ass wasn't what got me excited."

"I thought you liked when I spanked you."

She grinned up at him. "Spank, not beat. There's a difference."

No shit. "Okay, then what got you excited?"

"I managed to ask her about the policies."

Brick's ears perked. "Without her getting suspicious?"

"Yes! I swear I should be an actress."

"Will you just tell me what she said?"

"She believes their policies are for only two hundred and fifty thousand."

"They were when Kramer opened them, then he bumped hers up as soon as they moved to Florida." He dipped his head and slid his lips over hers briefly. "Good job."

"Do you think that means he'll kill her for that settlement?"

"It could. There's no reason to have the amount of coverage he has on her. None. They have no kids and she's not the main breadwinner in the household. It's just not a common amount. Why the insurance company granted it, I'll never fucking know."

"Maybe he knows someone who works for that insurance company?"

"And the person gets a cut?" Brick asked her. "Damn, that could be. Someone could fudge the paperwork... I don't know. I don't know enough about insurance to know if that's even possible."

"Okay, that aside, it *is* possible Kramer is giving Barb something to cause her headaches. He could be poisoning her."

"Makes sense if he wants to kill her." He sighed. "I need more time in their house. Especially in his office. He's got a safe in addition to the locked cabinet. I don't have any safe cracking skills."

She tugged on his shirt. "You can't just blow it up?"

"That might give me away."

She did a cute snort-laugh and face-planted into his chest. He wrapped his arms around her and held her tight. She felt so good there. Perfect, actually.

They stood there for a few quiet moments before, "Can you imagine that you love someone, trust someone, and without your knowledge they're planning your demise?" came muffled from his shirt.

"It's sick. I wonder why he needs the money?" Besides just being greedy, what did Kramer need millions for?

"I don't know if I can trust falling in love with a man again," she mumbled. "First Kevin and now Kramer. Why can't there just be decent men out there?"

He twisted his fingers into her hair. "There are."

"Well, I've yet to find one."

His chest tightened. He tried to convince himself it was because she didn't include him among her definition of "decent," not the fact that she would be looking for someone else. "You'll find someone."

"I just want what my parents had." She lifted her head but didn't pull away. "Do you know anything about our parents?"

He glanced down into her upturned face. "Do you think Mercy sits around like a real human being talking about Rissa?" Though, he did occasionally bitch about Londyn, but he wasn't telling her that. There didn't need to be more tension between the two.

"No. And I don't get what she sees in him."

"She's perfect for him."

"But is he perfect for her?"

His eyebrows shot up. "Has she said something?"

"Just that she loves him."

"Then he's perfect for her."

She shrugged in his arms. "I have my doubts."

"Don't. And don't put doubts in Rissa's head, either. Mercy's the best he's been in years. He's the cornerstone of our team. Diesel might be our boss, but Mercy's our leader. We don't talk about it, but we recognize it." It was so fucking true. Mercy was the glue for their team. He was the one who stepped into the leader role right from the get-go, which was something they needed, especially when they went out in the field on an assignment.

"What about you?" she asked.

"What about me?"

"You don't want to lead?"

"I'm just a grunt."

She fisted his shirt tighter. "A Navy SEAL sniper is not a grunt. Even I know that."

"This former Navy SEAL sniper is fine with being a grunt. He prefers it."

"Why?"

He looked over her head, seeing both nothing but everything at once. "I prefer to be the one receiving the orders, not giving them."

"You could've fooled me." She pressed a kiss into his neck and pulled from his arms. "Speaking of, I told Barb that you insist dinner be on the table at six."

He grinned. She was so fucking good at playing his wife that it was scary. "That's true, muffin. But dinner is going to be a snack since it'll be your ass on the table."

She patted him on the chest in a placating manner. "Oh, Seamus, honey, I'm not a snack, I'm an all-you-can-eat buffet."

That she was. And he was suddenly starving.

Chapter Sixteen

BRICK PRESSED his eye to the scope and surveyed Kramer's backyard. Like most times when he checked, it was empty. He pivoted his rifle on the stand toward the house and every nerve in his body began to vibrate.

Where his rifle was set up in the spare bedroom, he could see not only Kramer's backyard but a corner of the house. And in one window he spotted the man himself standing with a pair of binoculars to his eyes.

Not birdwatching. Fuck no.

Kramer was looking into Brick's backyard.

Where the pool was.

Where Londyn was swimming.

"Fucking motherfucker," he whispered.

He adjusted his rifle until the crosshairs of his sight were set perfectly between Kramer's eyes. His finger hovered over the trigger for only a second before he caressed it lightly.

He forced all the air out of his lungs and stilled, focused on the man focused on Londyn.

He shouldn't blame Kramer. Brick had pushed him to it. On purpose. He'd used Londyn as a tool as part of this job.

Over the past couple of weeks, he'd been fueling that interest.

The man's obsession was his fault.

And it was that very second when it hit him upside the head like a... brick. He was fighting the same obsession.

Because of that, the interest Kramer had in Londyn was causing his gut to burn and his blood to boil.

That fucker wanted what was his.

He shifted his finger away from the trigger, closed his eyes and pressed his forehead to the cold metal of his MK-11. The only thing he could count on besides his team. And now Londyn.

After the blood stopped rushing into his ears, after the pounding stopped in his temples, he straightened, closed the curtains and turned to stare at the weapon.

A weapon he'd taken many lives with, and one night, long ago, almost his own.

Somehow in the darkest, lowest moment of his life he realized that if he went through with it, the man who had strapped an IED onto that innocent, little boy would win. He would've achieved his goal. He had wanted to take out American troops and he would have been successful if Brick had taken his own life.

And just like that day near the Pakistan border, there was no fucking way Brick was going to let that monster be successful. Even if it cost Brick for the rest of his life.

But without solid proof of Kramer killing his wife, doing the same to him would make Brick no better. He never took what he did lightly. Not once. Every pull of the trigger had a reason. A valid one. The target had to deserve it.

A threat. A child molester. A cold-blooded murderer.

A suicide bomber.

A person in which the world would be a better and safer place if they were no longer a part of it.

Brick needed to believe that because it was the only thing keeping him whole. The only thing which kept him from disintegrating into a million particles of dust.

That day when a five-year-old changed his life forever, it made him question everything.

Where he came from. What he was doing. Why he was doing it. Where he was going.

Because the very millisecond he pulled that trigger, a piece of him went missing. Never to be found.

But then, that was his punishment. His cross to bear. A choice which would haunt him forever.

As it should.

Even though he couldn't kill Kramer for spying on Londyn, he could stop it without giving himself away.

He jogged down the stairs and outside, stepping up to the pool's edge. He watched her for a few minutes doing laps as he tried like hell not to twist his head and stare right up at Kramer. Maybe even give him the fucking finger.

Instead, he concentrated on how Londyn's body moved through the water. Smooth and steady. Bringing his blood pressure down a few points.

After a couple more laps, she caught sight of him at the edge and swam over. "Is something wrong?" she asked, blinking up at him with damp, spiky eyelashes.

"Why would you think anything is wrong?"

Her long dark blonde hair appeared light brown when it was wet and plastered to her head, but it made her blue eyes pop. Her lips were still a bit puffy from the sex they'd had less than an hour before. After his run and before her swim.

That made him believe Kramer now knew their schedule. He got up early to run, he came back, they had sex. She swam and then they had breakfast.

It had become a habit. A comfortable one that Brick had easily slipped into.

"One reason might be you standing at the edge of the pool being a creeper."

"I'm not the creeper."

She blinked. "What does that mean?"

"Act natural," he told her.

She twisted her face. "You know those words cause the opposite effect, right? Like telling someone to relax when they're upset?"

Brick squatted by the pool and freed a wet strand of hair clinging to her cheek. "We're being watched. Correction, *you're* being watched."

Londyn's head snapped up and her spine stiffened. "I assume by Kramer?"

Brick nodded, keeping his back to the neighbor's house to block the man's view of Londyn.

She bugged her eyes at Brick. "What should I do? Play with myself?"

"What?" he shouted, then cringed before hissing, "Why the fuck would you do that?"

"To send him into a frenzy? I thought that was the point, to keep him on the hook."

"You mean so his obsession drives him to kill me and kidnap you?"

She made another face and playfully splashed water on him. "You've been teasing him all this time. Making me call you Daddy. Smacking my ass in front of him. Should I go on? If he goes overboard, it's your fault."

That fact was already weighing on him. "If the man killed his wife for the insurance money, he already went overboard."

"Right." She sighed, still clinging to the side of the pool. "I feel sorry for Barb."

"Barb's not going to be the one tied up and... taken advantage of. Though, I'm starting to wonder if you'd enjoy being tied up."

"Hey!"

He cocked a brow. "Am I wrong?"

"Doesn't matter if you're right or wrong."

"Let's get it straight right now. I'm always right."

Londyn snorted. "*Soooo*, anyway, you came out to tell me to put on a show? Do you want me to get out of the pool?"

"*We* are going to put on a show. To do that you need to get out of the pool."

Her luscious mouth formed a tempting *O*. "*Ooooh*. And how are we going to do that?" She began moving toward the pool's steps but stopped suddenly. "Wait. What kind of show? The good kind or the bad kind?"

Good question. He could either "discipline" Londyn and hope Kramer was watching, or claim her and hope he got the hint that Londyn was his.

Or both.

LONDYN CLIMBED out of the pool and watched Brick's face. It was the first time she ever saw him lost with indecision.

Because of that, she made it easier for him. Instead of grabbing her towel, she walked directly to him. He rose from his squat and kept his eyes glued to her as she approached.

That look.

Every time he looked at her like that her breasts began to ache, and she wanted to jump his bones. Every single time. With all the sex they'd had in the past couple of weeks, she'd think they'd get tired of each other.

But hell no, it just fueled the fire.

No woman in her right mind would get tired of having sex with the man now standing before her. Unless he sucked in bed.

She could attest to the fact he didn't.

"Is he still watching?" she asked under her breath.

After a quick flick of his eyes, they landed back on her. "Sure as fuck is."

Color rushed into Brick's cheeks, which surprised her. No way was it from embarrassment. It had to be pure anger since even his blue eyes had a sharp glitter to them.

"You're not wearing your glasses," she whispered.

"That's the least of my worries. He's paying more attention to you than me."

"What do you want me to do?"

He set his jaw. "I'm going to smack you in the face and I'm going to do it hard."

"What?" she squeaked. Smacking her ass was one thing, but in the face?

"I'll barely miss you but you're going to act like I hit my target. Do you think you can do that?"

Ah, he was going to test her acting abilities. "I think I can handle that." At least she hoped so, otherwise she would end up with another bruise.

"It's got to look real, Londyn. I want you to fall to the ground, to play it up but not fight back." He tipped his head down and his eyes were just as hard as his jaw. "But let me make something really fucking clear. If a man ever strikes you, I want you to claw that fucker's eyes out, knee him in the nuts and stomp on his face in those ridiculous heels of yours. You got me?"

Did he think she wouldn't fight back? No man was striking her out of anger. She wouldn't knee the asshole in the balls, she would use her high heels to skewer them. Did he forget what she did to Kevin when he backhanded her? But before she could remind him of that, he continued.

"For right now, you need to act like you're giving me some sass, so I have a reason to discipline you."

"Well, I won't have to dig deep to give you sass."

It was obvious he was fighting a grin at that answer and

trying to keep his expression serious and his attention on her. "Ready?"

She nodded again, but just enough so he could see it.

"Game time."

And action! Planting her hands on her hips, she tilted her head and took a step back. Then she threw in a little chicken-necking for good measure. She had no idea what she was spouting for the most part, she was just throwing out random insults. Anything she could think of. Loud enough for someone to possibly hear her raised voice two houses away but not enough so Kramer could decipher those words.

Brick's eyebrows shot up his head and his expression became thunderous, but not one word crossed his tightly pressed lips.

She shook a finger at him, continued to yell, and when she spun away, Brick seized her wrist, spun her back to him hard enough to give her whiplash, and as he lifted his open hand, she actually cowered out of instinct.

She dug deep, followed the swing of his arm and as the rush of air brushed along her cheek, she jerked her head as if she'd been struck hard. She began to drop to the ground like he wanted, her hand pressed to her cheek, her hair in her face, but before she could hit the ground, he yanked her back up by the wrist he had never released.

"You fucking backtalking bitch!" he shouted, spit coming from his mouth.

Londyn's heart was racing. And so was her mind.

She knew women dealt with this kind of thing every day for real. Luckily, she never had. She couldn't help to think how horrific it would be to be so beaten down by someone who was *supposed* to love you that you were paralyzed with fear. Paralyzed to the point where you were too afraid to even leave and get out of that situation.

It not only caused a lump in her throat, but it churned

her stomach. While this was all acting, watching the feigned fury on Brick's face scared the shit out of her.

Her thoughts were interrupted when his other hand wrapped around the front of her throat and he roughly shoved her. If it wasn't for him holding onto her wrist, she would have stumbled to the concrete. He was shouting in her face, his own distorted with anger.

He kept pushing her backward by her throat until her back hit the post supporting the roof of the covered lanai. It was only then that his fingers loosened, though he didn't release her throat completely, and he dropped her wrist.

His face got even closer to hers. "That was fucking awesome, baby. He can't see us where we are now. But you gave him a show he won't soon forget."

She wouldn't, either. "We gave him a show, but you actually scared me." Her heart was still thumping heavily in her chest.

His thumb swept gently up and down her pulse. He had to feel it racing. "Sorry."

"Are you sure he won't call the cops?"

"I doubt it. He got worked up about me hitting you. And it wasn't the kind of worked up that meant he was concerned with your well-being." He brushed a light kiss over her lips. "I didn't hurt you, right?"

"No. Did I win an award with my acting?"

He grinned. "Yep. And I'm about to give it to you to make up for me manhandling you."

That sounded promising. "I need to wash the chlorine off first."

"I can help you with that and then I'll even make you breakfast."

Her eyes went wide. "*You're* making breakfast this morning?"

"Well, it might end up being brunch."

"I prefer brunch."

"I figured that." His mouth crushed hers and a few minutes later he was dragging her upstairs to the shower.

———

"ALMOST FOUR GODDAMN WEEKS. Ten searches of the house. You spending time with Barb just about every fucking day. Me spending too much time with that man who takes every fucking opportunity to eye fuck you, not only in front of his own woman, but me. We even spent goddamn Thanksgiving with them! We haven't gotten shit. It's time to end this fucked up bromance and go home."

Walker had even helped him hack into Kramer's computer and they'd found nothing. The hard drive was squeaky clean. The browser searches were clear. Walker suspected and confirmed the computer was purchased after Kramer's wife died. Probably with the settlement. Brick ground his teeth.

"What did your boss say?"

Brick stopped his pacing, raked fingers through his hair and blew out a loud breath. When he called Diesel to tell him he was ready to end this, to inform him this was a failed mission, the fucker not only laughed at him but hung up.

The man was the reigning King of Assholes.

He'd called Mercy next. That didn't go much better.

Mostly because he didn't think Mercy wanted Londyn coming back to his house to stay any time soon.

Then Brick started to wonder if the job was a whole set-up just to get Londyn out of the man's house. That Mercy knew the job was impossible from the beginning but told Diesel to accept the job anyway.

Because almost a month later, Brick was still only holding his own dick in his hand and not something concrete to give to the client.

The client needed indisputable evidence since he wanted

to hand it over to law enforcement to get justice for his daughter. Suspicions without hard evidence weren't good enough to get Kramer charged with homicide. Or to get any kind of charge to stick.

Even without solid proof, Brick had no doubt the asshole was guilty.

Londyn turned toward him after she finished loading the dishes from their once again very late breakfast. She was wearing some sort of light blue summer dress—a sun dress she called it—that matched her eyes, but with no bra and he seriously wanted to bury himself in those tits.

Fuck. He had a difficult time not touching her constantly.

Another reason they needed this going-nowhere job to be over.

Especially since he had caught himself several times—while searching for any kind of evidence—hoping he didn't find it so this assignment wouldn't end any time soon.

And that was just fucked up.

He hated Florida and couldn't wait to get back to colder weather so his fucking balls would stop sweating and he'd stop getting swamp ass when he ran.

Even though he wasn't a big fan of snow, right now he'd love to do a snow angel in a foot of it, in zero-degree weather while naked.

Londyn, with a concerned look, stepped up to him and fisted his T-shirt like she always did when she was standing so close. She tilted her face up to him, her blue eyes searching. "Well?"

Well?

Ah, fuck. She had asked a question and he got so caught up in his own fucking thoughts, he never answered.

Not that he had a solid answer to give her.

In the end, Mercy had told him that D was leaving the decision to throw in the towel up to Brick. The client was still willing to pay the fees for another week.

While he wasn't thrilled with staying one more week, if they left now...

Once they got back to Shadow Valley...

Everything between him and Londyn would be over.

He squeezed his eyes shut.

"Brick."

That husky voice saying his name...

It did things to him he didn't know what to do with. He didn't know where to compartmentalize all of it in his head. Things, like *feelings*, he didn't want to explore caused by hearing his name on her lips during sex. His name on her lips when they joked around or teased each other. His name on her lips as she smiled at him.

Or when she breathed his name right before their lips touched or he slid his cock home.

This needed to come to an end. Not just the job but whatever was developing between the two of them.

Because life was so much fucking easier when he only had to swipe right.

Uncomplicated.

Simple.

Steady.

Londyn was complicated.

Complex.

And made him unsteady.

Especially when he caught Kramer staring at her tits or ass. Or making conversation with her when he thought Brick wasn't within earshot.

All of that, while he knew it was necessary for the job, drove him bat-shit crazy.

And that was a problem.

They were playing husband and wife, but sometimes he'd forget it was only pretend. He'd have to remind himself Seamus and Gertrude didn't exist.

"Hey," she whispered, going up onto her bare toes and getting right in his face. "Why are you ignoring me?"

"I could never ignore you, muffin," he teased, though it came off as flat. He needed to let his frustration of the situation settle. He sighed, hoping that would help. It didn't. "The client is willing to pay for one more week."

"So then... Another week of the bromance? Or are we packing our bags and heading back to winter?"

"It's not officially winter in PA for another couple of weeks."

"Well, it wouldn't hurt to work on my tan for another week." A small smile curved her lips but he could see it. In her eyes. They spoke volumes.

The second they stepped off that plane in Pittsburgh, their made-up life was over. They had promised not to touch each other and because they hadn't kept that promise, they would have to keep the secret.

Because, while Mercy had wanted Brick to take Londyn out of his hair for this job, when she had shown up in Shadow Valley it was due to heartbreak. The man didn't want her to return to his house for the same reason, which was to lick her wounds. This time because of Brick breaking her heart.

And, like it or not, once this job was over, if she expected more than what they already had... That hurt could very well happen. Which was why they never should have touched each other in the first place.

Her knuckles grazed his jawline and he tipped his face down to hers. It was obvious she wanted to stay the extra week. He'd give her that much. "You have another week to work on your tan. Then we're leaving Satan's sweaty armpit."

That also gave him one more week to try to get a confession from that fucker. So far he'd done everything he could to get Kramer to trust him. To get Kramer to slip. To get Kramer to joke about it.

Something. Anything.

But he'd gotten nothing.

In the end, he might not be able to complete his assigned task. It might end up being a failed mission.

And failure was not in a Shadow's vocabulary.

Chapter Seventeen

LONDYN MENTALLY GROANED WHEN, after ringing the doorbell, Kramer opened the front door. His face went from annoyed to overjoyed in a split second.

"Hi!" she chirped.

"Hey," he purred.

Yuck. "Barb here?"

His smile spread and he jerked his chin over his shoulder. "Fighting a migraine again. She's up in bed."

Damn. She never knew *anyone* who had that many migraines. How did Barb or her doctor not think that was suspicious?

And now it was to the point where Barb was hardly ever getting out of bed.

She didn't have to plaster a concerned look on her face since she really was concerned with the woman's health and safety. They only had a week left for Brick to find something on Kramer and Londyn was starting to wonder if Barb would make it that long. She was torn with what to do about the woman. They had no "solid proof" that Kramer killed his wife and none that he was causing Barb's migraines.

Not only was Brick frustrated and on edge, but so was she.

Hence, why she was currently standing on their doorstep. She felt helpless and needed to do *something*, even though she wasn't sure what.

Her mind kept going back to somehow using the abused wife angle. It really was the only thing she had.

"Oh, I'm sorry to hear that. Can you tell her I stopped by, please?" She turned to go, hoping Kramer would stop her.

"Wait!" he shouted, then dropped the volume to just above a whisper. "Don't go. Come on in."

She mentally pumped her fist in the air.

Her gaze slid past him to the darker interior of the house. "You're probably busy making money hand over fist with the stock market."

He opened the door wider as if that would make it more inviting. "I'm taking a break for lunch. Why don't you come join me?"

"We had a very late breakfast." She patted her stomach, which drew his attention there. Which she noticed on its way back up to her face it got stuck on her chest for a long moment before breaking free. "While I appreciate the offer, Seamus will wonder where I'm at." She shot a glance over her shoulder back at their house to make her point.

"You're visiting Barb. That's where you're at."

Oh, he was a sneaky shit.

Londyn let a little smile toy with her lips. "Yes, but she's unavailable, so I need to go home to my husband."

As she turned to leave again, his sharp, "Does he always keep you on such a short leash?" stopped her.

Londyn chewed on her bottom lip for a second, wondering how she should play this. "No, of course not. He didn't mind me spending time with Barb. But he *would* mind me spending lunch with you alone."

"You wouldn't be alone with me. She's right upstairs."

Right. She's right upstairs and you not caring makes me want to stab you in the nuts with a rusty fork.

"*Soooo. Anywhooo.* I need to get back."

Londyn took a step back when he took one step out onto the front stoop.

She wanted to move out of his reach when he dragged a knuckle down her cheek. The one where she used makeup to make it look like a new bruise. Now she wasn't only an expert actress, she was a great makeup artist. Two more things to add to her resume for her job search when they were done in Florida.

She winced at his touch to pretend it hurt. Though, she would've winced anyway, just from his creepy touch.

"He could be watching," she whispered, acting afraid of getting caught.

"I can help you," he whispered back, dropping his hand and returning to the shadows of the house.

"How?"

"Come inside, Gertrude."

The forcefulness of his tone surprised her. He'd used the same one that Brick did when he was playing a bossy Seamus. Kramer must think that she was some spineless twit and did whatever any man demanded.

Was he fucking wrong.

She squeezed her eyes shut for a second. Though, today she needed to play one. It might be their last chance to discover the truth.

"Let me help you."

There was so much to unpack in those four little words. "You haven't said how."

He lifted his gaze over her shoulder to Seamus and Gertie's temporary home behind her. "Come inside before he sees us."

Aaaah, he was going to use her own fear to manipulate her.

Brick had mentioned several times that a confession from Kramer would be the easiest way to tag the murder to him. But he also said it would be the hardest way to get what they needed.

However, it could very well be the only evidence that may pin it on him because if any physical evidence existed, Brick said he would've found it. They also had to assume none existed because law enforcement hadn't found any, either.

But—and it was a big but—if Londyn could get a confession from him—since he wasn't spilling his guts to Brick no matter how hard Brick tried—she may be able to convince Barb to leave him, which would save the woman from whatever nefarious plans Kramer had for her. And she could give the information to Brick for his client. What the client, Teresa's father, did with it from there, she didn't care, as long as Barb was safe and Brick's assignment was successful.

His stress level was dialed to a level ten and Londyn could see the effect it was having on him, plus his night terrors, which hadn't popped up in the last couple of weeks, had returned.

After his thrashing around in bed last night, she was lucky the bruise on her cheek wasn't real. He had jerked awake drenched in sweat and moved to the spare bedroom in the middle of the night, against Londyn's wishes.

This morning Brick was right. It was time to end this and go home. But she could see that giving up would cost him, also. So, she might be the one who could coax that confession from Kramer. *If* she played the man right.

Only, she knew Brick would not like her plan in the least. No matter what, she was a part of this assignment and if she was the only one who could get it done, she was going to do whatever she could to help him.

That meant her plan was about to go into play.

"Game time" whispered through her head. It was what Brick said whenever they were about to stage a scene as an abusive husband and a battered wife.

With a last nervous glance behind her, she stepped inside and squeezed past Kramer, barely avoiding his touch as he closed the door. The hairs on the back of her neck prickled as she heard him turn the deadbolt.

"I can only stay a little bit." Unfortunately, the shake of anxiety in her voice was not acting.

"How long?"

"I told him I'd only be gone a half hour. Otherwise, he would've insisted that I wait until later when he could come with me."

As they stood in the foyer, Kramer glanced up the steps, then jerked his head toward the back of the house.

Wringing her hands, Londyn followed with nervous excitement. Kramer was most likely a cold-blooded murderer and she was going to try to out-play him. Without Brick.

"The bruises on your face... He hits you, doesn't he?" He was playing dumb. Like he hadn't watched multiple "scenes" through his binoculars over the past few weeks.

She slammed on the brakes. "I need to go."

Kramer turned and held out his hand in a reassuring manner. Londyn eyed it suspiciously, which, again, was more reality than acting.

"I can't talk about this," she hissed.

"He won't know," Kramer insisted.

"He'll know."

"You're safe here."

She struggled not to roll her eyes. She was a million

times safer with Brick than with a man who murdered his wife for money. "Where are we going?"

"Into my office where we can talk and it won't disturb Barb."

"It's soundproof?" That thought caused imaginary spiders to walk across her skin.

"No, but our bedroom's at the front of the house. My office is at the back."

"She won't mind?"

"Of course not. I'm just trying to help her friend. She came to me with her concerns a couple of weeks ago. She's worried about you."

Barb might be, but Kramer was only concerned with one thing.

And it wasn't Londyn's safety.

As soon as they entered the office, he closed the door, but, thankfully, he didn't lock it. Since she was wearing shorts and a casual V-neck top, she had donned flats. She doubted beating Kramer with a sandal would have the same effect as cracking him with a three-inch spiked heel.

He walked to the front of his desk, turned and perched his ass on the edge. "We've known each other for a few weeks now. I don't want you to only think of Barb as your friend, but me as one, too."

Gag. "So, you think you can help me."

"I know I can help you."

"How?"

"I can give you everything you want, Gertie."

Gah, she hated that nickname and it made it worse coming from his lips.

"I can give you anything you desire and you wouldn't have to get smacked around to get it."

Like she would voluntarily take abuse just to get material objects. *Fsst.* "And how can you do that?"

"It might not be apparent, but I have plenty of money. I'm sure a lot more than your husband."

Arrogant ass. She was dying to ask him outright how he got that money, but she bit it back. "You have Barb."

His gaze dropped to her chest and didn't he lick his damn lips? "But I want you. I told you that several times."

And each time she'd ignored it, playing "hard to get" to keep him on the hook. To keep him inviting her and Brick over to their house. A play that had worked well.

She frowned. "Yes, you've told me that but... Are you only wanting an affair?"

He shrugged one shoulder and lifted his gaze again to meet hers. "To start. Then see where it goes from there."

"Right. Me six feet under when Seamus finds out."

Kramer tilted his head and studied her for a moment. As if he was weighing what he should say next. A clock ticked somewhere in the otherwise dead silent room. Once. Twice.

A third time.

Then... "I can take care of Seamus."

Ice skittered down Londyn's spine, even though she should be rejoicing from his statement. But it was only a start to what she hoped he'd reveal to her. The confession Brick needed. "What do you mean?"

"Gertie, how about you just take some time and think about it. You would no longer be controlled, or 'disciplined' as your husband likes to put it when he puts his hands on you. You'd be free of all of that. And, like I said, I'd give you what you want. I promise I can make you much happier than him."

First of all... Kramer could never make her happier than Brick. Not even close. She was overrun with joy every time he simply wore those silky little shorts of his.

Second... Take some time? They didn't have more time.

She needed to encourage him to reveal his secrets.

"Again, I don't know how Seamus would accept me leaving him." She lifted a hand. "Yes, I do. He wouldn't accept it. He's told me time after time he'd kill me before he'd allow anyone else have me."

Kramer's brown eyes narrowed. "Again, I can handle Seamus."

How? Just say it, you shit! "By buying him off?"

"You just let me handle that once you decide this is what you want. Think about it."

Damn it.

He pushed off the desk and took a step toward her. "How about a taste of what I could give you?"

Londyn fought her grimace and her first instinct to say no. More like scream, "Fuck no!" She swallowed down not only that but the bile that had risen.

"You're a handsome man, Chris. And Barb's a lucky woman..." *Lie!* "But I can't risk Seamus finding out."

"Just a kiss," he insisted. He wasn't asking, he was insisting.

Oh fuck. Oh fuck. Oh fuck.

She knew this was one of the risks with going one on one with Kramer. She knew this might be the game she'd have to play... But she needed to avoid it, if at all possible. Or at least put it off as long as she could.

As he took another step closer, she panicked and lifted a palm to stop him. "I... I... can't."

"No one will know except us."

And that was two people too many. "He knows everything," she whispered.

"I know you're scared, but you don't have to be." Another step closer. "I can take care of you. No allowance. No strict rules. No calling me Daddy."

She forced her feet to remain in place. "I hate when he makes me call him that."

"Never again."

Her bottom lip trembled as she asked, "Do you promise?"

Kramer was now toe to toe with her. He tucked a thumb under her chin and lifted her face. His soft answer of "promise" made her want to puke.

"But Barb—"

"Don't worry about Barb or Seamus right now. I just need you to say yes."

He dropped his head until his lips were right above hers.

Abort! Game over!

She pushed a hand against his chest and stepped back quickly, breaking his hold. "Let me consider it. Give me a day or so?"

His face was full of disappointment, and maybe a little impatience, but he nodded. "A couple days. If you say yes, I promise you won't regret it."

Suuure. "I have to go. I'll be back to visit with Barb tomorrow. Hopefully, she'll be feeling better."

His disappointment quickly fled and heat filled his eyes. "I look forward to that."

So did she, but for not the same reason he did. However, right now, she needed to get the hell out of there and figure out a solid game plan on how she would work this. How to get what she needed without giving up a part of her soul by dancing with the devil.

And that's what he was, now that he confirmed he could "handle" Brick and Barb so the two of them could be together.

She also needed to decide if she was going to tell Brick.

Her fear was, if she told him, he'd shut her mission down completely and immediately. But, even though he wouldn't like it, it might be the only way to finish this job successfully.

If she had to sacrifice a little to save Barb's life and to help Brick, so be it.

Chapter Eighteen

LONDYN WIPED her sweaty palms down her shorts then lifted her fist to knock lightly.

The door opened immediately.

Of course it did.

She had managed to tell Kramer last night, when she and Brick were hanging out with them after dinner, that she was considering his offer and needed to talk with him about it.

Luckily, she had communicated that to him without either Brick or Barb—who looked horribly pale and weak—hearing her. Because if Brick had heard, it wouldn't be Seamus's feigned fury she'd be dealing with, it would be Brick's real rage.

She needed to avoid that at all cost to continue with her plan.

She had her cell phone tucked in her front pocket and planned on recording Kramer's confession. *If* she could get him to spill it.

She was going to try her damnedest.

If she didn't get it today, she'd keep trying until Brick pulled the plug and they packed their bags.

So, once again, she told Brick she was heading over to check on Barb, even though she knew Barb wasn't home. Or at least, that's what Kramer had said. But she couldn't imagine Barb—with how she looked last night—had the energy to go anywhere by herself.

The only problem with Barb not being home—if it was true—was no one would hear her scream if Kramer tried anything crazy.

The man greeted her with a smile that made her stomach churn, but she ignored it and followed him inside. Once again not liking the fact he locked the door behind them.

She felt like a dead man walking as he trailed her on their way to his office.

There, he once again closed the door and looked like the cat who ate the canary. Too bad that canary wasn't poisoned with whatever Kramer was giving Barb.

Allegedly.

She had no facts to back that up, so that was why she was alone with a man she didn't trust.

If Brick knew she was going to be alone with him, he never would've let her leave the house. In fact, he got anxiety at the thought of her being there at all without him, even if she was with Barb.

As she opened her mouth to start, Kramer was there, in her space, his fingers digging into her biceps, his mouth curved upward, his dark eyes intense. "It didn't take you long to decide."

"No. Not after what happened last night."

His eyes narrowed. "What happened last night?"

Londyn shook her head. "He got so out of control, I had to lock myself in the bathroom until he calmed down." She chewed her bottom lip nervously.

"I'm surprised he allowed that."

"He didn't. Tonight after dinner, I'll be disciplined for my actions."

"Why tonight?"

"Because he wants me to suffer all day with the wait, with knowing what's coming."

Instead of concern, his face showed a sick sort of excitement. This man was whacked. "How bad will it be?"

"Bad. Because it's planned, he'll do things to me that won't be detectable. It's only when he strikes out impulsively that he creates bruises where others can see them. Since we've moved to Florida, his temper has gotten worse and his patience a lot shorter. I can't do anything right no matter how hard I try." She dropped her head and blinked, hoping it looked like she was fighting back the tears.

"I can make that all end for you."

She managed to push a couple tears out before lifting her face. She whispered, "I need discipline, but not like that."

"I can give you the discipline you need." Excitement shook his voice and she was sure if she looked, he'd be sporting an erection.

She pushed herself to keep going. "If we do this, I want to be your one and only. I don't want it to be an affair. You'd have to break up with Barb."

The hands on her biceps squeezed tighter. "I can handle Barb."

She needed him to say how. Her phone would only record for so long, he had to confess soon.

She discovered she was right about his erection when he suddenly pulled her against him and wrapped his arms around her, brushing his nose against her hair while inhaling deeply.

Her late breakfast was about to reappear. And not in a pleasant way. She had to fight her shudder of disgust.

She needed him to keep talking. "He's so possessive.

He'll never let me go. I'm worried he'll actually kill me first like he has threatened."

"Unless we kill him first."

Londyn shoved him away with wide eyes. Her heart was beating so hard in her ears at his answer that she was sure she misunderstood him. "What?" Did she hear him right? Did he actually say what she heard? She needed to be sure.

"If you want it done, leave it to me."

"You mean by killing him? How? Won't you be arrested?"

Without even a hesitation, Kramer said, "Not if it's ruled an accident."

Shit. Fuck. Shit!

She was getting it! It was working. She only hoped her phone was actually picking up the conversation. "Chris, that sounds risky."

"It can be if you don't know what you're doing."

Her blood rushed through her veins at what he was revealing. "And you do?"

She was so close to solid proof. So. Damn. Close.

He needed to answer her!

Londyn shook her head. "No, you won't go through with it."

"I will."

"How do I know that? This is not only risky for you, it's risky for me. If you fail and Seamus finds out..." She shuddered.

"I won't fail. I'll make it look like a car accident. Screw with his brake lines or something. I'll figure it out, do some research. Don't you worry. If you want this, I'll make it happen."

"What about Barb? How would you get rid of her?"

"It's already in the works."

Her heart did a flip, but she stayed in character as she tilted her head. "How? The headaches?"

Something flashed behind his eyes. Maybe surprise. "Is it obvious?"

Londyn quickly shook her head. "No, but I've noticed they've been getting worse."

"Because I'm doubling the amount."

She bit back a scream of mixed horror and excitement, and did her best to ask calmly, "Amount of what?"

That scream almost turned to one of frustration when he shook his head. "That's not for you to worry about. I'll take care of you. I promise."

"How do I know that you'll keep your promise? Seamus also promised me that in the beginning. You're a good guy, Chris, but how do I know you'll be able to follow through? Give me some reassurance so I'm not risking everything for you to only fail."

Suddenly his eagerness turned to what looked like annoyance. He took two steps toward her and captured her face within his hands. And he wasn't gentle about it. "I won't fail."

Her bottom lip shook for real when she asked, "How do I know that?"

"Tell me!" she screamed in her head. *"Just say it!"*

"Because I was successful in making my wife's death look like an accident."

All the breath rushed out of her. The look in his eyes was terrifying. Completely, utterly terrifying.

Zero emotions were behind his words. Nothing. His wife's biggest mistake, which cost her her life, was loving a man who loved money more than her.

Cold.

Blooded.

Killer.

"That's between you and me, Gertie. If you tell anyone, Seamus will be the least of your worries. I'm telling you this only so you believe I can do what I'm saying. Do you believe it?"

Fuck yes! Fuck yes, I believe you're a psycho murderer!

She didn't scream any of that, instead she whispered, "Yes, thank you for trusting me enough to tell me. I won't tell a soul." She let out a sigh of relief. "I'm happy that my nightmare will soon be over." That this whole nightmare would soon be over!

Her phone beeped a warning in her pocket and she bit back her panic. "He's texting me. He's wondering where I'm at. I need to go."

"Gertie..."

"No, Chris, I need to go before Seamus gets suspicious, comes looking for me and finds me here alone with you. We need to act normal for this to work, right?"

Kramer frowned. "Right. But I was hoping..." His fingertips trailed over the exposed upper curves of her breasts.

She stepped away and gave him a beaming smile. "This will all be yours soon and if you do what you say you're going to do, I can be all yours without worry. No Barb. No Seamus. Just me and you."

His hand slid down his erection which was pressing against his zipper. "Just give me a few more minutes, Gertie."

Fuck no!

"I just want a taste."

Hell no. "He'll know."

Londyn gasped as Kramer shoved her hard against his office door, grabbed a handful of her hair and ripped her head back, arching her neck painfully. "He said you don't listen because you like to be disciplined. He was right."

His unmistakable erection was now pressed into her lower belly. She was starting to fear that his "taste" would end up being more than a kiss.

"Women like you love to be shown who's boss, don't you?" Not a question.

Her voice shook for real when she said, "I do. I just don't like when he hurts me."

"I'm not going to hurt you. I'll only give you what you want."

His lips crushed hers and Londyn fought to keep hers closed. Acting was one thing, but she had her limits and pretending to enjoy his kiss was past that limit.

He forced her mouth open and his slimy tongue swept through hers. A scream bubbled up her throat, but she swallowed it down.

Stay calm. Stay calm. Stay calm.

Think!

By her not participating in the kiss, he pulled away and stared down into her face. Irritation wrinkled his brow and the corners of his brown eyes. "You don't seem interested."

"I'm just scared. Until Seamus is no longer a threat..." She pressed her hands into his chest, trying to push him away. "Seriously, I need to go. If he catches us, he'll not only kill me, he'll kill you, too."

Kramer had the nerve to chuckle. It wasn't a ha-ha chuckle, it was one that sliced through Londyn. "I seriously doubt he'd be able to kill me. He might be in good shape, but I doubt he has the balls to kill a man."

Oh, if you only knew.

"Cowards hit women."

One thing they could agree on, but...

Psychos killed their wives.

"I won't be able to relax until it's done," she said.

He reluctantly released her and nodded as he stepped back, freeing her from the door. "Soon. I promise."

She reached behind her, feeling for the doorknob. Her fingers wrapped around the cool metal and she turned it. "Okay," she whispered because she didn't know what else to say, she only knew she needed to get the hell out of that office, out of that house and away from the man who just promised to kill two more people for his own selfish reasons.

She rushed from the house and then ran back to theirs, not looking back.

———

"You fucking did what?" he roared. His blood was screaming through his veins and he swore his eyes were about to explode from his head.

And she had the fucking gall to just stand there and shrug, holding her damn phone out in front of her.

"I got his confession. You said it's what you needed."

"You."

She bugged her eyes out at him like he had lost his marbles, when it wasn't him who had lost them. No fucking way. "Yes."

"You."

"Yes, Brick."

"*You* got his confession." He snagged the phone out of her hand and spun away from her. He stomped to the other side of the kitchen and stared at the phone in his fist. He spun back around. "How did you do that, Londyn? What the fuck am I going to hear on this? What did you do?" The last part came out in a growl.

He felt like a pissed off lion about to rip the head off an antelope that just gored him with his antlers.

What fucking lengths did she have to go to with Kramer to get him to confess?

"What. Did. You. Do?" He tried not to snarl each word. He failed.

"I got what you needed."

Well, fucking-A. That simple. *She* got what *he* needed. "By doing what?" If she let him touch her...

"We had him convinced that you were abusing me. I used that."

"How?"

"I just let him believe..."

Oh no, she needed to finish that.

"Believe what?" He strode across the kitchen, grabbed her chin and tipped her face up. "I didn't give you that bruise."

"No. It's makeup."

"So, you lied to me when you said you were going over there to visit Barb." Was she running her own plays without him knowing it?

"No. I was going over there to check on her. She was again in bed. Kramer saw the bruise yesterday and offered to help me."

Yesterday? And she said nothing to him? "Help you do what?"

"He was going to help save me from you. Just listen to the recording."

"You didn't think I'd have a problem with you doing this on your own? You're lucky you didn't get raped."

"He... I..."

His eyes narrowed at her floundering.

"There was no risk of that. I handled him."

Holy fuck. She *handled* him. That probably meant he *handled* her.

"Listen to the confession, Brick," she insisted in a hiss. "It's why we're living in this house. It's why we're Seamus and Gertrude. It's the whole reason we're here."

Oh, was she getting angry? Well hell, welcome to the fucking club.

"I know why the fuck we're here." It was his job to do, not hers.

"Brick." She walked up to him and fisted his shirt. Like she always did. Like he loved. He closed his eyes and pinched the bridge of his nose, taking long inhales. Long. Deep. Inhales.

She was here now. She was safe. Kramer didn't hurt her. That was all that mattered.

But she had put herself at risk.

And he had no idea she had done it.

None.

Something could have happened to her and he would've been too late. And then how the fuck was he supposed to live with that?

"Brick. Just listen to it."

He dropped the phone onto the counter, grabbed her face and dropped his forehead to hers, closed his eyes and just breathed her in.

"This is why I didn't tell you," she whispered.

"No fucking shit. Don't ever do that again."

"I won't have to. With what I recorded, the job is over."

The job is over.

Because of her. Because she got what he couldn't.

Failure might not be an option for him but losing Londyn wasn't, either.

She had put herself in a situation that could've gone sideways quickly.

Her fingers trailed up his neck, where his pulse was still pounding, to his jaw. "I'm okay."

He pressed a kiss to her forehead, then to her lips before turning her around, pulling her back to his chest and leaning back against the counter, his arm wrapped tightly under her breasts to hold her there. He grabbed the phone and handed it to her.

She fiddled with it and her voice along with Kramer's filled the air.

He pressed his face into her hair, breathing in the floral scent of her shampoo as he listened, trying to settle his disappointment, fury and fear at what she did. Of what could've happened.

As soon as the actual confession was over, and the second Kramer demanded "a taste" from Londyn she shut off the recording.

"No. Play the rest."

"You promise not to get angry?"

"No." He couldn't promise because he was once again there. Kramer's words burned in his gut. *I just want a taste.*

"Then I'm not playing it."

He snagged the phone from her fingers and pressed play. And with everything he heard, with everything he could imagine that went along with what the man was saying...

It took Brick everything he had not to run upstairs, grab his Glock, go to Kramer's and when he opened the front door, plug a hole in the center of his forehead.

Kramer had touched his woman.

Worse, he kissed her.

He fucking kissed her.

That was undeniable in the recording, so he didn't even ask her. He'd heard it.

And while he wanted to smash the phone, he didn't do that, either.

He needed to keep his head on straight. He needed to make some phone calls. He needed to make plans.

They needed to get their shit packed and out the door before he did something he regretted.

Or didn't regret, but would pay for in the end if he lost his shit.

Shooting Kramer right on his front doorstep would not go unnoticed.

He put his hands on her shoulders and gently pushed her away. "Pack your shit, we're heading out of here as soon as Jewel can book us flights."

"But Barb—"

Right now he didn't give a fuck about Barb. He only cared about Londyn. She was his priority. "Not our problem. You got what we needed for the client. I'm handing that shit over as soon as we land. But in the meantime, I need to call the boss man and let him know what we have, then see what he wants me to do." No matter what D wanted, they were still heading home ASAP.

"We need to save Barb."

"No, I need to get you away from Kramer. Once that's done, we'll worry about Barb." He'd give her that much. Barb was a good woman and she didn't deserve whatever Kramer was dishing out to her.

"It could be too late, Brick! He said he's doubled the dose."

"Of what?"

"I don't know. You heard him tell me not to worry about it, so I have no idea what he's feeding her."

"Let me find out what the client wants done with Kramer first. We can't just go in and evacuate her. Questions would be raised and Kramer could ghost. Then we did this all for nothing. Once we get a handle on Kramer, we'll deal with Barb."

"But—"

"Londyn. You already did enough. Let it go and let me handle it, damn it." With that, he took her phone and he went upstairs to make the calls he needed to make and to get away from her, to give himself some much needed space.

She was pushing him and he was already struggling with keeping his shit together. If she kept pushing, he might take it out on her. And that was the last thing he wanted.

Because that would not make either of them happy.

Chapter Nineteen

LONDYN CAREFULLY WORKED her way up the stairs, trying to avoid causing any creaks on the wood steps.

She had no idea where Kramer was. She hoped in his office, but she wasn't about to check.

Her goal was to get in and get out without him knowing.

Getting in had been a bit nerve-wracking, as she had to make her way through the fenced back yard, past the pool and into the unlocked sliders, all without being caught. Now she just needed to get to Barb.

When she got to the upper landing, she went directly to the bedroom at the front of the house where Kramer said it was. She only hoped it was true, because with his office at the back, he shouldn't be able to hear them.

Even so, she was going to be as quiet as possible.

While she did have an excuse to visit Barb—to check on her well-being—Kramer had never allowed her upstairs to do that. And she had already knocked on the front door once today to inquire about Barb. Kramer would find it odd if she did it again, not even a half hour later. Especially after she rushed out of his house earlier, using a jealous Seamus as the excuse.

One door was closed at the end of the hallway. She didn't bother to knock, instead she turned the knob slowly and pushed it open.

The curtains were drawn, the lights off, and there was a lump under the covers.

Londyn's heart thumped wildly. If the woman was already dead...

She carefully made her way through the dark room and sat on the edge of the bed. She almost jumped out of her skin when Barb groaned.

"Barb," she whispered. She put a hand on the woman's shoulder and shook her gently. No response. "Barb!"

"Gertie?" The woman sounded like she had one foot already in the grave. And the way she had looked last night had frightened Londyn.

This was exactly why she was going against Brick's order of not helping Barb until they were out of Florida. She could not, in good conscience, allow Barb to suffer at the hands of that monster. She had to do something, otherwise she'd never be able to live with herself.

"Yes, it's Gertie. I'm worried about you."

"I'll be okay... I just need... rest."

"No, Barb, you need more than rest." *You need a hospital and a battery of bloodwork. And a man who doesn't want to kill you for the money.*

"I'm surprised he... he let you up here."

"He didn't. He doesn't know I'm here. So, we need to keep our voices down." Though, Barb's voice sounded so faint, Londyn wasn't worried Kramer would hear her.

"Did you... sneak up here? Why?"

God, every word for her was a struggle. She was not only weak, but she was fading. There was no way Londyn was leaving Florida without helping Barb first.

"Because..." Londyn sucked in a breath. "Because I'm concerned that Chris is trying to hurt you."

Not trying. He was. But she had to convince Barb that the man she loved was harming her and not after her best interests. However, she had to do that carefully. She didn't want Barb just shutting her down and out.

"How can you say that?"

"This is more than migraines, Barb. Your skin is yellow, your eyes discolored. You can't even get out of bed. This is not normal!" She cringed at the rise of her own voice.

Barb's hand barely lifted from the mattress. "I... I have a doctor's appointment... scheduled next month."

"You might not make it to next month."

"Chris loves me... Why would he hurt me?"

Because he's a murdering psycho who's a greedy bastard, who doesn't give two shits about you. Londyn reworded that carefully. "Because you dying would make him two million dollars richer. And allow him to pick his next victim."

"What?" Barb asked weakly. "His next victim?"

"Barb, listen. He has two life insurance policies out on you. For a million dollars each."

"No," she whispered. "He would've told me that."

"Right. Just like he had taken the same type of policies out for Teresa before she *slipped* in the tub and died." She air-quoted "slipped."

Barb's breath rattled in her chest. "It was an accident... a freak accident."

Londyn wanted to shake the woman but was afraid of breaking her. "No, Barb, it wasn't. He told me it wasn't."

Barb's eyes went wide.

"Do you want to sit up?"

The pale woman nodded.

Londyn gently lifted Barb's shoulders and tucked a couple pillows behind her head. That was as good as it was going to get. The woman had no strength left.

Jesus. She wasn't that bad last night. She could at least

get around, though, somewhat weakly. What the fuck did Kramer do?

Hell, what did she do? Did she cause Kramer to rush his process of poisoning Barb?

Was this all her fault?

Londyn bit her bottom lip. Did she sacrifice Barb to get the information Brick needed?

"Please, let me get Seamus over here and we can help you get out of the house and to the hospital to check you for toxins."

"What... what did Chris tell you?

"He told me he killed Teresa, made it look like an accident and he's poisoning you. Did you know he got two million for her 'accidental' death?"

"Why would he tell you that?"

Shit. "Because I played him, Barb. He fell into my trap and confessed. I'm sorry. I'm sorry I had to do it, but I needed to get the truth. Let me help you now. You need to get out of this house and away from him."

"How do I know it's not you lying to me? Maybe it's you who's trying to steal Chris away?"

What? Had she seen what Brick looked like? She had no reason to steal Kramer away.

"I know Seamus abuses you. Maybe you think Chris will be your savior."

Ugh! "No, Barb. Seamus... doesn't abuse me. It's all fake. He... he..." He what? What the hell *did* Brick feel about her? *Good grief.* Now was not the time to worry about what Brick felt about her. "It was a ploy."

"Why? Why would you do that? It doesn't make sense."

"I know... Please," she grabbed Barb's hand and gave it a gentle squeeze, "just trust me."

"I've only known you for a month. I've been with Chris for over a year. He loves me."

"And why did he move you guys down here?"

"To get away from the memories of his late wife... He was devastated."

"He wasn't. He did it, Barb. He moved you down here to isolate you from your friends and family. Please believe that. You are his next victim."

Barb managed to drag her limp hand from Londyn's and covered her eyes. Her whole body jerked as a sob wracked from her. "I... I don't know what to think," she said thickly.

"I know. I'm sorry."

"I'm too weak to get out of bed myself. Even if this is all true, how can I leave?"

Was Barb finally beginning to believe her? Relief flooded her. "I'll be back. With Br— Seamus. I swear. We're getting you out of this house and to safety." Even if Brick had to carry her the hell out of this house.

Or she had to get the police involved.

Something was going to happen today to get Barb out, either way. No matter if Brick liked it or not. No matter if Kramer ghosted because of it.

The client would get his information and he could hand it over to law enforcement. Let them track Kramer down. It wasn't up to Brick or Londyn to see justice served.

"I'll be back," Londyn assured her again. "In the meantime, don't eat or drink anything Chris gives you, okay?"

Barb gave her a weak single nod. "Thank you."

Good grief, those two words shot a shiver down her spine. Londyn pressed a hand to her shoulder, squeezed and then rose from the bed.

As she left the bedroom, she mentally bolstered herself for Brick's reaction. She was sure it would be worse than earlier when she gave him the recording.

He was military through and through. Not only had she broken "rank," she disobeyed a direct order.

She crept back down the steps.

Her scream, which turned from surprise to terror, was muffled when a large hand covered her mouth, and another grabbed her hair almost ripping her from her feet. Her knees buckled and she couldn't catch her balance.

Her eyes went wide, and she tried to scream again but it was impossible as Kramer dragged her through the house, not saying a word.

Not having to.

Londyn could read the rage on his face.

He had heard them talking.

She wasn't sure how much. But whatever it was, was enough.

She couldn't swallow, she could hardly get a full breath. She couldn't make a sound.

Brick didn't even know she was there.

Nobody knew but Barb. And since Kramer was being quiet, she probably thought Londyn had left the house already.

He dragged her through the kitchen, her nails digging into his skin, trying to pry his hand off her mouth and pull the other one out of her hair. She kicked at his shins, but he avoided the contact.

Every time she began to catch her balance, he jerked her off her feet again.

He was taking her outside.

She had no idea why.

Why? Why the hell was he going outside?

If she could get his hand off her mouth when they were outside, she could scream her head off and maybe Brick would hear it.

It was her only hope.

Once they were out back, Kramer's words struck her like bullets from a machine gun. "You fucking lied to me, you bitch! You set me up! You're a lying cunt! No wonder he hits you. You deserved it. You deserve more. I could've given you everything, you bitch. Now you get nothing. Now, instead of Seamus dying in an accident, it will be you."

He dragged her across the concrete toward the end of the pool.

Brick could see the pool if he was looking. But he probably wasn't. He was most likely still on the phone making arrangements and sharing the info she provided. She needed to scream to get his attention.

She needed to fight free of Kramer to be able to scream.

When he got to the entry steps to the pool, she realized what sort of "accident" she was going to die of.

Drowning. Like Teresa. But this time in a pool, not a tub.

She squeezed her eyes shut. They would eventually find her at the bottom. Possibly with her hair caught in the filter. Something that would hold her under until her lungs filled with water. Until she could no longer breathe. Until she could no longer fight.

Until she was... no longer.

Panic made her struggle even harder. She would not let this asshole kill her.

She tried biting his hand and her teeth scraped his palm but she couldn't get a good grip.

And because of that, he jerked her hair even harder, making her eyes water. And not just with tears of panic. From the pain searing her scalp.

He dragged her down the steps into the shallow end of the pool. And as the water rose around them, she began to float. She kicked hard to try to escape.

It was futile.

The man was strong.

She was not.

This was the first time she ever regretted not being that gym bunny.

Not having the strength to break free.

But she had a set of lungs on her she could use. She just needed the opportunity.

That opportunity came when he slipped in the pool as he was moving toward the deep end and his hand shifted enough that she could chomp down on his finger.

Instinctively, he jerked his hand away from the pain and yelled out. And when he did, she did her own yelling. She screamed Brick's name as loud as she could. Once.

Because as she sucked in oxygen to scream it again, a fist flew. And she couldn't avoid the impact to her temple.

It rattled her brain and made her see stars, and as she gasped, he shoved her under the surface.

She inhaled out of instinct, but she only breathed in water.

She clawed at him helplessly until she saw spots in her vision.

She kicked, pulled and scratched until everything went dark.

Chapter Twenty

THE HAIR on Brick's neck instantly stood. With his phone to his ear, he raced down the second-floor hallway and into the spare bedroom.

Jerking the curtains open, he glanced out and saw movement in Kramer's pool. What the fuck was the asshole doing?

He saw the man close to the deep end, fully clothed, but with his back to Brick. He put his eye to his sight and his heart stopped.

Dark blonde hair swirled around in the water. But he couldn't get a good look at who it was.

Was it fucking Londyn?

What the fuck? Did she leave the house after he told her to pack?

"Fucking motherfucker!" he screamed.

"What?" Mercy's deep voice came from his phone. He was on a three-way call with him and the boss man. He had played the confession for them and they had been discussing their next steps.

"I told her to pack and she went back over there."

A rumble of a chuckle came through the phone. "Think she listens?"

He saw Kramer's body jerking and something splashing as he shoved whatever it was under the water. "Oh fuck."

"What?"

No. Not something.

Someone.

He tucked the phone between his jaw and shoulder as he put his eye to the sight again, adjusting the rifle until the crosshairs were at Kramer's head.

"I'm taking him out, D."

"Don't got the greenlight for that from the client," Diesel barked.

"Fuck the client! He's got Londyn. He's drowning her!"

Mercy's voice exploded from the phone. "Fuck—"

"I'm taking him out!" Brick screamed again, dropping the phone to his feet. He threw the window open and with a trembling finger on the trigger, he put his eye to the sight and tried to slow his breathing.

He couldn't.

He couldn't empty his lungs.

But he also couldn't breathe.

He had to be careful. Kramer was blocking Londyn but that didn't mean she wouldn't get hit.

The man needed to move away. Brick needed to wait until Kramer had finished what he was trying to do. And every microsecond Brick had to wait seared his gut, tore at his heart.

It would take him longer to run over.

He needed to wait it out.

Wait.

Breathe.

Wait.

Kramer turned to head back to the shallow end and now faced Brick.

Thank fuck.

Everything inside him screamed as he had to ignore the lifeless body floating in the water face down. Hair floating around her like a dark cloud.

He had to ignore it.

He needed to concentrate on his target.

Kramer.

Focus on Kramer.

He sucked in a breath. Blew it out. And squeezed the trigger.

Kramer's head kicked back and he toppled into the water.

Brick didn't wait another second.

He had less than four minutes.

Less than four because he wasn't sure the moment her lungs had filled. Wasn't sure when her world went black.

He snagged the phone at his feet and ran.

Down the hallway, leaping down the stairs and almost breaking his neck.

He tore the front door open and sprinted the distance between the two houses.

It only took six fucking minutes under water before the brain was dead.

Six.

He had six fucking minutes to get her out of the water and get her breathing.

Six minutes until he lost her.

Six minutes until she was gone forever.

But he had to do it in less than four.

After four minutes without oxygen, brain cells began to die and irreversible damage occurred.

Four.

Less than four to be safe.

He lifted his boot and slammed it into the gate, splintering the wood by the latch. He sprinted to the pool and jumped in, ignoring the blood and brain matter which swirled around Kramer's head.

He turned off his brain, the part that wanted to scream, the part that wanted to kill. He let his training kick in. He set everything he knew, everything he learned as a SEAL, on autopilot.

Because if he didn't, then his brain might just splinter into jagged unrecoverable pieces.

He hooked Londyn under her armpits, turned her over until her face, already turning blue, was up and he dragged her as fast as he could out of the pool and onto the concrete.

He checked for breathing and a pulse.

None.

He turned her head to drain any water from her mouth, then quickly gave her five rescue breaths. He began chest compressions.

One... two... three...

"Fucking breathe, goddamn it! Breathe, Londyn," he yelled, his voice breaking, his heart thumping in his ears as he did them. He shouted each number out until he reached thirty.

He gave her two more rescue breaths before beginning chest compressions again. "C'mon, baby, don't you fucking give up. Stay with me."

After the third set of breaths and compressions, he checked her pulse one more time. It was weak. But her face was beginning to regain color.

Her eyes were still closed but, *thank fuck*, she was starting to breathe.

He rolled her to her side as she began to cough out water.

"That's it, baby, cough that shit out. Keep breathing. That's it. Breathe. Breathe for me." He rubbed her back as her body convulsed and she kept expelling the water from her lungs.

And then she vomited more water mixed with her breakfast all over the pool deck.

He cleared her mouth with his finger and kept her on her side for what felt like forever until her coughing slowed and her eyes opened.

They were unfocused but there was life behind them.

She tried to say his name.

"Just wait. Concentrate on clearing your lungs first, baby. Just keep breathing for me."

Her fingers weakly squeezed his, she took a deep inhale that rattled in her chest, then coughed again.

After a while, when her breathing was almost back to normal and she no longer expelled water from her stomach or lungs, he pulled her into his lap, drew her tight against his chest, buried his face into her wet hair, and did his best not to cry like a fucking baby.

He continued to hold her as he dug his phone out of his pocket, thankful it was waterproof, and called Mercy back to give him the lowdown.

He didn't envy the man who needed to tell Rissa they nearly lost her sister.

But that was the least of his worries.

Because now he had to get Londyn out of Kramer's backyard and figure out a plan to cover up what he just did.

It didn't take long to formulate that plan with the help of Mercy.

They both agreed.

There was no better way to hide the evidence of a kill shot than by making a larger hole at close range. One that couldn't be traced back to Brick.

———

HE HATED to leave Londyn alone back at the house, and she begged him not to, but he had no choice. He needed to finish the job and do it in a way it would not be linked back to them.

As soon as she was settled on the couch under a blanket and he made sure she wasn't suffering from secondary drowning, he gave her a kiss on the forehead, went upstairs to change out of his damp clothes and grab gloves from his duffel bag. Then he headed back to Kramer's house.

He made his way through the broken gate, which luckily was still on its hinges, and carefully wedged it closed as best as he could behind him. It only needed to block the view from any nosy neighbors.

He donned the gloves as he made his way into the house through the wide-open sliding glass door, imagining Londyn struggling as Kramer dragged her outside through it.

He set his jaw and headed to Kramer's office, closing the door behind him. After plugging in the password for the computer, the one that Walker had hacked, he pulled up a blank Word document.

It took a bit longer due to his gloves, but he typed out a suicide note confessing to Teresa's murder. Brick worded it so it sounded as if Kramer's guilt had been eating at him and he couldn't live with it anymore. He added an apology to Teresa's family. It was the least that fucker could do. Apologize to his wife's family for being a lying, greedy fucker who stole their daughter's life. He also had Kramer confess to poisoning Barb.

When he was done, Brick read it over, then clicked on the printer icon. Grabbing it off the printer, he set it directly in the middle of Kramer's desk. He only stared at it for a second before he grabbed the Mossberg from the closet. He checked the chamber to make sure at least one round of buckshot was racked.

There was.

He headed back out to the pool, the shotgun heavy in

his hand, the thought of almost losing Londyn heavier in his heart.

His hatred of Kramer searing his chest.

His brain was once again on autopilot as he grabbed the leaf skimmer that hung on the side of their shed and went to the edge of the pool. Catching Kramer's body with it, he pulled it over to the side. Using Kramer's hair, he lifted the man's head out of the water, placed the barrel of the shotgun directly into the man's slack mouth, pushed him under the surface to muffle the sound...

And pulled the fucking trigger.

He let the shotgun drop to the bottom of the pool, shoved the now headless body farther towards the deep end, blood, brain matter and worse trailing behind it. He pulled out his cell phone and dialed 911, calling in a possible suicide as a "concerned neighbor."

And then he waited.

———

BRICK SCRUBBED a hand down his face just as the uniformed officers rushed through the broken gate.

Show time.

He went from wanting to kill Kramer a second, third and even fourth time to an upset and alarmed neighbor in a split second flat.

With one hand pressed to his forehead and the other planted on his hip, he shouted, "Thank God you're here!" and stopped his pacing, his eyes wide.

One cop rushed directly to the side of the pool, taking in the carnage—Brick might have even heard a gag—while the other approached him. "What happened?"

The one on his knees next to the pool spoke into the mic on his shoulder, using code speak Brick recognized for a DOA. No reason to take a pulse to confirm it.

Two more cops hurried through the gate.

And now it was a party.

Brick gave the cop who was questioning him his full attention. "I'm concerned about his girlfriend."

The cop, whose name tag said Woods, frowned. "Have you been in the house?"

"No. After I heard the shot, I looked out of my window and saw Chris," he made a strangled sound, "or what remained of Chris floating in the pool. I panicked and ran over here and had to kick in the gate to get to him. I was afraid to pull him out but figured it was too late and couldn't save him anyway." Hard to do CPR on a corpse with an exploded melon. Brick sucked in a shaky breath. "I wasn't sure what to do, so I called 911." He covered his face with both hands for a moment. After making a noise which he hoped sounded sincere, he dropped his hands, sniffling and wiping at his eyes and nose, even though they were bone dry. "I... I have no idea where Barb is and I'm worried. I hope he didn't hurt her like one of those murder-suicides."

Hook.

"We'll check the house." The cop turned his head and yelled out to another one, ordering him to check inside.

Another cop, a woman, pointed to Londyn's breakfast chunks on the concrete. "Why is there vomit there?"

"That was me." He sheepishly pressed a hand to his stomach and made a face. "I've never seen a dead body before... except on TV and in movies." Brick covered his mouth and gagged a little. "And Chris... *it* doesn't look anything like the ones in the movies."

Woods patted him on the back. "First one's always the hardest."

Right.

"Can I go now?" Brick knew it wouldn't be that easy, but he had to act like an average Joe citizen, who would be not only clueless in this type of situation but upset about seeing a man with his head blown off.

"I need to get some information from you first. I know this is probably difficult, we can step outside the gate, if needed."

Fuck no. He needed to hear and see what the cops were doing while he was stuck there answering their questions.

"I'm okay now, I think. What do you need to know?"

Woods, the middle-aged cop with a belly that hung over his duty-belt, hiked it up, then pulled a notepad from his back pocket and a pen from his shirt pocket.

He opened the pad, cleared his throat, and squinted up at Brick. "Name?"

"Seam—" He swallowed that down. They'd want a valid identification and would check it. "Shame this happened. Byron Williams."

"You have ID on you?"

He shook his head. "I ran out of the house without my wallet." He knew what came next.

"Sosh?"

He rattled off a false social security number the Shadows used for this exact purpose.

The cop scribbled it down. "Any outstanding warrants?"

Brick raised his palms up. "Nope. Just a concerned neighbor. Me and my wife live two doors down."

"Okay. Give me a phone number, in case we need to contact you."

He gave him the number to a burner phone at the warehouse, also kept for this very reason.

"She see anything?" Woods asked.

"She?"

"Your wife."

"No, she was taking a nap when I heard the shot."

"How long have you known the victim?"

Victim. Brick fought his sneer and stayed in character.

"Only for about a month now. We're new to the neighbor-hood, but we were becoming close friends." He needed to add that bit in case his or Londyn's DNA or fingerprints were found in and around Kramer's house. But hopefully Kramer's death would be an open and shut case of a self-inflicted gunshot wound.

And if it went any further and they dug deeper, Seamus and Gertie would be long gone.

"Had he seemed depressed? Down on his luck? Did he mention suicide at all or even hint at it?"

"He always mentioned his wife who died a couple years ago in an unfortunate accident. I don't think he could move past it. Because of that, I felt bad for his current girlfriend."

Line.

The cop nodded and jotted something down.

"A bus is en route for the woman upstairs. As soon as it gets here send them up," a male voice came from the open doorway. "She's not looking good."

Woods arched an eyebrow at Brick. "Has she been sick?"

"Yes, we were worried about her, especially after we had dinner with them last night. My better half watches a lot of the Discovery ID channel, so she began to come up with some crazy scenarios."

"Like?" Woods prodded.

Brick leaned in and whispered, "Like Chris was poisoning his girlfriend. Like maybe his first wife didn't die of an 'accident.'" Brick air-quoted that last word. "Wouldn't that be crazy if that was true?"

Sinker.

"Right," the cop mumbled, staring toward the door. "Crazy."

"I hope she's going to be all right."

"As you heard, an ambulance is en route. Plus, the coroner."

Sirens could be heard in the distance. At least Barb

would be getting some help. That meant Londyn could stop worrying and they could leave with a clear conscience.

"Can I go? I need to break the news to my wife. She's close friends with Barb. She'll want to head to the hospital to check on her later and to comfort Barb on her loss. Hopefully, that'll be all right?"

Woods, distracted with whatever he was writing, nodded again. His head shot up when another yell came from inside the house. "There's a note."

"We'll be in touch if we need anything further," Woods said, then headed inside.

Brick smiled as he walked out of the backyard through the broken gate.

They were getting the fuck out of Dodge while the getting was good.

He wouldn't be answering any more questions or making any more statements. They needed to split before the cop ran his information.

On his way back to the house, he decided that he needed to have a serious discussion with Londyn about the risk she took. About how she almost died.

How the people who loved her almost lost her forever. Like her sister.

And the perfect time to do it was when they were on the plane and she couldn't escape.

Because she was not going to like what he had to say.

Chapter Twenty-One

LONDYN PULLED UP THE FT. Myers news on her laptop, searching the top stories. Every day for the past week, she checked the local network affiliate's website for updates about Barb and that whole situation they left behind in Florida.

She'd sighed with relief when, the day after they arrived back in Pennsylvania, she read that Barb survived. Toxicology reports had shown she was slowly being poisoned by Kramer using small doses of arsenic and a cocktail of household products. All detectable, so that was stupid on Kramer's part. Maybe he was arrogant enough to think he'd get away with the second murder since he got away with the first.

The list of toxins wasn't in the news, but Mercy had Walker hack into the hospital's lab records to find out the specifics. Londyn was surprised Mercy had taken her request into consideration, but then, maybe her sister had something to do with it.

Today the online article said the case was officially closed; the coroner ruled Kramer's cause of death a suicide. Law enforcement also speculated that it might have ended up a case of murder-suicide if Barb hadn't been found when she was.

Luckily, Barb would recover and was currently surrounded by family, so she was in good, caring hands.

Londyn wished she could talk to Barb herself, but she was strictly forbidden by Mercy not to have any contact with her. They couldn't risk Barb finding out who they really were or why they had been in Florida.

Mercy also proceeded to tell her, in not so nice terms, that she already risked herself and Brick enough by disobeying him and that result was almost deadly, so she needed to "listen" in the future.

And while she wanted to argue that fact with the dead-eyed jerk, she knew he was right.

Damn it.

But, no matter what, she had saved Barb. And Kramer was dead. In the end, it all worked out.

Well, everything except for her and Brick.

Because instead of waking up in Brick's bed every morning, she'd been waking up alone in one of Parris's spare bedrooms.

That would soon have to change. She couldn't stay there forever. And Mercy made it quite clear that he didn't like having her there. He acted like she was some pimple irritating his ass.

In fact, he'd offered her money several times to move to a hotel until she decided what her future held and where.

But right now she was floundering. Just like she had been when she first left New York and arrived in Shadow Valley.

At least in Florida she'd had a purpose.

Now she had nothing. Not even Brick.

On that plane ride, after he was done reaming her out for putting herself at risk. Informing her that she could've died. Telling her she actually *did* die, and she was lucky that he could *save her ass...*

After he was done reminding her that if her heart hadn't started beating again, Parris would've killed him. And then Mercy.

And possibly even Diesel.

After he said she would've had those deaths weighing on her soul, even as a ghost.

During and after all that spiel, what she noticed most wasn't his words, it was his face as he said them. It was his body, his expression, the look in his eyes that told her he would've been affected by her loss—maybe would've even been lost a little bit without her—if he hadn't gotten to her in time.

So, she got it.

She got that he'd been angry, upset and worse because she had gone against his orders and went back to try and save Barb.

What she didn't get was why they were pretending not to care about each other. Why they weren't spending time together.

Why the second the job was over, so were they.

It was that she was having a hard time swallowing.

"That's it, then?" she had asked before walking out of the airport and climbing into Mercy's bulletproof SUV on steroids.

"What's it?"

What hurt the most was, he wasn't confused about what she was asking. Even with dark sunglasses covering his eyes —even though they were still inside the terminal—she could read it on his face. But he wanted to play it like the last month meant nothing to him.

"Us."

A muscle ticked in his jaw and he adjusted his sunglasses. "Londyn, we promised not to touch each other and when we broke that promise, we swore we'd keep it to ourselves, remember?"

How could she forget?

But even so, while that was true... So many things had happened since they said they'd keep it quiet. She thought things between them had progressed past that point. Was she wrong? "Did we fuck up?"

"What do you mean?"

Again, he wanted to avoid this talk, but she wouldn't let him. She needed to know.

Maybe he could fight his feelings, fight his emotions. Bury them deep to hide them. But she couldn't.

She'd never been able to and probably never would.

Her mother used to chide her about her wearing her "emotions on her sleeve." But Londyn got it honestly. It was passed down from her parents.

She reached into his open leather jacket to his T-shirt underneath and fisted it. Her knuckles brushed against his dog tags which were now back where they belonged, around his neck and tucked under his shirt. And, since he was back to wearing his contacts, she was sure his prescription glasses were now buried deep in the duffel bag he had flung over his shoulder.

"Do we like each other?" She cringed internally at the question she was sure she'd asked when she was twelve on the school playground.

His eyebrows shot up, then dropped so dangerously low they disappeared behind his sunglasses. "Well, I sure as fuck hope so, since we fucked. And more than once. In fact, I lost count with how many times. So, yeah, I'd say we like each other, Londyn."

She ignored his irritation and pushed on. "But do we *like* like each other?" *For crissakes*, she was acting like a desperate fool but couldn't stop that train wreck.

He twisted his neck to turn his face away, biting out a growled, "Fuck."

"That's what I thought. We fucked up. But the last I checked, we were both adults."

His nostrils flared as he turned back to stare down at her. She wished he didn't have his blue eyes covered.

"Last I checked, I was breathing. I'd like to keep it that way." He jerked his chin toward the automatic doors ahead of them, where, just on the other side, Mercy impatiently waited at the curb.

"So," Londyn lifted a shoulder casually, reached up and removed his sunglasses, "we don't tell anyone."

He snatched them from her hand. "No one can ever know."

But *they'd* know.

They'd always know.

"So, that's it," she said finally, disappointment bubbling up from deep within her belly.

Using his thumb, he tipped her face up to him and stared down into it, but said nothing.

And that silence said it all.

"It was fun while it lasted," she whispered, hoping he'd insist he didn't want it to end, that they could continue what they had, even if they had to hide it.

"It was definitely fun," Brick echoed softly, then his jaw got tight. "Except the part where you almost died."

Londyn plastered a grin on her face. If he could hide his true feelings, then so could she. "Right. Except that part."

He didn't return the grin. "You're the only one I've ever spent more than a couple of days with let alone a whole month, Londyn."

It was a simple statement which meant a whole lot more.

In his world a month was a record. Especially since he stuck to one-night stands. A whole month was probably a lifetime for him.

For Londyn, it wasn't long enough. "Do you get the trophy, or do I?"

The corners of his lips curled up finally and he released her chin. Sliding his sunglasses back on, he jerked his head toward the exit and said, "C'mon. Mercy's waiting. I'm surprised he's not lobbing grenades at us to get us moving."

"That thing has a grenade launcher?"

Brick shook his head and they headed out into the crisp early December air. A far cry from the sticky, boob-sweat causing heat in Florida.

After loading his own stuff into the Terradyne, Brick loaded hers and helped her into the back seat of the huge vehicle. That was the last time he touched her.

As he rode shotgun, he proceeded to give Mercy a detailed rundown of the last month—skipping all the sex she and Brick had, of course—as the big man took him home.

And all that time he never once looked back at her or included her in on the conversation.

He was cutting ties.

Making it a clean break.

As they sat in the driveway of a cute little Cape Cod-style home in town, Londyn was surprised Brick lived there. But even more surprising was the simple "Thanks for your help," he said to her without meeting her eyes, before barking out, "Sergeant Major," as he saluted Mercy and then disappeared into the house with his duffel bag, ruck sack and rifle case.

That was a little over a week ago.

She'd heard not a word from him since.

She hated sleeping alone.

She hated not having anyone to make breakfast for but herself. Mercy and Parris were gone every morning by the time she forced herself out of bed.

It was getting closer to Christmas and she wasn't in any kind of holiday spirit.

Bah humbug.

The "sisterhood" was getting together for a baby shower tonight. She had no idea which one was squeezing out a kid this time since she hadn't met them all yet. But Parris had insisted she come along to get her out of her funk. And maybe talk to the other ladies about a job within one of their businesses, even if temporary, since her sister also insisted Londyn needed a reason to get dressed and get out of the house every day.

Which she interpreted as: Londyn needed to get out of her PJ's and slippers, brush the knots out of her hair, go cold turkey on the ice cream and rejoin the real world.

She'd been looking online every day at job listings, after she scanned the Ft. Myers news. But no one in the Pittsburgh area was looking for a substance abuse counselor, at least not a paying position. The ones she saw were for volunteers. And that would not get her a car, a roof over her head and something other than Rocky Road in her belly.

Parris suggested she open her own office, but until the house in New York sold, she didn't have money for a rental deposit for office space or even an apartment.

But her sister was right, Londyn needed to get her shit together and formulate a plan, just like she had done to get Kramer's confession.

It was time to put on her big girl panties and become her own woman. Get her own place and stop hoping for a man to make her happy.

Like Brick, she needed to learn to "swipe right" for company when she needed it but not expect anything more.

Be independent.

Have no expectations.

Just sex.

Lots and lots of random, sweaty, naughty sex.

But the thought of having anyone touch her, kiss her, even spank her, other than Brick, turned her stomach.

With a long, loud sigh, she closed her laptop, decided

not to change out of her comfy flannel PJ's and headed downstairs.

As she hit the kitchen, she slid to a stop in her fuzzy socks, almost doing the Tom Cruise slide in Risky Business. Only she wouldn't have looked as cool doing it and probably would've skidded across the floor on her derrière.

Her sister, in her typical *heading-to-the-office* attire and makeup, was sitting at the table sipping, what Londyn hoped, was fresh-brewed coffee.

"What are you doing here?"

Parris lifted a perfectly manicured eyebrow. "I live here, remember?"

Londyn rolled her eyes and shuffled in her thick socks toward the half-full coffee pot. "No shit. I thought you had appointments this morning."

"I do. But my first one canceled and this won't take long."

"Oh shit," Londyn muttered under her breath and grabbed a mug from the cabinet above the coffeemaker. Filling it with coffee, she added a splash of vanilla-flavored creamer and three spoonfuls of raw sugar until it reached the very brim. She had a feeling she'd need every sip of that damn coffee.

She sucked enough down so it wouldn't spill over the lip and then turned, leaning her butt against the counter.

Parris shook her head and pointed to a chair across from her at the kitchen table. "Sit down."

What felt like a ghost whispering along her skin caused her to shiver. "Yikes, you sounded like Mom there."

A sad look crossed her sister's face, but it quickly disappeared.

"I miss her," Londyn whispered as she settled in the chair and swallowed another dose of caffeine, wondering if she'd need to add some Bailey's to get through this "talk."

"I miss them both."

"I want what they had, Riss." She hadn't used that nick-name since they were kids. But the thoughts of her parents took her back to when they were a family. Complete. Whole. The four of them. She missed that. The closeness. The love. The happiness.

"I know."

"I thought Kevin was it for me. I thought he was 'the one.' That he would give me what I've been searching for. Undeniable, unbreakable love. And eventually a family."

"And you were wrong."

Those simple and to the point words twisted the knife already seated in her heart. "As I always am. Maybe I don't know what true love is. Maybe because of Mom and Dad, I expect too much. Maybe what they had wasn't realistic. I mean, who dies of a broken heart? Doesn't that only happen in the movies?"

Not long after their father died of a stroke, their devas-tated mother went to bed one night and never woke up. Her sister swore it was from a broken heart since there was no other medical explanation. She had been perfectly healthy.

"She couldn't live without Dad. They were everything to each other. Their hearts and souls were one. I want that, Riss." Londyn tried to blink away the sting in her eyes.

"I wanted what they had, too."

"Do you have it?"

Parris gave her a small smile. "You might find this hard to believe, but yes, I have it. Our love isn't soft or warm, or even typical, it's intense and unpredictable, even sometimes explosive. And now I wouldn't want it any other way. I'd never expect Ryan to change or even ask that of him. I love him the way he is. Always will."

"But is it an 'I'll die without you' type of love?"

The creases at the corners of her blue eyes smoothed out. "He's my heart and soul."

"As long as you're happy, then I'm happy for you. I'm

not sure if I have what it takes to live with or love a man like Mercy."

"Well then, luckily, you don't have to."

Londyn took another sip of her coffee, then studied her sister over the rim of the mug. Parris didn't wait for her this morning to discuss their parents. This was about something else.

She also didn't waste any more time getting to it. "You broke your promise."

Shit. "No."

"I'm your older sister. I know when you're lying to me. There was a reason Ryan and I wanted that promise from you two. I couldn't tell you then, but I'm going to tell you now. When I first met Brick, I didn't know his secret. In fact, I didn't know it until Ryan had no choice but to tell me. And that wasn't until a little over a month ago when it was decided the two of you were heading to Florida together. Believe me, I love Ryan with everything I have, but I would not wish his issues on anyone. And once I heard what Brick's were, I didn't want that for you. Maybe that's because what you said earlier is true. There's a little bit of Mom in me. But Brick isn't as he seems on the outside." Parris took a deep breath as if she was about to reveal something devastating. "He's tortured on the inside."

Londyn already knew that. Brick hid it well, but his nightmares gave it away. "I know."

"Then you know being with a man like that would never be easy. He's good with covering it up. An expert actually. And because of that he can hide a lot of things. Not just his past, but his feelings. He's emotionally damaged like most of the Shadows. He did not escape his time as a sniper unharmed. He might not have any visible scars on the outside, but it's the ones you can't see that mess with him."

"I know." She just didn't know the details.

Parris shot her a surprised look. "Did he tell you about it?"

"No. I know he has demons, but he wouldn't talk about it. The fact is, he didn't trust me enough to share those memories." And that hurt, too. But she never told him that.

"Or maybe it wasn't about you, Londyn. I doubt it had anything to do with trust. There are many reasons why men like them keep that shit bottled up inside. So, don't take it personally."

She expected him to eventually reveal what caused his night terrors. But he hadn't. And she didn't feel as if she was in a position to push, though she wanted to.

They had been on a job, not there to reveal all their secrets. While they had broken their promise not to touch each other, there had never been any expectation of more than that time in Florida.

None.

Brick owed her nothing.

So, Parris was right. Londyn shouldn't take it personally. But it was difficult not to. Mostly because of how she felt about him.

"He may never share them. And that's what might make it more difficult. He wears his armor of an easy-going, fun-loving guy to hide the fact that something eats at him from the inside. That armor is how he gets through his day-to-day." Parris ran the pad of her index finger around the edge of her mug. "My point of all of this is, we know you two broke your promises. I had a feeling when you were in Florida and we talked on the phone. I could hear it in your voice. But my suspicions were confirmed once you returned and began moping around. It's not because of Kevin. In fact, you haven't mentioned Kevin once since coming back from Florida. But I watch you check your phone constantly. For a missed call, a missed text. I know it's not about a job, or Kevin, or anybody other than Brick."

Londyn put her coffee down and closed her eyes. "I fell in love with him," she admitted on a broken whisper. She opened them when her sister grabbed her hand across the table, giving it a squeeze. "Does Mercy know?"

"He doesn't miss much," Parris admitted. "I kept it to myself until he came to me about it last night."

"Was he pissed?"

"Surprisingly, no."

Parris wasn't the only one surprised about that. Londyn expected the big man to go ape shit.

"Why?"

"He has his reasons," Parris stated simply.

"That he didn't share."

"He did. With me. I can't tell you everything he said, but Brick is a vital part of his team. Ryan's loyalty is unwavering to each and every one of them. While he might not show it, he cares about them. And he knows their stories, knows their struggles. He's lived it all himself. He only wants what's best for them."

"And what does that all mean?"

Parris pursed her lips and studied Londyn for a few seconds, looking like she struggled with something. After a few silent moments, she reached into her purse, which was sitting on the chair next to her and pulled out a small slip of paper with torn edges. The handwriting on it consisted of sharp slashes, not her sister's delicate cursive.

Parris slid the paper across the table to her. "Here. He wanted you to have this."

"What is it?" She took it and saw it was an address, one that looked sort of familiar. Londyn lifted her eyes and met her sister's. Her heart began to thump in her chest. "He's not just doing this to get rid of me?"

"The boys are having a poker game tonight at the warehouse. It'll end once the baby shower is over. Once the women head home, the guys all go home, too."

"But... I... I don't have a car." It was a lame excuse since she could get an Uber.

Rissa dug into her purse again and pulled out a set of keys. She tossed them at Londyn, who barely caught them in time. She stared at them in her palm. Car keys. A Lexus to be exact.

"I can't take your car."

"They don't belong to my car. They belong to yours. Ryan got it for you."

He did what? He bought her a damn car? And a Lexus to boot? Had he finally completely lost his mind? This couldn't be because he was feeling generous. He had to have an agenda. Mercy did not do things impulsively.

Then it hit her. "Damn, he must *really* want me out of your house."

Parris's eyes crinkled at the corners as she laughed. "I'm not going to lie and say that's not true. Because so do I. Having you here puts him on edge, which puts me on edge. And though I want you to stay in Shadow Valley, if you remain in our spare bedroom for much longer, he might just strangle you in the middle of the night."

"Oh, thanks. Now I'm going to have to sleep tonight with one eye open."

"Hopefully, you won't be sleeping here tonight at all."

Huh? Were they kicking her out into the cold right before Christmas?

Wait.

Ooooooh. Damn. "Does Brick know?"

"No."

Londyn pursed her lips. "I'm not sure he's going to like your plan."

"Maybe, maybe not. But if things don't work out with Brick, there's an empty house in the compound that Nash will rent you."

"I can't afford to rent a house in this neighborhood. Not yet. I need to find a job first."

"You can afford that house. It's sitting empty. Ryan and I spent a little time there and Michael furnished it. It would be perfect for you. It might be a little large for one person, but the rent will be cheap. As for your job, yesterday I signed a lease on the office space next to mine. I'll pay the rent until you're established and then you can pay me back. But I want you to be happy. You'll find it here, Londyn, I promise. This whole community—the MC, the Shadows and their women—while very unconventional, are a family. They have embraced me and will embrace you. I want you to find happiness in Shadow Valley, however you find it."

So did Londyn. She only hoped that was possible.

Her sister wasn't finished yet. "The two of us are the only real family we have left. And family helps each other. But the bottom line is, you need to get the fuck out of our house." With that, Parris shot her a grin. She scraped her chair back, went around to Londyn's chair and pulled her up into a hug. "Now, eat a big breakfast and go take a nap because I have a feeling you're going to be up late tonight."

Chapter Twenty-Two

"CLIENT'S HAPPIER THAN A FUCKIN' pig in shit. Wanted the fucker arrested. Dead's even better in his book." Diesel's deep rumble echoed through the warehouse as he approached the corner where the Shadows were playing poker.

"Mine, too," Brick grumbled, placing his cards face down on the table. His gaze caught on his left ring finger. The one that no longer had a noose circling it. He'd thought about taking the wedding band to Shadow Valley Pawn, but hadn't found the time.

Right.

"'Specially since he thinks the fucker offed himself. Everybody's fuckin' happy an' got a nice chunk of scratch out of it."

Everybody was happy except Brick.

Diesel rapped his massive tattooed knuckles on the table, making the poker chips jump. "I'm outta here. Got some shit to handle."

By shit he probably meant diapers full of it.

"Then get gone," Steel said. "You're fucking up our game."

Their beast of a boss man cocked one dark, dangerous eyebrow at Steel. "Thought you were done gettin' your ass kicked."

Steel gave him a cocky grin.

"He gets off on his woman kicking his ass every fucking night," Hunter said with his own grin. "Fucked up foreplay."

Steel shrugged. "Don't be a hater."

"I'll take soft over hard any day," Walker said under his breath.

"That's not what Ellie told me," Steel said, his toothpick bouncing from one corner of his mouth to the other.

"Shame havin' a woman in your bed who actually likes you hasn't changed you from bein' an asshole," Ryder said.

"We're all assholes," Steel reminded him.

"Won't fuckin' argue that." Diesel shook his head and lumbered away, leaving them to get back to their game.

"Whose turn was it to bet?" Walker asked.

"Yours," Mercy grunted.

"I call." Walker tossed a couple chips into the center pile, then shot a look at Mercy who gave him the slightest chin lift.

What the fuck was that about?

But it was Steel who asked Mercy, "Now that the assignment's complete, Londyn going back to New York?"

Mercy's scarred face twisted, making his face scarier than ever. "Fuck no. I swear we ain't ever gonna scrape her the fuck off." He grabbed the bottle of Jack sitting in the middle of the table and filled his lowball glass halfway. He downed it, wiped the back of his hand over his mouth and said, "Only hope I got is if she finds another man online and moves across the country again. Hopefully to California. Or Australia. Know any Aussies?"

Brick's ears perked up.

Ryder stole the question right out of his mouth before he

could ask it. "She's lookin' online again? She didn't learn her lesson the last fuckin' time?"

"Guess not."

Steel elbowed Brick. "You should've given her some pointers during that month you spent together. Swipe right, wrap it tight and escape in the middle of the night. Keep it simple, right?" He sat back in his chair and grinned.

"Right," Brick growled.

"Rissa wants her to stay in the Valley. Don't give a shit where she lands, long as it's not in my house."

"The Sergeant Major still finding it hard to launch his missile with her in the next room?" Steel's toothpick bounced up and down as he smirked.

"I'm not missing hearing that shit since I live next door," Walker griped and took a long pull from his beer.

"That's one good thing 'bout winter, y'all keepin' your windows fuckin' closed," Ryder said, the smoke from his cigar rising in a thin white line toward the dark ceiling of the warehouse.

"Like you and Kelsea don't make your own fucking ruckus," Walker growled. "Damn, I'm in the fucking middle and some nights it's like hearing it in stereo. How many headboards have you two broken?"

As Ryder opened his mouth, Mercy interrupted him. "*Any-fucking-way*, she must've learned some hookup pointers from dickhead since she's got a date tonight. Thank fuck."

Brick didn't miss all eyes landing on him. He picked up his beer and took a long swallow. And then another. Once the brew cooled off the burn in his gut, he wiped his mouth and said, "Can we get back to this fucking game and stop chatting like a bunch of women? If I wanted that shit, I'd have worn a dress and gone to Frankie's baby shower." Exactly where Londyn should be, not on a fucking date with a stranger.

Steel grunted his agreement, but when Brick glanced at

him, he noticed the man had his head down and wore a sly smile.

Fuck them all for fucking with him.

But for the rest of the night he couldn't concentrate on poker. So much so, he lost all his fucking money and Steel had to spot him a fifty.

Instead of the game, all he could concentrate on was the fact that Londyn had a goddamn date.

And if she used a hookup app, it could be just for sex.

Thinking about someone else lying between her soft thighs, someone else sinking into her wet heat, some asshole having her lips around his cock, some bastard spanking her fucking ass while watching it ripple with each smack and then turn red...

Fuck no.

Just fuck no.

Sleeping next to her had become a strange addiction. Surprisingly, something he'd gotten used to. Comfortable with.

In Florida it had become expected, a habit.

Since returning to Shadow Valley, something had been missing.

It was Londyn in his bed. By his side.

No, it was more than her just being in his bed.

So much fucking more.

She was so much fucking more.

He couldn't let her date other men. He couldn't let other men touch her.

She couldn't make cookies without dead grapes for anyone but him.

Nobody else could eat raw brownie batter off her body but him.

She was his.

Fuck the promise.

Fuck the secret.

Fuck breathing.

Because if he couldn't have Londyn, he didn't want to breathe.

He shot up from his seat, almost knocking everything off the wobbly, second-hand poker table. "I fucked Londyn," he shouted and winced when it echoed through the cavernous warehouse.

Dead silence around the table greeted him.

His heart thumped furiously in his chest as he slowly turned to face Mercy at the end of the table. His asshole might have even puckered a little.

The man's chin was tipped down and his silver eyes bore into him. "You think I don't know that, dumbass?"

"I didn't mean to. It just happened," he said quickly.

"Yeah, right. Oops, my fucking dick accidentally slipped into your future sister-in-law," Steel said with a smothered chuckle.

Brick shot him a frown before facing Mercy again.

"You promised me you wouldn't touch her and you broke that fucking promise. Which means you broke my trust, brother."

Brick filled his lungs with air and then choked when he inhaled cigar smoke.

"I'm thinkin' this poker game's over," Ryder mumbled, grounding out his cigar into an ashtray.

"I'm thinking Brick's life might be over," Walker said, counting his chips stacked in front of him. "Anyone wanna make a bet on that?"

"Yeah? Well, fuck it. It was worth it," Brick said.

"Was it?" Mercy growled, rising to his feet and jabbing a finger in his direction. "Is it you who has her fucking moping like a kicked puppy around your house? Fuck no. I knew that shit would happen if you stuck your dick in her. I was right because I'm always fucking right. Bad enough that asshole fucked with her head. Then you had to follow up and fuck with it some more. Somehow *I* got stuck dealing with it all. I got all the fucking headaches without getting the fucking benefit."

"What did you expect when we had to live together for a fucking month?"

"I expected you to keep your dick in your pants. I expected you to keep your fucking word."

"You're only as good as your word," Steel mumbled under his breath.

Brick twisted his head toward Steel and shot him a glare. "This shit isn't funny."

Steel lifted his palms and pressed his lips together.

"No, what's funny is, Mercy expected Brick to keep his dick in his pants," Hunter muttered next to him, also rising to his feet. "So really, it's not Brick's fuck up, but Mercy's."

"Did you fuck her because she reminded you of Rissa?" Mercy asked, his voice as sharp as broken glass.

A whole lot of groans and "oh fucks" circled the table and everyone was now on their feet. Though, Brick managed to contain his "oh fuck." Barely.

"Brother," Ryder murmured to Mercy, reaching out for him.

Mercy jerked his arm away, his ice-cold eyes not leaving Brick. "Answer."

Brick pulled his shoulders back, inhaled a deep breath and cocked his head to the left and then to the right, flexing his neck. "Is that an order, Sarge?"

"That's a fucking order."

"No. I didn't fuck her because of that."

"Because you were bored? Because she was convenient?"

"No."

"Then why?"

Brick's nostrils flared as he sucked in another breath and as his world teetered before him, he tried to explain. And, fuck him, if he wasn't forced to admit things he didn't want to think about. Forced to see what he'd tried to ignore.

And at the end of it all, he survived to live another day, with a now empty wallet, and the truth striking him directly between the eyes like the kill shot that took out Kramer...

That truth being, he'd messed up not by fucking Londyn, but by letting her walk away.

———

Londyn swung her gaze from the *new-to-her* Lexus minivan in the driveway back to the door as she knocked again. Yes, Mercy probably thought it was funny that she'd be driving a minivan, simultaneously being generous but also sticking it to her at the same time.

Well, the last laugh was on him. Because here she was, standing on Brick's doorstep, with plans on being in Mercy's life *forever*.

Living close enough to visit Parris *all the time*. Being close enough to sit at his table for *Christmas dinner*. And Easter. And Thanksgiving. *And* bringing a damn crockpot full of pork and sauerkraut over to ring in the new year.

Even better, being close enough to drop her future kids off for them to babysit.

She huffed out a breath, wiped her damp palms down her snug black pencil skirt, wiggled her aching toes in her obscenely high red heels and ran a hand over her perfectly styled hair.

It was too bad the weather was cold and she had to don a coat, otherwise she'd be able to show off her cleavage, which was framed perfectly by the red, deep V-neck angora sweater she had squeezed into.

The man would see it, just not right away... As long as he didn't slam the door in her face.

Her heart pounded a crazy beat as she heard footsteps, a

pause, a longer pause, an even longer pause and a muffled curse before the door swung open.

She dropped her gaze from his mouth, which was sagging open to the beer hooked between two fingers. She snagged it, downed the remainder, not caring if it had his backwash, and then tossed the empty bottle over her shoulder into the yard behind her.

His eyes followed the arc of the bottle's path until it thumped in the dead grass, then swung back to her.

She planted her hands on her hips and announced, "I want a divorce."

His gaped mouth snapped shut and his eyebrows pinned together. "We aren't even fucking married!"

"Then why does it feel like we are and I can't move forward until we get a divorce."

Brick shook his head. "You're crazy."

"I must be. It's the only good excuse for why I'm here."

His blue eyes narrowed and his jaw shifted like he was grinding his molars as he raked his gaze from her loose hair, over her faux fur coat and then he took his time letting it slide over her skirt before settling on her shoes. The ones he insisted she wore in bed that one night. "I thought you had a date."

So, Mercy *had* set the bait. "I do."

"Then why are you here?"

She raised her eyebrows and tilted her head. "Are you that dense?"

Didn't he realize the date was him?

His lips twitched as he grabbed her wrist and yanked her inside, almost pulling her off her feet. He peered out over her shoulder toward the driveway. "Why is there a minivan parked out there? *Fuuuck*. Is that the mom mobile Mercy bought? Is he here with you?"

"What? No." She sighed. "Close the door, Ramsey W.— whatever that stands for—Briggs."

"Damn. You used my full name. Am I in trouble?"

"Do you want to be?"

He tilted his head and smirked. "Depends on the trouble." He reached behind her, slammed the door shut and twisted the lock. "Will your skirt slide up?"

"Over these hips? Nope, that would be a miracle. But that's not why I'm here."

"It isn't?"

"Okay, it is, but we need to talk first."

Brick groaned.

She opened her coat and slipped it off her shoulders.

He pursed his lips at the bounty she just revealed. "Okay, we can talk first."

"That's what I thought."

"You know how to bring out the big guns."

"If anyone knows about guns, it's you." With a hand to his chest, she pushed him out of the way and headed into his open concept living room which clearly proved his place was a bachelor pad. Black leather sectional, enormous flat screen hanging from the wall and large speakers flanking it. A video game console sat in the center of the coffee table with a stack of what looked like shoot-em-up war games.

Empty beer bottles riddled the room as well as dirty cups, open snack bags, a pizza box with one slice of pizza remaining, and free weights scattered on the floor. Londyn imagined him curling a dumbbell in one hand while lifting a piece of pizza to his pie hole with the other.

Holy smokes, he was a pig. She saw no sign of that in Florida. She might have to rethink her plan.

At the center of the room, she turned on her heels to face him where he was still standing by the front door. She waved her hand around, indicating the trash dump. "Seriously? You bring women here?"

He didn't look embarrassed at all. "I don't give them any reason to stay."

Fair enough. "Then I can only imagine what your bathrooms look like." She cringed. "I can only imagine what your sheets look like. Yuck."

He gave her a crooked, but hot as hell, smile. "I change them often."

"As often as your women?"

That smile slipped and slowly turned upside down as he made his way to her. He didn't stop until he stood toe to toe with her. Until his intense blue eyes held hers. Not letting her go.

In her heels they were almost eye to eye, but he still had a couple inches on her.

"I'm sorry," he said softly.

"For what?"

"For being a stupid fuck."

"About what?"

"About us."

They were close, but he wasn't touching her at all. Maybe that was a good thing right now. They had things to work out first.

Before she could respond, he continued. "But there's shit I haven't told you and it's shit I don't want spread on you. I didn't want to dirty you with it. And... and... *Fuck*." He closed his eyes and shook his head before opening them again, showing a pain so deep that it even hurt her.

"So tell me. I can handle it."

"There are things I'll never be able to forget, no matter how hard I try. Things that will haunt me for the rest of my life."

She fisted her hand in his T-shirt, the warmth of his skin touching her even through the worn cotton.

"We need to get one thing out of the way first... Kevin was a piece of shit. He didn't appreciate you, baby."

"And you did?"

. . .

AND YOU DID?

He deserved that.

"You don't know how much I fucking appreciated you. How much I *appreciate* you. And that's my fault. At the airport, when you asked if we fucked up, I agreed we did. But really, it was me who fucked up. And not because we broke our promises to my brother and your sister. I fucked up by thinking I could just walk away and let you go. That you meant nothing more to me than any other women I'd had in the past. I was wrong. I knew I was wrong. I just didn't want to admit it."

"Are you admitting it now?"

She was so goddamn beautiful. So smart. So funny. So fucking perfect.

She had done it. She had slayed him.

"That day... *Christ*... I almost lost my mind. It scared the living hell out of me."

"The one from your night terrors?"

"No, the day you almost died, Londyn. That day. If I hadn't been able to revive you..." He tried to swallow down the lump, but he couldn't. Because her blue face, her cold skin, her lifeless eyes... That would haunt him for the rest of his life, just like that day in Pakistan.

"When you began breathing again. When the life came back to your face, when your heart began to beat again..."

It was when he was holding her he realized he'd gotten caught up in something he never should have. The mistake he made by allowing it.

He realized losing her might have destroyed what piece of sanity he had left.

He realized how invested he'd become in her.

How much he cared.

How much he needed her.

How much he... fucking *loved* her.

He never even thought it would be possible.

It had been hard to wrap his head around it. And, at the time, he didn't want to.

But he needed to deal with it now.

This last week without her had been so fucking empty.

He never cared about finding what his teammates had found. He thought he could live without it.

Until it became clear, he couldn't.

"I realized that moment... When I pulled you from that fucking pool. When I thought you... when I thought he had taken you from me. When I thought I might have lost you forever..."

"What?" she whispered, shaking her fistful of his shirt. "What did you realize?"

He wrapped his fingers around hers, holding her hand against his chest. "You feel that?"

Her palm flattened over his heart and he knew his heart was beating furiously because he could feel it all the way up his neck.

"Yes."

"That belongs to you."

"That's my trophy." She tilted her head, and stared up at him with blue eyes that held tears. "Are you going to say it?"

"Are you?"

"I love you, Ramsey W.—whatever that stands for —Briggs."

"And that's *my* trophy."

"Why did you make me fall in love with you?"

He wiped away the single tear that hovered at the corner of her eye. "Because I didn't promise not to. Why did you make me fall in love with you?"

He grinned when she echoed, "Because I didn't promise not to. But you still haven't said it."

"I love you, Londyn..." He whacked his forehead with his palm. "I don't know the rest of your fucking name." He groaned. "Fuck me."

"Well, it certainly isn't Gertrude 'Muffin' Ramsey."

"I guess it's not important until it's Londyn Briggs." Both of their eyes widened. "Oh fuck."

"Oh no. I may have to keep my maiden name."

"Or hyphenate."

"Or just keep my maiden name."

Which he still wasn't sure what it was. Whether it was the same as Rissa's. "Londyn Briggs is kinda catchy."

"No."

"It's growing on me."

"No."

"So, now can I get that skirt off you?"

"No. We're not done yet."

"Fuck," he muttered. "Really, I just told you something I never told any other woman in my life."

"Again, that's my trophy. But we need to figure out where we go from here."

"Where do you want to go?" His only regret was that it should've been him that went to her. Not the other way around.

Though after his confession at the warehouse earlier, he had planned on it. Just not tonight since she had her date.

Wait.

Oh fuck, the date was him.

Mercy set him the fuck up. *Bastard.*

"Well, I think you still have something important to tell me. I get that you don't want to talk about it but I need to hear it."

The half-chub he'd been sporting due to her outfit, and how tightly it hugged her curves, completely deflated. "Londyn..."

"No secrets, Brick. None. Because if you plan on keeping them, tell me now and I'll walk right back out that door. I lived with and loved a man who kept secrets. I won't do it again."

"You have to swear to me you won't hate me afterward."

"I could never hate you."

He cocked a brow at her. "Do you hate Kevin?"

Her mouth twisted. "I strongly dislike him."

He tipped her face up to him. "Londyn, swear it."

Her mouth parted and she breathed, "You're scaring me."

"Swear."

"Okay."

"No," he shook his head, "I need you to say it and mean it."

"I swear I won't hate you."

For fuck's sake, he wished he could believe that. He loved the woman standing in the middle of his messy living room. And she loved him.

He knew he needed to tell her. It was only right.

And the last thing he wanted was for the woman to walk out his front door. Not because he was keeping secrets but because of that secret. "Sit down."

"Oh shit. This day started with me being ordered to sit down. Now this day is going to end the same way."

"What?"

Londyn waved her hand in an unspoken "never mind," and moved away from him toward the couch. She stared at it for a second, then twisted her head to look at him over her shoulder. "Is your bed cleaner than this couch?"

"Yes." He hoped the fuck it was. He thought back to what it looked like this morning when he rolled out of it. "At least, I think so."

"That's promising."

He snagged her hand and dragged her back toward the entryway to where the steps were. She stumbled in her heels. "Hey! Let me slip my heels off first before I break my neck."

"Fuck that. Those aren't coming off until I take them

off." He turned, flexed his knees and put his shoulder to her middle, hauling her up over his shoulder with a grunt.

She squealed. "You're going to kill yourself!" She screamed as he headed toward the bottom step, "I'm too heavy for you to carry me."

"Never," he bit out as he hoofed it carefully up the stairs. He grunted with each step until he reached the top. The master suite took up the whole second floor, so there wasn't a door or hallway. As soon as you hit the top step you were in his bedroom. It was great for a single guy or a couple, but privacy was lacking if someone had kids and was trying to make more kids.

Or *practice* making kids.

He let her slide down his body but didn't release her. Instead, he circled his arms around her and held her closer. "I love you, baby, but I'll need some sexual therapy after what I tell you."

She buried her face in his chest. "I think I can help with that. But, again, while I know it's bad, you're scaring me."

He needed to just get it over with. He brushed the hair away from her face. "Can you sit in that skirt?"

"I'll manage so you can concentrate."

"That fucking sweater and those heels are distracting me. It would be better if you take them all off."

She pulled her face away. "Nice try."

He sighed and tugged her over to the recliner in the corner instead of the bed. Without letting go of her hand, he tossed the pair of cargo pants that had been thrown over it onto the floor. "Sit here, then."

She settled in the chair, her eyes holding worry as he sank to his knees at her feet.

And he told her his story. His nightmare.

The ghost that haunted him which might never go away. And, in truth, shouldn't. Because no one should forget the innocent life who had been forced into becoming a tool of war.

No one should forget the little boy who woke up one morning, ate breakfast with his family, played with toys. Not knowing his father, uncle, brother, whoever the man was that day—the man he should be looking up to—valued him as a weapon more than loved him as family.

He told her about how that very moment changed his view on "Guns, God and Country." About how afterward he would embrace the first. His one true steady and the only thing solid he could hold onto. He lost faith in the second. And the love for his country? Dented and tarnished from that day forward.

When he was done, he tipped his face back up to her and met her blue eyes, which once again held a sheen of tears. But this time not one had escaped. Her bottom lip was crushed between her teeth, probably to keep her from crying out while he spilled his guts, while he told her his secret.

Because she couldn't live with secrets between them.

She sniffled once and wiped at her eyes, doing her best to keep her shit together. Most likely so he'd keep his shit together, too.

Her strength became his.

Once he was finished, he waited, his hands squeezing hers in her lap. Hoping she wouldn't hate him the same way he sometimes hated himself.

Hated what he'd been forced to do.

But one thing he hadn't told her was, what made him put away his MK-11 the day he thought he needed to end it all—to kill the burning hatred, to rid him of that ghost forever—was by remembering when all the spouses, children and family of the troops he saved thanked him.

The cards, the letters, the phone calls. All of it.

Simple words expressing how they knew how tough it

had been to do what he did. How they knew it would affect him.

But even so, despite all of that, he had nothing left to give.

He wanted out of the Navy.

That day, he was done.

He packed his rifle away and he also tried to tuck away that memory as best as he could.

Some days were better than others.

Some nights his thoughts were clear.

And then there were the nights he lived it all over again.

But Londyn was right. She needed to know. Because for her to sleep safely by his side every night, she needed to be prepared.

And he wanted her there.

He only hoped after hearing his story, she still wanted that, too.

He continued to remain silent because he didn't want to influence her decision. That whatever her decision was, she made it honestly and it came from her heart.

"Many men wouldn't have survived something like that. Especially if they had children of their own."

He shook his head. "I didn't survive it. It crushed me. It crushed my career. Everything I worked hard for, everything I bled for, ended that day. That moment. That second. I walked away, Londyn, a defeated, broken man."

"You had no other choice, Brick."

"We all have a choice."

"And your choice was to sacrifice one to save many."

A shiver swept through him and caused the little hairs on the back of his neck to stand. She had repeated a saying he told himself over and over again to live with what he had to do, with what he had done.

But he hadn't mentioned it once during his story. "Where did you hear that?"

"In Florida. You'd mumble it in your sleep sometimes when you had your nightmares."

He wondered what else he had said, what else she had heard. How much she already knew, but still insisted on hearing it directly from him. "I do everything I can to wake up every fucking day and not let that moment, that single fucking sliver of time crush me. Because if I let it, it will. And I don't want to be a miserable fuck."

"How many lives have you saved?"

"That day?"

"In your lifetime."

"I don't know."

"You saved mine. In the end, you saved Barb's, too. How many lives would've been lost that day in Pakistan if you hadn't done what you did?"

"At least thirty."

"Including the boy?" When he didn't answer, she said, "His destiny was to die that day. His unfortunate fate was already determined when that man strapped those explosives on him."

"Doesn't make it easier."

She brushed fingers through his hair. "Anybody would have a hard time living with it. If they didn't, then they'd be the one truly broken. They would be the one who'd lost all humanity. That's not you. That can never be you. I never would've fallen in love with a man like that and you'd never be able to love me back. Sacrifice one to save many. That *one* was you, Brick." She stood and held out her hand to him. "Thank you for telling me. If you never want to talk about it again, I'm okay with that. If you do, I'll listen." She pulled him toward the bed. "But now, I'm done talking. How about you? I think it's time for a little sexual healing."

"I can get on board with that." She turned and gave him her back. He stared at her, confused. "What?"

"I not only need you to unzip my skirt but I need you to peel me out of it."

He snorted. "I can do that."

She pointed to the zipper at the small of her back. "Don't tell me, just do it."

He stepped up to her, one hand going to the tiny tab at the waist of her smoking hot skirt, the other arm snaking around her, his fingers wrapping around the front of her throat.

He drew her head back until it rested on his collarbone. Then he pressed his mouth against her ear. "You're keeping those fucking heels on."

"That's why I wore them."

"Good girl," he whispered and felt her shiver at his words.

His fingers flexed on her delicate throat as he worked her zipper down slowly, only to discover she hadn't worn any panties.

"Fuck," he groaned into her loose hair which caught on his beard and tickled his nose. But he didn't give a fuck.

"That's the plan," she murmured. "Should I inspect the sheets first?"

He worked her skirt down until it fell around her heels. "No need, muffin. You're going to be on your hands and knees first."

"Maybe *you're* going to be on your hands and knees first for all those times you made me call you Daddy."

He kept one hand on her throat as the other dipped into the V of her sweater and directly into her bra to find her rock-hard nipple. "You said we're not keeping secrets from each other. And I saw how excited you'd get when you'd say it." She gasped when he twisted it roughly between his fingers.

"I'm good at faking it," she said on a pant.

"Now, I know that's a lie."

"Do you?" She gasped as he tightened the fingers on her throat and ran his tongue round the outer shell of her ear.

"Do I need to prove it?"

"If you must."

He grinned into her hair. "That's one sacrifice I won't mind making."

Nothing he did that night was a sacrifice.

It was the most solid night of sleep he'd had since Ft. Myers. He didn't fool himself by thinking it wouldn't be like that every night.

But he'd take what he could get.

And, in turn, he'd give Londyn everything she ever wanted.

Especially the undeniable, unbreakable love that was as strong and as deep as her parents'.

And that wasn't a sacrifice, either.

Epilogue

6 months later

"Fuck," Brick muttered as his phone "grunted" on the nightstand. He had recorded the tone directly from the source and assigned it to the boss man.

He was pulling on his boots to head to the warehouse for their monthly poker game, so at least the Shadows were getting ready to head in that direction if something was going down.

He finished lacing up his left boot, snagged his phone and glanced at the mass text Diesel had sent out.

Church. Now.

Church? Was there a problem at the clubhouse the Shadows had to handle?

Every 1. Women, kids 2.

That sounded like a lockdown. Which could mean a threat to the MC.

Fuck. Things had been peaceful for a while now since the Dirty Angels' rival, the Shadow Warriors, was no more.

All thanks to him and the rest of his team.

"We gotta go!" he shouted over his shoulder as he stood,

gathering his wallet and Glock and everything else he need to strap on in preparation of something big going down.

Londyn peeked her head out of the open bathroom, her hair still partially up in curlers. "You don't need to yell, I'm right here."

"Get ready to go. Double-time."

"Double-time means I have twenty minutes instead of forty. You do know that, right?"

Brick shot her a frown. "Londyn. Just throw on some jeans and boots, or flip flops, whatever and let's go."

"Go where? I have a baby shower to go to and I don't need you to drive me."

These women needed to stop getting pregnant. They were going broke with buying shower gifts, then baby gifts once the kid came screaming into the world. How much shit did they need? The women should all just be sharing the same shit and passing it around.

Recycling, right?

"You did. Now you don't. D wants us all at the club-house right away."

"Why?"

"If I knew, I'd tell you. He's not good with providing details. He says show up, we show up."

"Well, that's crazy. How is anybody supposed to plan?"

"You plan after the fact." He turned to see her pulling out the rest of the curlers. Way too slowly. He snapped his fingers at her. "Less chatter, more movement."

Her mouth twisted. "Damn, I thought I left bossy Seamus in Florida."

"If you did, your ass cheeks wouldn't be red and hot right now, would they?"

She smiled in a way that made his dick twitch. "I like Seamus sometimes."

So did he. But now was not the time.

"Londyn," he growled his warning.

She lifted hands full of curlers up in the air. "Fine. It's June. I'll throw on shorts and sandals."

"Whatever," he muttered under his breath. "Just hurry."

"Fine."

"You know the rule."

"Fine!" came from inside the bathroom.

Brick grinned. The "rule" was every time Londyn gave him a sassy-mouthed "fine," he added one strike to her growing "spank bank." This spank bank wasn't a typical one. It was one they both got to enjoy.

Especially since she used "fine" a lot.

"I'll be waiting in the Tank," he called out.

"Can't we take my Benz?"

It only took less than a month for Brick to buy her a badass Mercedes AMG GT Coupe and drop that mom-mobile back off in Mercy's driveway. The fuck if he was driving around in a minivan when they couldn't take his TUV or Indian Scout.

"No."

"Fine."

Brick shook his head as he jogged down the steps, out of the Cape Cod and climbed into his TUV.

Ten minutes later, he was still waiting.

He sighed as he kept his gaze glued to the front door and tapped his fingers impatiently on the steering wheel. Once they moved into the compound, both the warehouse and DAMC's church would be a shorter drive.

He loved this house, but Hawk wouldn't sell it to him since renting it put steady cash in the man's pocket. So, Brick bought the last lot in the cul-de-sac. The one that had been set aside for him and also the one Londyn insisted on. The one directly to the left of Mercy and Rissa's house. Despite the fact Mercy kept suggesting other "better" lots elsewhere in the neighborhood.

Like on the other side of the walled neighborhood, next to Nash's still empty house.

In the end, Londyn got what she wanted.

Like always.

The grin that thought brought quickly disappeared after waiting another five minutes.

He grabbed his phone to text her and realized something. Something he neglected to do.

He swiped right and found what he was looking for. The multitude of "hookup" apps he had on his phone. Tinder. Happn. Fling. And more. *So* many more.

One by one he deleted them all and when he was through, he blew out a breath, glanced up and still didn't see Londyn.

He pulled up his text app, typing out: *Hurry.*

He quickly followed with: *And don't u fuckn answer w/ fine. Fine!*

And then there she was, backing that caboose of hers out the front door, pulling the door shut behind her and locking it. Then she strode toward the vehicle wearing not only a tight pair of shorts and a V-neck shirt that showed off way too much of *his* tits, but also a hell of a sassy smile.

THE PARKING LOT WAS OVERFULL. Bikes, cars, trucks and SUVs parked in every space and even in the grass surrounding the pavement. And due to Londyn's lack of respecting the order "double-time," Brick wouldn't be surprised if they were the last ones to arrive.

"Down & Dirty 'til Dead?" Londyn whispered as she read the carved wooden sign over the metal door Brick was holding open for her. "What does that mean?"

"Baby, they're bikers. It's their motto. The code they live by, you could say."

They stepped into the common area of church and were greeted by complete silence.

Not one person was inside. Which was weird. And because of that, the hairs on the back of Brick's neck stood. "Yo! Anyone in here?"

"Been waitin' on you." A large, Black biker wearing a worn black leather cut followed the deep voice through the swinging double doors of the commercial kitchen that separated the private club area and the public bar, The Iron Horse Roadhouse.

"For what?" Brick asked as they approached each other, pulling Londyn along with him. "And why the hell are you here, Magnum? Shit must really be going down." Especially if D called in the Dirty Angels' allies. That meant he needed numbers. A huge show of force.

This couldn't be good.

The big, bald-headed man nodded, his dark face a mask of *way-too-serious*. "Fuckin' big shit. Shit we never expected."

Londyn grabbed Brick's arm, her nails digging into his skin. "Parris is okay, right?"

Brick lifted his gaze in question to Magnum, who nodded. "She's out in the courtyard with everyone else for this crazy-ass impromptu meetin'."

Did the Sergeant at Arms for the Dark Knights MC just use the word "impromptu?"

Damn.

"Okay, so what the fuck is going on?" Brick asked, following Magnum toward the door that led outside, but to the courtyard instead of the parking lot.

But before they stepped outside, the sound of the kitchen doors swinging again made Brick glance over his shoulder.

Dawg's daughter, Caitlin, came from the same direction Magnum had come and her feet stuttered to almost a complete stop when she saw them.

"What—" Brick began, but Magnum pushed open the side door and jerked his chin, indicating they should head outside. As soon as they stepped out into the fading light of the day, he heard a bellowed, "'Bout fuckin' time, asshole!"

Brick found his boss, Diesel, standing on the stage at the other end of the courtyard, which was packed full of people. Every fucking Dirty Angel, every ol' lady, every one of Brick's team, and all of the children. Too many bodies to count.

His first thought was, if there was a threat, having them all standing outside was not safe. Any sniper, like him, could start picking them off. "Stay behind me," Brick murmured to Londyn.

Cait moved past them, not saying a word to any of them, and headed over to the pavilion where she began talking with one of the younger bikers named Coop.

Two seconds later, Magnum also veered off to their left and headed in the same direction as Cait. Brick wasn't the only one who noticed. Dawg's head swiveled that way and his eyes narrowed.

"What's going the fuck on?" Brick asked the bearded, heavily tattooed biker.

Dawg didn't pull his gaze from his oldest daughter who now had her pretty—but *young*—face tipped up to Magnum, while wearing a very large smile.

Oh fuck.

"That's what I'd like to fuckin' know," the DAMC member grumbled, shifting his youngest daughter, Emmalee, also blonde and pretty like her momma, in his arms.

Diesel bellowed to someone out in the crowd. "Get 'er."

Get who?

Brick snagged Londyn's hand and fought his way over to Steel, who was leaning back, his knee cocked, and the sole of his scuffed, pointed cowboy boot planted on one of the pavilion's posts.

He had Kat pulled against his chest, one arm around her shoulders, holding her tight against him.

"What's going on?" Brick asked him.

"Hey, Kat," Londyn said, already sounding weary of the situation.

She wasn't the only one.

Kat, who was sporting a swollen, discolored eye from her latest MMA fight, greeted his woman with an answering, "Hey."

Steel grinned, his toothpick waggling between his lips as he jerked his chin back toward the building. "Well, fuck me with a—"

Brick didn't hear the rest of it because the loud shouts, hoots and hollers became deafening and swallowed Steel's words when everyone began to clue in on why they were there.

And why they were there not only stood on that stage by himself but also included the woman being escorted out of the side door, blindfolded.

Jewel.

The boss man's ol' lady.

The mother of his three baby girls.

The woman D would die to protect.

The only woman on the face of the planet who could tame the beast.

Holy fuck.

Following behind a confused Jewel was her mother, Ruby, and Diesel's mother, Janice, with D's three daughters in hand.

Brick's head swung from Jewel to Diesel, who had moved to the very edge of the stage, with eyes only for his woman.

But he looked a bit pale. And that was not good.

Because when the man went down, he went down hard. Just like he did for Jewel.

"Someone better make sure he doesn't topple off that fuckin' stage and crack his fuckin' head open, because that will fuck everything up," Ryder said, sidling up to them with Kelsea by his side.

"There's nothing hard enough to crack open my cousin's thick skull," Kelsea said.

"What the hell is going on?" Jewel yelled, still blindfolded as she was led through the parting crowd by her sister, Diamond. "I'm taking this blindfold off."

"Don't you dare!" Diamond yelled at her, smacking her hand away. She stopped Jewel in front of the stage, moved behind her and waited for Diesel's signal.

The Dirty Angels' enforcer's massive body heaved as he took a deep breath. Then he nodded to Diamond.

Her sister untied Jewelee's blindfold and it fell to her feet. She blinked, glanced up and her mouth dropped open when she saw her ol' man. "Holy shit! What is this?"

D got to his knees—slowly and with a curse and a grunt —and held out his sledgehammer-like hand.

"What did you do?"

"Woman!" he barked. "Just grab my fuckin' hand!"

She did and he hauled her up onto the stage like she weighed nothing. Once he rose to his feet, he turned toward everyone on the ground. His deep voice boomed over them. "Jewelee kept givin' me surprises I didn't ask for. Wanted to give her one."

Even from where Brick and Londyn stood, he could hear Jewel say shakily, "I never asked this of you."

"Know it." D jerked his chin up at someone else near the stage and another Black man, also wearing a Dark Knights cut, hopped easily onto the stage. Brick had no fucking clue who he was, but the man moved to stand behind D and Jewel.

"Um, is this a wedding or something?" Londyn whispered, leaning against Brick and giving him a squeeze.

He wrapped his arm around her waist and pulled her into him, trying not to laugh too loudly. "Yeah. Or something."

"This is messed up," she said under her breath.

Brick shook his head. "No, it's fucking perfect."

The Dark Knight mumbled some shit Brick couldn't hear and then asked D and Jewel, "Got any vows you wanna say?"

"Oh, this should be good," Hunter laughed behind them.

"Should we record it?" Steel asked.

"Fuck yes," Brick answered. "I want this playing on a loop when he's being a cranky fucker."

"You ain't fucking recording it. Let the man have his moment," Mercy said from somewhere in the shadows of the pavilion.

"Your wedding going to be like this?" Brick asked him, smothering another laugh.

"No," he heard Rissa answer.

"Parris?" Londyn whispered loudly.

"Behind you."

"Will y'all pay attention? Jesus fuck," Ryder grumbled. "Man's gotta be shittin' his pants about now. And y'all are missin' it."

Everyone shut up and turned their attention back to the stage.

Did they miss the vows?

Fuck no.

D's was a simple, "You're fuckin' mine, woman." His nostrils flared and his throat worked a couple times. "This makes it legal. Happy?"

Jewel turned to look at each one of her daughters, then she scanned the crowd. She shot everyone a big smile, then turned back to D. "You've already made me happy because you've already given me everything I've ever wanted... and more."

A gagging sound came from somewhere in the distance, followed quickly by a "shut the fuck up."

Brick rolled his eyes.

"Not everything," D grunted.

Every one of them—every single person in that courtyard—hung on what the man just said. Every single one of them knew what he meant.

"You don't have to," Jewel breathed. "It can remain between us."

"Oh fuck, he's going to do a Brick," Steel chuckled.

Kat punched his arm and frowned at him. "You're ruining the moment."

"We already know he fucked her," Walker said. "We've not only caught them several times doing it, but they have three kids from it."

On stage, D whispered something to Jewel.

Everyone... every-single-one... yelled out, "What?"

D rolled his eyes toward the sky and shook his head before yelling, "Fuckin' love 'er."

"What?" was echoed around the courtyard again.

"Fuckin' Christ!" he barked. Then yelled, "Fuckin' love you, woman!"

"Is he going to pass out?" Kelsea asked, not even bothering to hide her excitement. "I hope he passes out."

"He's not gonna pass out," Ryder answered. "Wait. Is he?"

"He can't pass out before the ceremony is over, otherwise it doesn't count," Parris whispered.

The Dark Knight hurried through the rest of the spiel.

"Is this even legal?" Londyn asked.

Magnum's deep voice came from beside them. Luckily,

Dawg's daughter was no longer anywhere to be seen. "It's fuckin' legal. Sully's an ordained minister."

Brick gave Londyn a squeeze. "Hear that, baby? Sully can marry us when we're ready."

"In your fucking dreams," Londyn told him. "In *my* dreams, my wedding looks nothing like this."

"You should just be happy to be with me."

"I've been waiting a long time to find the right man, so I'm getting the wedding I've always dreamed about."

"Did you find him?"

"I'll let you know."

As Sully finished on stage, making it official, Jewel Jamison was now legally Jewel Dougherty. Amazingly enough, D stayed upright through the rest of it.

Then as the party kicked off and Nash's band, Dirty Deeds, took the stage, he spun Londyn around in his arms to face him.

"Think D realized something." He glanced around him at his fellow Shadows who were all holding onto their women tightly. "Think we all did."

She tilted her head and gave him a soft smile that made his heart squeeze. She wrinkled her nose at him. "What's that?"

Damn, D wasn't the only lucky fucker there tonight.

He pulled her close and when she curled one arm around his waist and fisted her hand in his T-shirt, he whispered into her hair, "'You're only given one little spark of madness. You mustn't lose it.'"

All of them now had their little spark of madness. And now they all needed to do whatever was necessary so they wouldn't lose them.

"Who said that?"

"One smart man."

"You're only given one little spark of madness.
You mustn't lose it."
~ Robin Williams, 1951-2014

Turn the page to read a sneak peek of
Blood & Bones: Trip (Blood Fury MC, book 1)

———

Sign up for Jeanne's newsletter to learn about her upcoming releases, sales and more! http://www. jeannestjames.com/newslettersignup

**Turn the page for a sneak peek of
Blood & Bones: Trip
Blood Fury MC, book 1**

Blood & Bones: Trip (Blood Fury MC, bk 1)

"Sometimes you have to burn yourself to the ground before you can rise like a phoenix from the ashes." ~ *Jens Lekman*

Prologue
Turn the key

TRIP STOOD in the middle of the deserted building, shaking his head, wondering if it was worth the fucking hassle to start the club back up. To reclaim its territory.

But what other fucking choice did he have?

He'd already had it set in his mind, not only to do it, but to do it right this time.

He wouldn't let his father's club, which died a violent death, just remain a memory. And a bad one at that.

But now that he had done his time in the Marines, done his time in prison, he needed something.

Because he had nothing.

Except his granddaddy's run-down farm, a barn full of farm equipment he had no clue how to use and didn't want to, and the abandoned warehouse he was currently standing in on the outskirts of town.

While he was in prison, his lawyer had shown up and read him his granddaddy's will.

Yeah. He got everything.

Sig got nothing.

Trip was sure his brother wasn't happy about that, if he even knew.

But most likely Granddaddy had made up the will when Trip was still doing time in the service and not doing it behind bars. Unlike Sig who had been in and out of county jail, or the state pen, off and on since he turned eighteen.

But now here he stood. In an empty building, feeling fucking overwhelmed. But still, it was something.

And something was better than nothing.

He also had new ink on his back and an old cut in his hand.

The leather was worn, the rockers and patches on it dirty. All except one.

One rectangular patch on the front had been torn off by his own fingers after using the point of his buck knife to loosen the threads. The patch that used to say "Buck" was now replaced with one that said "Trip." But above it, the patch that had deemed Buck as president remained. That now belonged to Trip.

He'd also used that same knife to remove the 1% diamond patch off the back. He wouldn't need that one anymore.

The club used to be outlaw. But Trip was determined to keep it above board. For the most part.

He'd spent many a night down in Shadow Valley talking with the members of the Dirty Angels MC, soaking up everything their prez named Z told him. Learning how to rebuild Blood Fury stronger than ever. How to keep the money flowing into the club's coffers.

One way to do that was to keep the members out of prison and, even better, keep them breathing.

Dead or incarcerated members weren't any good to a club.

And there had been too many of those in the Blood Fury MC in the past. It had been its downfall.

Trip didn't want that mistake to happen again.

So, they had to play the game. Keep shit on the up and up as best as they could. Become a powerful force, strong enough to withstand the occasional bump in the road.

He had no fucking clue how he was going to pull it off, but he would take the advice he was given and do his fucking best.

He scrubbed a hand through his long hair before tucking it up under his baseball cap, blowing out a loud breath and shrugging on his cut.

His cut.

It wasn't his father's any longer.

This club was no longer his father's, either.

This world, even as broken as it was, now belonged to Trip.

It was his and he wouldn't let anyone destroy it again.

The Fury was about to rise once more. This time stronger and smarter.

Get Trip and Stella's story here:
mybook.to/BFMC-Trip

If You Enjoyed This Book

Thank you for reading Guts & Glory: Brick. If you enjoyed Brick and Londyn's story, please consider leaving a review at your favorite retailer and/or Goodreads to let other readers know. Reviews are always appreciated and just a few words can help an independent author like me tremendously!

Want to read a sample of my work? Download a sampler book here: BookHip.com/MTQQKK

Also by Jeanne St. James

Find my complete reading order here:

https://www.jeannestjames.com/reading-order

* Available in Audiobook

Stand-alone Books:

Brothers in Blue Series:

The Dare Ménage Series:

A Daring Journey *

The Obsessed Novellas:

Forever Him *

Only Him *

Needing Him *

Loving Her *

Tempting Him *

Down & Dirty: Dirty Angels MC Series®:

Down & Dirty: Zak *

Down & Dirty: Jag *

Down & Dirty: Hawk *

Down & Dirty: Diesel *

Down & Dirty: Axel *

Down & Dirty: Slade *

Down & Dirty: Dawg *

Down & Dirty: Dex *

Down & Dirty: Linc *

Down & Dirty: Crow *

Crossing the Line (A DAMC/Blue Avengers MC Crossover) *

Magnum: A Dark Knights MC/Dirty Angels MC Crossover *

Crash: A Dirty Angels MC/Blood Fury MC Crossover *

Guts & Glory Series:

(In the Shadows Security)

Guts & Glory: Mercy *

Guts & Glory: Ryder *

Guts & Glory: Hunter *

Guts & Glory: Walker *

Guts & Glory: Steel *

Guts & Glory: Brick *

Blood & Bones: Blood Fury MC®:

Blood & Bones: Trip *

Blood & Bones: Sig *

Blood & Bones: Judge *

Blood & Bones: Deacon *

Blood & Bones: Cage *

Blood & Bones: Shade *

Blood & Bones: Rook *

Blood & Bones: Rev *

Blood & Bones: Ozzy

Blood & Bones: Dodge

Blood & Bones: Whip

Blood & Bones: Easy

Beyond the Badge: Blue Avengers MC™:

Beyond the Badge: Fletch

Beyond the Badge: Finn

Beyond the Badge: Decker

Beyond the Badge: Rez

Beyond the Badge: Crew

Beyond the Badge: Nox

COMING SOON!

Double D Ranch (An MMF Ménage Series)

Dirty Angels MC: The Next Generation

About the Author

JEANNE ST. JAMES is a USA Today bestselling romance author who loves an alpha male (or two). She was only thirteen when she started writing and her first paid published piece was an erotic story in Playgirl magazine. Her first romance novel, Banged Up, was published in 2009. She is happily owned by farting French bulldogs. She writes M/F, M/M, and M/M/F ménages.

Want to read a sample of her work? Download a sampler book here: BookHip.com/MTQQKK

To keep up with her busy release schedule check her website at www.jeannestjames.com or sign up for her newsletter: http://www.jeannestjames.com/newslettersignup

www.jeannestjames.com
jeanne@jeannestjames.com

Newsletter: http://www.jeannestjames.com/
newslettersignup
Jeanne's Down & Dirty Book Crew: https://www.facebook.
com/groups/JeannesReviewCrew/
TikTok: https://www.tiktok.com/@jeannestjames

facebook.com/JeanneStJamesAuthor

amazon.com/author/jeannestjames

instagram.com/JeanneStJames

bookbub.com/authors/jeanne-st-james

goodreads.com/JeanneStJames

pinterest.com/JeanneStJames

Get a FREE Erotic Romance Sampler Book

This book contains the first chapter of a variety of my books. This will give you a taste of the type of books I write and if you enjoy the first chapter, I hope you'll be interested in reading the rest of the book.

Each book I list in the sampler will include the description of the book, the genre, and the first chapter, along with links to find out more. I hope you find a book you will enjoy curling up with!

Get it here: BookHip.com/MTQQKK

Printed in Great Britain
by Amazon